Crazy Is As Crazy Does
Part 2

Crazy Is As Crazy Does

Part 2

A Novel

Eva S. Pinkney

Cover design by Demont Pinder, Pinderstory@gmail.com
Back Cover Photo by Derrel Todd, www.footprintfotos.com
Makeup by Kelsey Williams, Williams.e.kelsey@gmail.com
Haircut by Garland Chapman, www.geethabarber.com
Editing by Kayode Kendall, kayode.kendall@gmail.com

First Edition

ISBN: 9798986250106 (Paperback)
ISBN: 9798986250113 (ebook)
Library of Congress Control Number: 2022909409
Talking Parrot Media
Camp Springs, Maryland

To God for making all things possible. You had my back every time I was ready to quit.

To Mommy and Daddy watching over me from above: Thank you for instilling in me the confidence to do and be whatever I wanted in this life.

To my family, extended family and friends, your words of encouragement meant everything to me. This has been a journey. I couldn't have done it without you.

To my daughters, Raquel and Nikki: I'm glad you both got to see me evolve and love me for who I am now. Nothing can break our bond.

To Jada and Chase: My heartbeats. Still my motivation to elevate.

To Trice: You remember how I always used to say that Rocky should have been JeJuan's and you should have been mine. I know JeJuan is smiling down on the both of us right now.

To Debbie and Johnny: Thank you so very much for reading the manuscript long before it became a book. I knew you both believed in me wholeheartedly.

To Mo: Thank you for talking me down off that ledge every single time.

To Chrissy and Terri: Thanks for being there, excepting my phone calls no matter what time, and providing much needed answers, and there were many.

To E: Thank you for checking on me constantly. It meant so much.

To @e.marieglamour on Instagram: Thank you for the makeup sessions, the private conversations and the laughter. You are one of the best in the DMV to do it!

To all my bonus sons and daughters. You know who you are and will always remain in my heart.

To Adrian: For always returning my calls and lifting me up when I needed encouragement.

To John Houston: Thank you for the critiques and open and honest conversations about the book. You always believed in me. I miss you my friend.

To Keyfi Houston: Thank you for all the laughs and being one of my most dearest friends. I miss you so very much. Most of all thank you for giving me, "My Mai." You know what you mean to me, unconditional love. Thank you for being one of my biggest cheerleaders.

To JL: Thank you for being my sounding board, listening intently no matter what time, day or night. Keeping it real when my ideas were as you say, "Too Hollywood." It's been a hell of a roller coaster ride. You believe in me and my dreams and you continue to be my ride or die.

1

Early summer, 1970

The ride up 95 North was silent. The sky was clear and the traffic was light. The cars to my left and right were just a blur, as I bounced from lane to lane, making my way back to D.C. I glanced in the rearview mirror and caught Chloe taking a hit of coke out of a dollar bill, creased and folded. Our eyes met. She looked away. I quickly rolled down the back window on Ms. Lola's brand-spanking-new black Cadillac sedan and pushed on the gas pedal hard. I heard Chloe curse, as her stash was now in the wind.

"Amber, slow this damn car down before you get us pulled over. You know your underage ass ain't got no driver's license."

"What the fuck!" Ms. Lola said angrily. She spoke for the first time since leaving the boys at the Lorton Youth Center. She did everything in her power to keep them from going to jail, even telephoned her man, the Judge, to see if he could call in a favor. Sometimes, palms can be greased, at least shave some time off the sentence. Fats and Desi were arrested and charged with assault. Allegedly, they beat up some pastor's son over a drug bill. He testified in court before his parents got him out of the country.

Ms. Lola asked with a raised brow and an eagle eye, "Amber, what you and Fats be talking about all huddled up in the corner?"

"He just wants to know about the goings on in the neighborhood," I answered quickly hoping to end further interrogation. I looked straight ahead keeping my eyes on the road. She could always tell when I was lying. I wasn't about to look her way.

Fats was schooling me one visit at a time to take over his and Desi's drug business. I had to be sharp, listening intently to his every word. I put it all to memory. He'd quiz me on what was said the week before and throw me a few more pieces to the puzzle. Six months later, I had the keys to the workhouses and a whole new life began to unfold.

"Fuck the Police" was written in large, bold black lettering on DJ's white tee shirt. He was my right-hand man, doing what he did best: serving a client on his black ten-speed bike, pocketing the crumbled currency, and peddling down the middle of the Avenue without a care. I had to give him credit; he had balls the size of New York, but that kind of stupidity was only going to bring him heat, and cause me unwanted attention. I pulled up beside his narrow ass and blew the horn. He turned his head slightly revealing that dead eye. He'd caught a bullet in crossfire around a year ago. He seldom wore the black eye patch. He didn't like being teased, as it brought out the worst in him.

"You know you can't see shit on your left side," I said. He laughed. "You need to burn that tee shirt!" I said with a hard glare. I proceeded to roll the window up and burned rubber before he could give me some nonsense rebuttal.

"Let me out," Chloe said, still irritated. I dropped her ass at the bottom of the hill. I watched her in the rearview mirror, walking hard and fast, as she disappeared around the corner. Cody, another one of my workers, DJ's protégé, was running toward the car. He was waving his arms in the air, trying to flag me down. I couldn't have missed him even if I tried. He always stood out from the rest with his unique style of dress, designer tee shirts costing several hundred dollars for everyday wear. Cody was ahead of his time with fashion and street sense. I was glad he was a part of my crew. I pulled the sedan over to the curb.

"Ms. Lola, I'll be right back," I said, opening the car door as I stepped into the street without looking, distracted, waving away a troublesome bee buzzing too close to my ear and circling around my head. I heard tires screech on the asphalt. I instinctively jumped out of the way. The white convertible Mercedes stopped right in front of me. The darkly tinted window on the passenger side slowly rolled down. I gazed at the woman staring back at me. She looked to be around twenty in a soft pink halter top, her complexion had a bronze glow. Her hair was very black, freshly done in an asymmetrical bob displaying a widow's peak, giving the style a little more edge. She had well defined eyebrows with a noticeable deep gash. You could only focus on that momentarily because her makeup was flawless with smoky gray shadow, winged black liner drawn with a steady hand and never-ending lashes with a cute button nose. Her lips were perfect, not too full, painted with a bright pink lip gloss that made her eyes twinkle. The woman was gorgeous in spite of the small imperfection that was easily overlooked.

With a flick of her wrist, she threw a handful of trash out the window landing at my feet. I looked down at the used tissue with several silver sheets of gum wrapper balled in a knot. My eyes darted from the trash then back to the woman. Thinking to myself, *Mommy said it's not nice to litter.* Unlike the gash, her behavior couldn't be overlooked. I mouthed the word, "BITCH" in her direction, looking straight into her eyes, knowing I couldn't curse out loud with Ms. Lola sitting in the car, smoking a cigarette with the windows rolled all the way down. I didn't have time to focus on the driver before he sped off down the street.

I continued walking toward Cody, meeting him halfway. He stepped in close, as if he didn't want anyone else to hear our conversation. His voice was just above a whisper, "Amber, Boogey got killed last night. Word on the street is he owed a drug bill and bought a Cadillac from Mr. Lloyds. They lit him up on New York Avenue, just as he was leaving town. He crashed into a tree. He was dead before the ambulance arrived. I thought you should know," he said, suspiciously eyeing any movement around us. He stayed ready.

"Thanks for telling me. Make sure to let DJ know," I said as I turned and walked back toward the car, shaking my head, thinking to myself, *He never should've stolen from me."*

I pulled into the cement driveway under the carport in the rear of the house. I was glad to have made it back to the city with no incidents. I noticed immediately that green ivy was attached to the redbrick. I wondered when Ms. Lola was going to have someone take care of that shit. It seemed sinister the way it grew in abundance and just took over. If the boys were home, it would've been handled.

Ms. Lola opened the car door and slowly exited, smoothing the wrinkles on her silk skirt. She always looked like the wind had been knocked out of her sails after visiting Fats and Desi. She hated seeing them confined. There was nothing to say to lift her spirits. I don't think she would be happy again until they were home.

Inside the house, I could hear the motor of the air conditioner working double time. I unbuttoned my navy denim dress and reached down to loosen my scarf tie sandals. The pastel colors of the silk material falling softly around my ankles like a rainbow. I stepped out both my dress and sandals on the way up the stairway. A hot bath was calling my name as I leaned over the tub, turned on the faucet, and adjusted the temperature of the water. I then removed my navy lace bra and panties, which I let delicately fall to the floor. The cool air was refreshing against my naked skin. As soon as I stepped inside the tub and felt the water on my body, I began to relax. I closed my eyes, dozed off, and began to dream.

"Come back here, Bitch! You didn't let me comb your hair," Mommy screamed as she chased me down the block with an oversized hairbrush with bristles that were elongated and reached out for me like huge blood worms.

"I did my hair already!" I yelled running speedily ahead of her. "I don't need you to walk me to school anymore!" I was embarrassed that she would show up anyway. I awoke from the dream overcome with panic, my heart was racing. I held on to both sides of the porcelain tub, gripping it tightly. Salty tears began to drip down my face. I wiped at my cheeks with closed fists. Tears were a sign of weakness. "Get it together, Amber," I said out-loud with a sigh. "No time for this emotional bullshit. I got somewhere to be."

Mommy was still in and out of St. Elizabeths mental ward. I dangled on the edge of depression myself. I just didn't understand my feelings. I didn't know what it was called, not having an appetite, the lack of sleep or too much, stuck with the covers over my head for days on end, or the sudden and unpredictable anxiety attacks that left me frozen in fear. As I got older, I realized why I didn't seek help. I didn't want to be labeled. That shit follows you for the rest of your life. Go-Go was my escape from the darkness. There was something special about the percussion, that strong African drum beat passed down from our ancestors. A blend of blues, soul, funk, jazz, and salsa. It was a mix of the music that complemented our variation in skin tone. A reminder of our journey. The drums were used as a means of communication. The call and response embraced the core of my soul. Masonic Temple, Byrne Manor, Panorama Room, Burgundy Room, Northwest Gardens, Squad Room, Knights of Columbus, the Maverick Room, Glen Arden. This was my life after dark. Just hit repeat.

It wasn't your typical balmy DC summer night; there was a cool breeze and no humidity. A line of cars and pockets of people were gathering down the entire block. I could hear Smokey Robinson and the Miracles "Going to A Go-Go" blasting from a car radio.

The salutations and group conversations now muddled as I approached the entrance to Northwest Gardens. I knew the guy on the door, so it was easy access. I entered the venue; the lights were dim with sparsely scattered tables seating six. I squinted, scanning the room for Chloe. Her ass was always in some niggas' face trying to get a free high. She had no drug of choice. Weed, hash, cocaine, heroin, dust, Quaaludes, LSD, Chloe loved it all. I appointed myself her protector. I knew I wouldn't always be there to intervene, but I did my best. Was I too young to be in the establishment? Hell yeah! Could anyone have stopped me? Hell no! I dressed the part to accompany the ass and titties, looking much older than my fourteen years of age, and carried myself like a mature young woman far beyond my years. I'd watched Ms. Lola for all of my life and I wanted to be just like her. Besides, my crew had fake IDs to be shown when needed.

I was drawn to what had become a "DC Thing," a growing movement. All the guys were clean as the board of health, and the ladies were dressed to impress. The crisp smell of new clothing, stale smoke and clean sweat engulfed the room. A quick hand to hand exchange of drugs and money was over in the blink of an eye. The cameraman was set up in full glory in the right back corner with several backdrops displaying money and luxury cars, the two things that were attainable if you got with the right folks and had enough nerve. I knew some teenage girls who were taking that trip overseas to bring back heroin, their payment on return was a new car. It was tempting, but I wasn't taking a chance on doing the jail time that went along with that move; besides, I was already involved in criminal activity.

The line wasn't too long. I probably should go take a picture to send to Fats before I sweat my hair out. I'd spent hours waiting my turn to get in the chair at the hair salon. Ms. Sonya was finally able to highlight my hair to a perfect shade of blond. Daddy was going to be mad as hell, but I'd deal with that shit later. I heard Chuck's voice on the microphone as the band finished the sound check and began to play the first set. On second thought, maybe I won't take a picture tonight, as I reached up and touched the loosely falling curls. I was ready to get on the dance floor.

You didn't need a partner. It would only take a few minutes for a total stranger to wrap their arms around your waist, pull you in close and start riding your ass. It was up to you if you allowed it or danced away. The women who were foolish enough to wear heels would more than likely be barefoot by the time the night was over. Even the men who were too cool to dance stayed on the perimeter in linen attire, sipping dark liquor, and bobbing their heads. "Excuse me. Excuse me." I moved through the crowd with ease, until I found a spot closer to the stage. My hips began to sway; I was cool but suggestive as my body gyrated to the beat. I unbuttoned the last four buttons on my Halston pale lemon blouse, tied it in a knot underneath my breasts, rolled up my sleeves as if I was about to put in some work, closed my eyes, and lost myself in the music. It was as if I was the only one in the room.

I felt his stare penetrate my body. I opened my eyes and there he was. He had the face of an Angel but was anything but. He was known as O. He was a living legend in the city. I'd only seen one picture of him, but I could never forget that face. Caramel skin with captivating grayish-blue eyes. His mustache and beard were freshly trimmed and laid like carpet. He had that rich exotic look, wearing a European cut summer sweater that matched his eyes, looking as if he'd just returned from a vacation in St. Tropez. I tried not to focus too hard on those arms, he was cut; I couldn't help imagining him lifting me instead of the weights. Those lips were so inviting, it made me lick mine. He looked to be at least twenty-one, way too old for me. I suddenly realized I'd stopped dancing. He never took his eyes off me as some guy in a Gucci shirt standing next to him was engaged in a one-sided conversation. My feet started moving in his direction as if he was willing me to him. My body felt as if it was on fire. I felt faint. I quickened my pace and headed straight for the ladies' room.

There were two women standing in the mirror holding idle chit chat, reapplying lipstick, and adjusting breasts that were barely hidden under a thin sheet of material. I splashed cold water on my face without stopping to get a piece of paper towel. The crystal-clear droplets ran down my nose and wet my blouse. I stood fanning my face with both hands.

"Hey, Sweetie. You okay?" asked the woman in the multicolored skin tight jumpsuit. "You look like you need to sit down." She sprang into action and got me a few sheets of paper towel.

"Thank you. I'm feeling better," I said while I patted my face. "Can I ask a question?" I said looking at both women not caring who replied.

"Go right ahead," the second woman spoke up, still making sure her makeup was perfect leaning into the mirror under the blinking fluorescent light.

"Have you ever had a man stare you down and your entire body felt hot?"

Both women laughed out loud. The woman in the jumpsuit responded, "Baby, whoever out there made your ass feel that way, you better go find him now and take that nigga home." They both laughed again.

I walked out of the ladies' room with a new air of confidence, but O was no longer there. I searched the room as if I wore night vision goggles to no avail. My heart sank just a little, but the music brought me right back to the dance floor. I smoothed my hair into a ponytail while I reached into my skirt pocket in search of a rubber band, wrapped it tightly around each strand, and then went right back to partying like there was no tomorrow. Chuck Brown and the Soul Searchers were in the pocket and had a way of making you forget all your problems. Go-Go saved my life, over and over and over again.

2:00 a.m. came too quickly. Still no sign of Chloe. DJ almost knocked me over as I walked out the front door. I could feel the dampness of his shirt. "Amber, O is waiting to talk to you around the corner. He paid me $500.00 to bring you to him." Panting between each word as if he'd ran a 100 yard dash in 6.5 seconds.

"I should make you break that shit down, taking money to deliver me to some nigga," I said gritting. "What he look like?" I asked with a scowl.

DJ could see I wasn't happy. "Don't take this the wrong way because you know I love me some women, but he looked like if he had a sister that looked just like him, I would bang her ass, right here, right now, in front of everybody."

My face began to soften. Curiously, I asked, "What's he driving?"

"He's in a sports car, a two-seater with no top," DJ replied. "One of them shits you don't see a lot."

I walked to the corner and looked down the street. There was only one car parked. I looked back at DJ and gave him a head nod. He knew not to follow.

O sat with the engine running, his foot on the brake. He rolled down the window, and our eyes met for the second time.

"Are you looking for me?" I questioned.

"You not scared, little lady?" he asked, staring a hole in my chest.

"You put your pants on one leg at a time just like I do," I answered with conviction.

"I got a business proposition for you. Would you like to take a ride?"

For a brief moment, the poem about the spider and the fly came to mind. *Will you walk into my parlor? Said the Spider to the Fly.*

I finally replied, "I'm good as long as you're not trying to kidnap me. My mama crazy and my daddy work a 9–5, so my folks ain't got no money to pay no ransom. Just letting you know before I get in."

He smiled with his eyes. "That means you're crazy too?" he asked with a smirk.

I opened the door and got in on the passenger side before responding. "Obviously. I just got in the car with you."

We both smiled. Mommy always said everything that glitters ain't gold. Right now, at this moment in time, that life lesson was totally forgotten.

O was listening to John Coltrane's "Equinox." The song was one of my father's favorites. I began to snap my fingers and move my head from side to side, remembering what Daddy would always say, "Just breathe it in, baby." That's just what I was doing while I let it invade my pores. Reminding me of the hours spent sitting on the floor while Daddy lay on the living room couch, neither one of us saying a word, appreciating the music.

"You like Coltrane, huh?" I asked, as I glanced in his direction. It was hard to look at the man, but I got in a quick once over.

"Yeah," he replied. "Jazz keeps me from overthinking. . . tend to do that a lot. . . What you know about Coltrane?"

"I grew up in a house with all types of music. Jazz is my father's favorite genre." Right about now, I found myself feeling really good about all those times Mommy made me look up the spelling and definition of new words on a weekly basis. I had a broad vocabulary and I had a feeling that I was really going to need it right about now.

We were definitely going across town. The South Capitol Street Bridge was a connection to S.E., but once we hit Suitland Parkway, the street lights were scarce and the street signs were few and far in-between. There seemed to be as many lightning bugs as there were stars in the sky. I had no idea where we were heading, but it was away from the city. I placed my hand on my knee to calm any shakiness before it began, rubbing in a circular motion. In my head, I was having a full blown conversation with myself. *Yeah, bitch! You wanted to play 'big girl' did you? Well look at you now, in the car with an infamous criminal. You don't even know if he's going to slit your throat and leave your ass in the woods to be eaten alive. Silly girl.*

Just then, O pulled off on the side of the road. It quickly brought me to the present and out of my head. "Here's the part where you're going to have to trust me," he said. "I don't bring anyone where I lay my head. I'm going to blindfold you for the rest of the trip. You got a problem with that?"

"It's a little late if I did have a problem," I replied. "Do what you gotta do so we can get to the business at hand."

O leaned in to tie the blindfold tightly around my eyes with a slight squint. *Damn! He smells good. Keep your composure, Amber.* I thought inwardly.

We were back on the road, now listening to Grand Funk Railroad, "I'm Your Captain." I now found myself wishing for the jazz so it could stop me from overthinking, as my mind began to race. We rode for the next few minutes with no conversation. O was quite content with pushing the car to its limit. He was shifting gears effortlessly, taking curves at the max. We had to be going 110 miles per hour, if not more. I held on tightly, gripping the edge of the seat as the high speed and wind velocity pinned my body against the seat like an insect to a windshield.

"What kind of car is this?" I asked loudly, turning my head in his direction.

"A 67 Shelby Cobra 427," he proudly stated over the growl of the engine.

"My brother Chris used to race down Aquasco Speedway. He would love to handle these wheels! He taught me how to drive but more importantly how to shift gears.

"Why did he stop racing?" O asked inquisitively.

"He got drafted into the Army," I said fighting back the tears. It was the first time I'd said it out loud. I missed my brother. Finally, I could feel O down shift. The car began to slow. I continued the conversation without yelling. "I had a near-death experience coming home from the track one night. You want to hear about it?" I asked hoping he would say yes.

"I'm all ears," he said.

Daddy refused to give me money to go to the track that morning. Maybe that was a sign. I paused for a few seconds; I could feel myself biting a quivering bottom lip as I remembered that day. Chris was just about to pull away from the curb. "Please let me go! I don't want to stay home with Mommy." He looked me in the eye, feeling my pain and said, "You can get in the trunk. I'll sneak you into the track once we're close."

"So did you get in the trunk?" O asked.

Yeah, but I wasn't alone. My brother met up with a friend named Jerry on the way down to the speedway. He had a young guy riding with him. He was short, fair-skinned, and thin as a rail with a crooked nose and teeth to match; I don't even remember his name. Both cars pulled over to the side of the road near the tree-line about a mile from the track. Chris told me to get in Jerry's car. I happily did as I was told. We both climbed awkwardly into the trunk.

I was cute that day in my blue and white seersucker midriff top and wide bell bottom pants that Mommy made especially for me. It was unbearably hot, close to ninety-five degrees, even hotter once the trunk was closed. It was tight quarters. Darkness fell on us as if daylight had disappeared. It felt as if the heat kicked up another few notches. Our knees touched, his sour breath gave a whole new meaning to halitosis. I was wondering what was taking so long to get us out. My bra and panties were damp, sticking like glue to my skin.

"What was the holdup?" O asked attentively.

Jerry got in the inspection line with the two of us still in the trunk. I could hear Chris' voice as he walked toward the trunk giving Jerry a vicious cussing out. The next thing I knew the trunk opened and we both climbed out in front of hundreds of onlookers. I just disappeared into the crowd, pulling a wedgie from in-between my butt, heading straight for the bleachers.

O began to chuckle.

Chris had a pretty good run that day. His friend Turk was just about to win a bunch of money when he threw a rod on his very last run. We had to tow his car all the way back to D.C. We left Aquasco with applause from the spectators, now on their feet as we slowly exited the speedway. I smiled and waved as if I was a prom queen on a float.

It was late and the road was dark. Chris was fighting to keep his eyes open. He let me shift gears while he drank Gatorade. James Brown's song, "Say It Loud—I'm Black and I'm Proud," came on the radio. He reached for the dial to turn up the volume and we both began to sing. Turk let go of the steering wheel to lay his son down in the front seat, he'd fallen asleep. Out of nowhere, the cars jackknifed across the highway. Chris was trying to steer with his left hand and hold me with his right. A tractor trailer was barreling down on us. All I could hear was brakes and a horn. The smell of burning rubber engulfed my nostrils. My heart was palpitating. I saw my life flash before my eyes. The truck stopped two feet away from hitting us. I guess it wasn't my time to go.

There was an awkward moment of silence before O began to speak, "Our fate is predetermined; we can't alter our own destiny. It's already written," he said as he placed his hand on mine. I felt the connection.

2

After what seemed like an eternity, we finally came to a stop. With my eyes covered, I was more in tune with the sounds of the night: the car door being closed, followed by footsteps, crickets chirping, birds singing high in the trees, the croak of a nearby frog. Then the air was filled with screams of torture.

"What the fuck is that?" I exclaimed moving too quickly, stepping on a rock, and twisting my ankle just a little as O grabbed me before I hit the ground.

"It's a fox," he answered. "That's their mating call. . . .I got you. Stay right here." O propped my ass against the car for support.

I heard a key unlock a door, the alarm system being disarmed. Next, he swept me up into his arms and carried me across the threshold like a brand new bride. The open door closed behind us. He carried me a few feet before laying me down on a silk chaise. I ran my fingers along the edge. The soft material felt comforting underneath my fingertips. He removed the blindfold. I blinked, trying to adjust to the light as I looked around and rubbed my ankle. He turned on the alarm and locked the door. We were in a pristine white kitchen, with stainless steel appliances and a black and white marble floor. The stove was spotless, as if it had never been used; the entire kitchen looked like a picture out of an *Architectural Digest* magazine.

O removed my shoes and proceeded to massage my ankle and foot. He stopped momentarily to fix a drink, straight Hennessy on the rocks. "Would you like one? he asked while holding his glass in the air.

"Water please," I replied. "I don't drink."

He walked toward me with both glasses, took a nice size gulp from his, slowly swallowing as if he was savoring the liquor. He handed me the water and then set his glass down on the granite counter. Reaching for my ankle, he continued massaging with light pressure. "I can offer you a better product at a wholesale price. I promise you'll have no complaints," he said, as he stared into my eyes.

"I have partners," I said reluctantly.

"I know, but I'll be dealing directly with you."

"How much do you know about them?" I asked.

"Fats and Desi are at college, shall we say?" he said sarcastically. "You took over the business. I'd like to help you."

"Why?" I asked, tilting my head with a quizzical look.

"I like your work. I think you have the potential to go to the next level in this game. If I allow that to happen, it should be with me and under my direction." He continued massaging my ankle. I sat back and closed my eyes.

This was a lot to digest. I would have to make a decision without consulting the boys. I reached up and ran my hand over my hair, smoothing the strands, an unconscious habit. Hell, if it was the other way around, they would jump at this deal. Fats left me in charge. This was an excellent opportunity to stack some real paper. Something for them to come home to. Opening my eyes, I began to speak, "I'm in."

"I knew you'd make the right decision," he said, reaching for the glass of liquor. "Let's toast to new beginnings." We raised our glasses in the air, touching briefly, taking a sip, sealing our agreement. A look of contentment crossed O's face.

"What time is it, please?" I asked.

"Too late for me to take you home," he answered bluntly.

I looked toward the window. The sun was rising and its reflection bounced off the water in the swimming pool just beyond the terrace.

"I'd love to get in the water," I said.

"Now?" He questioned. My eyes widened in anticipation.

"What about your ankle?" he asked.

"I'm sure the water will make it feel better," I answered.

"Can you swim?" he asked.

"No," I admitted with disappointment, dropping my head, thinking this was a done deal.

"I guess I'll have to get in with you. Can't have your tiny ass drowning in my pool. I'd have to dump your body in another state. . . .and I'm too tired to take that drive."

He was hard to read. I couldn't tell if he was serious or joking.

"I don't have a bathing suit." O was already disrobing.

"You've never been skinny dipping?" he asked.

"No!" I exclaimed, my cheeks beginning to blush. I didn't know whether to look or turn away from that chiseled physique.

"Get naked if you trying to get in the pool! There are towels in the pool house."

Turning my back to O, I quickly stripped, juggling my weight so as not to put too much pressure on my ankle. When I turned around, he was right there. All up in my personal space, looking down on me. I could smell the liquor on his breath, but not in a bad way. He was close enough for our lips to touch if I stood on my tiptoes. I closed my eyes and with one quick swoop I was in his arms again. I was a little disappointed, more than ready for that first kiss. He carried me out the patio door and into the heated pool, one step at a time.

"Relax. Can you float? Big as those titties are, you'll be alright!" he said letting me go before I could answer, but staying right next to me, as I let the water carry me out to the middle of the pool. My ponytail began to fan out around my head like a halo crown. I'd forgotten all about the recent blond highlights. All I could do now was pray that they didn't turn green.

I closed my eyes and began to enjoy the sun playing hide and seek with the clouds. I flipped over on my stomach and swam toward O under water. He pulled me up toward him, studying every aspect of my body.

"So where is my birthmark?" I asked flirtingly.

"Your upper left thigh . . . Did that butterfly tattoo hurt bad?" he asked, focusing on my bare breast.

"Hell, yeah!! I went to a shop on the Avenue with some hardcore biker boys, just before closing. I was the only customer left. They were throwing back beers and toting some real big guns. Once the tattoo artist started with the outline, I felt light-headed, realizing too late that my breast was a sensitive area and that I'd made a mistake."

O smirked as I continued my story.

"I fanned my face, and asked him to give me a few minutes. He told me he'd had grown men pass out getting tattooed, like that was supposed to make me feel better. There was no way I was passing out with a shop full of half-drunk men and I was the only female. I got it together real quick."

"I thought you couldn't swim?" he asked with a little suspicion. I could feel his breath on my neck as he spoke.

"Only a little. I'm scared to go in the deep end," I responded.

"Bam!"

I jumped at the noise. "What was that?" I asked looking back toward the house holding on to his neck a little tighter.

"A bird. They sometimes fly into the windows."

I looked at him and then looked back toward the house once more.

"I know. It took me a minute to get used to that shit," he said with a little chuckle.

"Okay," I said, still a little uneasy, looking back toward the windows again.

"Come on; let's get in the shower. Time for us to get some shut eye."

O carried me from the pool to the outdoor shower. He shampooed my hair and his, rubbing the bar of soap rapidly over my body, cleansing me with his hands. That lustful look he'd given me all night was gone. He then washed off and we both stood under the water washing the soap away. After drying off, he carried me into the house, up the stairs to a guest room. It certainly wasn't the master. He handed me an oversized black tee shirt and said, "Get some sleep," before leaving the room, closing the door behind him.

I tossed and turned, landing on my back staring at the ceiling, eventually discarding the tee shirt. My mind was tumbling. All I kept thinking about was what the woman at the Go-Go said to me in the bathroom. *Find the man that made your body feel like it was on fire and take him home with you.* Here I was under the same roof with that man, separated merely by walls. The wind picked up and the sky turned dangerously dark. A bolt of lightning made contact somewhere nearby, followed by a loud crash of thunder. I ran toward the room with the music playing. I knocked before entering but entered unheard.

Awakened from a deep sleep O pointed the 9mm Luger between my eyes.

"It's me Amber! Don't shoot!" I screamed. "I'm afraid of storms!"

Lowering the gun, O replied, "Your motherfucking ass is scared of a lot of shit! Are you sure you are in the right business?" He took his hand off the trigger and placed the gun back on the nightstand.

There I stood shaking, naked and humiliated.

O pulled the covers back and said, "Get in."

I damn near broke my neck hobbling to his bed, his warmth and the safety of his arms. "Go to sleep."

I awoke around 4 p.m. to a hard dick rubbing against the crack of my ass.

O whispered in my ear while massaging my nipple, "You going to be able to keep this separate, business and fucking? I didn't invite you into my bedroom. You changed the dynamics of this relationship. So, if I stick my dick in you right now, fuck the shit out of you, I don't have to worry about no sudden attachment. Correct?" He grabbed my chin and turned my head so he could look into my eyes, searching for an honest answer.

I looked him right back in the eyes and said, "I can handle it; let's get this money."

O spread my legs wide and entered me with an unexpected urgency, as he wrapped my legs around his neck.

I was receptive to his every stroke. Chills and heat. The combination was about to drive me crazy. I waited until we were cheek to cheek before grimacing, the size alone on top of the deep thrusts was almost too much to bear. The buildup to the climax was filled with suspense and wanting. He made sure I was drained before he came. We collapsed, entangled as one. Sweaty, lustful, and satisfied. One hour later, we were at it again.

Ms. Lola warned me about that third leg. "Always remember that you are in control. Never slip. It can be a powerful force if you let them penetrate you. If it's good, they can smack you upside the head with it and you won't say a word. Foreplay can be enjoyable, but keep a clear head. It's a method to the madness. Always guard your heart."

Lord, help me.

I was lightheaded. I could hear the rumbling in my stomach. My stirrings awakened O. "I'm starving!" I exclaimed. "I can fix us some dinner. Can you go to the grocery store?"

"I don't eat everybody's cooking," O said as he turned back over pulling the covers off my naked ass.

"Negro! I can burn! Get up!"

O gave me that look like I was overstepping my boundaries, but I didn't care. I got real bold when it came to my stomach being empty.

He just left the bed spewing orders, "There are cameras everywhere. Don't be stupid," he growled.

"You're a man of very few words. I got it! I'm on Candid Camera," I said as a joke. There was that cold stare again as he walked toward the bathroom. I sat up in bed and looked around. "So, did you record us fucking?" I asked, a question left unanswered.

I watched him get dressed, trying not to drool as I wrote out a list. "I need to call home if that's okay," I asked out of respect.

"Go right ahead," he said matter-of-factly. "Don't talk no nonsense on my phone." I stared at him while sucking my teeth and rolling my eyes to the ceiling, and then back toward him as I reached for the phone on the nightstand, thinking to myself, *This negro talking to me like I'm green.*

Chloe answered on the second ring.

"Hey, girl! What are you doing?" I asked, wishing I could fill my good girlfriend in on my adventures, but knew I needed to save that conversation for another time and place.

"Chillin," she replied.

"Where did you disappear to last night?" I asked. Slowly, she continued sounding high off that smack, "I left with this cute guy I met."

"I should've known. Next time, can you give me a heads up? Do me a favor and tell Mommy and Daddy that I'm down the beach with Ms. Lola. I met someone too." I was trying to sound like it was no big deal.

"Sure will. Have fun! Check you later." The phone line dropped. I guess I was blowing her high with frivolous conversation.

O took longer than I anticipated to return from the store.

"Did you forget where you live?" I asked jokingly as he came through the door.

"I needed to meet somebody while I was out. Enough said?" he responded with a frown.

"It's all good. I'm getting ready to put a smile on your face."

I went about my work in a cook's apron and nothing else. I had a lot of skills but cooking was at the top of my list of attributes. Besides, Ms. Lola said the way to a man's heart is through his stomach.

"Why do you keep walking past and touching my neck?" I asked. "That shit sends a signal straight to my pussy and I'm trying to cook!"

This time, he walked up behind me playing with my nipples and rubbing his hardness against me.

"Can you please stop?" I said, playfully pushing him away.

"What do you expect me to do?" he asked. "I'm sitting in the chair watching that ass prance back and forth in front of me. To me, it's like an open invitation. My dick is hard."

With a smile on my face, I turned off the stove and walked to the kitchen island, untying my apron along the way. I laid the palms of my hands on the cold granite with my fingers spread before asking O provocatively, "So what you gonna do?"

I could hear him walk toward me, unzipping his shorts. He spread my cheeks and entered me slowly. I was quickly learning to respond to his every movement.

I felt as if I'd known him for years. The rhythm was intense. This time, we climaxed together. Once we were done, I hurried off to the bathroom to take a ho's bath, and then returned to the kitchen to continue preparing the meal.

"How did you learn to cook like this?" O asked while licking his fingers and cleaning his plate.

"My daddy taught me how to cook at a young age," I replied. "My mommy was in and out of the hospital. There would be times that she was institutionalized for up to six months. He worked a lot; Chris worked, but ran the street more. I made sure we all ate."

"I didn't know you were serious about your mom being crazy. That must've been really hard for you to deal with."

"I still deal with that shit! That's why I seldom go home. Mom and I butt heads on a regular. I love her and I know she's sick, but it's hard to remember that when she's calling me out my name. I've been called a bitch more times than I can count in this one lifetime. I decided that if I was going to be labeled a bitch by my mommy, then I was going to be a bad ass bitch! Give motherfuckers something to talk about! Ya dig?" I giggled at my own words.

O laughed out loud. It was the first time I'd heard him laugh.

"We've been fucking like rabbits and I don't even know your name," I said thinking how absurd that sounded.

"You mean my government name?" he asked as his eyes began to squint. "What, you the police?"

I held my hand out to shake his. "Let's start over. My name is Amber Hayden."

He reluctantly took my hand as he replied, "My name is Anjelo Dominquez Jones. It's a pleasure meeting you, Amber." He held my hand tightly as he shook it.

"You part Spanish?"

He laughed before responding. "No. My mom named me after the man that raised me. He was from Cartagena. She said the only thing she would do for my biological is give me his last name."

"Do your parents live here?"

There was a brief pause as he looked away from me and stared out the kitchen window as if he was suddenly lost in memories of the past. "They were killed in a car accident a long time ago."

"My apologies," I said. "How did you get in the game?" I asked not knowing if he would answer or not.

"I was a stickup boy for a while. I robbed a few banks, stacked my money, got introduced to a few people and that's how it happened. I always rolled alone. The one thing that I know for sure is that I'm not telling on myself.

"Can I ask. . . "

He cut me off abruptly. "No more questions."

I walked over to his album collection and pulled out *In the Groove* by Marvin Gaye. There was a cut I liked a lot, titled "Heard It through the Grapevine." I placed the needle on the vinyl and walked back toward O. Marvin's sultry voice came through the stereo shifting through the airwaves out the patio door, settling on the leaves like sugar on cake.

"Can you hand-dance?" I asked, thinking he would say no.

"How's your ankle?" he asked as he rose from the kitchen stool and grabbed my hand.

"It's much better. Thank you."

We began to dance. He was smooth as shit on his feet, about as smooth as that brown liquor he was so fond of drinking.

I didn't miss a beat, although he threw some back-to-back turns on me trying to show off as if he had an audience, but I was good. He seemed to enjoy himself, as if he didn't get a chance to do this too often. When the song concluded, he walked over to his collection and picked out one of his favorites. A slow cut by Barbara Mason, "Yes I'm Ready." I was well acquainted with this song.

I used to bop with the older guys in the neighborhood at St. Gabriels' playground on Friday nights, and I could dance far better than most of the teenage girls. I never had to stand against the cement wall unless I was taking a breather.

O pulled me in real tight.

I purposely didn't slow drag when I was out at parties or the Go-Go. Didn't like some strange guy rubbing all up against me. O was no longer a stranger. I wrapped around his waist, closed my eyes and followed his every move, instantly learning exactly what it meant to slow drag.

There was no air between us. He ravished my lips with deep kisses. My nipples were hard and my sweet spot was wet.

He let go of me momentarily to remove his clothing.

I untied the apron, slipping it over my head, letting it fall to the floor.

He then took my hand and led me to the kitchen chair where he took a seat and lifted me on top of his manhood.

I gasped, not knowing if I could handle the ride down.

He was far gentler than I expected. He slid his hands underneath my hips and raised me up and down slowly, until I could feel his balls underneath me.

O whispered in my ear, "Hold on."

As he lifted me into the air, I wrapped my legs around his waist and my arms around his neck and held on tight as he walked me across the room, never missing a stroke before he nailed me against the wall with such intensity, the art shook. My hair was dangling and wet. Beads of sweat ran down his chest onto my midriff. There was that feeling of ecstasy again as we slid down the wall, spent.

I vaguely remember him waking me up to go upstairs to bed. He cuddled me in his arms and I fell back into a deep slumber.

I could feel the sunlight through the partially open drapes as it licked my skin. It was morning. He took my hand and led me from the bed to the shower. He turned on the water and adjusted the temperature. He sat on the bench and pulled me toward him. "Get on your knees," he said in a throaty voice.

There was his shaft, standing at attention right in front of my eyes. I licked the sides like an ice cream cone.

"Put it in your mouth," he continued, as he leaned back against the wall of the shower with his eyes closed.

I moved in closer and took him into my mouth, terrified of not being able to please him. I gagged and began to cough; tears began to well up in my eyes. I couldn't help scraping his skin with my teeth upon a quick exit from the shower. I lay on the bed in a fetal position, sobbing, not knowing what to expect next, waiting for him to announce he was taking me home.

O came into the bedroom, and lay down on the bed spooning me from behind. He caressed my face as he gently pulled away my wet and tangled hair. He planted soft kisses on my neck, as he held me tightly. "Baby, I'm not upset," he finally said. "I couldn't be happier. All I need is for you to trust me completely. I'll teach you everything you need to know." We laid there on the wet bedding, neither one of us caring.

* * *

I was humming while cooking lunch. He was reading the newspaper and drinking a mimosa. I reached for the spice and there was something small wrapped in newspaper with a string tied around it. Turning toward O with that something small in my hand, I asked, "What is this?"

"Why don't you open it and see," he said as he watched the excitement in my eyes.

I tore into the newspaper catching the diamond tennis bracelet as it fell out of the wrapping, examining it as if I was a jeweler. "Is this for me?" I asked, admiring the bracelet even closer.

"Why don't you walk over here and let me fasten it on your wrist."

I didn't waste any time walking across the kitchen, sitting on his lap, and allowing him to put the bracelet on my arm.

Watching me beam, he asked, "You like it?"

"It's beautiful. Thank you." I proceeded to kiss him on the lips. I eventually got up from his lap, twirling around in circles on my tip toes.

"I don't have any clothes to wear; I guess it's time for me to go back to the crib. I'm tired of wearing this apron."

He looked up without smiling, folding the paper in two and reading the next page, and casually said, "There's some clothes upstairs that you might be able to fit into."

"What makes you think that I would want to wear some other woman's shit?" I replied, folding my arms signaling my exasperation. "Who would leave without taking their clothes anyway?" I said just short of showing my ass.

Nonchalantly, he replied, "I paid for those clothes and most of that shit still got tags on them. Look. It's just a suggestion."

"Which bedroom?" I asked, more out of curiosity than anything else.

"Next to the master, on the left." He rose from his seat and placed the newspaper on the counter. Without looking in my direction, he raked the scraps from his breakfast in the trash.

For one fleeting moment, he made me feel like I was worthless—something that could easily be discarded because I'd asked too many questions.

I walked up the stairs and opened the door to a brightly colored bedroom. The harvest gold walls were adorned with modern paintings, a queen size bed with a white comforter, five pillows strategically arranged, two nightstands on each side of the bed with brass lighting and an eight-drawer wooden dresser. I went straight for the closet. I pulled out some bell-bottoms and tie-dyed shirts, frayed jeans, and a cotton midi skirt along with a Mexican peasant crop top for starters, and laid them on the bed.

Every piece of clothing still had the tags attached. Bergdorf Goodman, Saks Fifth Avenue, and Lord & Taylor, just to name a few. Time slipped by quickly as I got caught up trying on the outfits. I didn't hear O enter the room. He was always on that ninja shit.

"Damn, Baby," he said, admiring my body in the crop top and little else. "You look good. Now you don't need to go home."

"So should I take that to mean you don't want me to go?" I asked with both hands on my hips.

"You're entertaining," he said, the lust was back in his eyes.

"Entertaining like when you watched me dance at the Go-Go? You already got my snatch without giving up no paper. You got to empty those pockets if you want to see me dance again."

"Long and short, if I got to pay to watch you dance, I'll just catch you at the Go-Go for free. I want you to put on something sexy tonight. We're going out to dinner."

"What time should I be ready?" I asked.

"Five should be good. Give us plenty of time to get into the city," he said while smacking my ass as he left the room.

I was back in the closet again, anxiously searching for the perfect outfit, slowly sliding the hangers with care, one by one, examining each piece, running my hands over the material. I wanted to look exceptional. I showered and dressed in a hot little beige jumpsuit that criss-crossed my chest, showing a slight hint of cleavage and fit like a glove. I was just about to leave the bedroom as I glanced back over my shoulder to make sure I hadn't forgotten anything, when I saw something wrapped in paper with a string tied around it sitting in the middle of the bed. I walked over and sat down on the bed, removed the string and watched the Cartier watch fall out.

It was 5 p.m. when I came down the stairs, wearing the diamond bracelet and the watch. O signaled his approval by the look in his eyes and the funny way he rubbed his beard.

We got in the Jaguar and once seated, he tied the blindfold tightly over my eyes and we headed into the city. Once again, I could hear the tires on gravel as he pulled over and removed the blindfold. "Thank you for the watch. I absolutely love it!" I said, kissing his cheek.

O found a parking space on F Street, just a few feet from the Old Ebbitt Grill. Chloe and I'd passed this restaurant on numerous occasions when shopping downtown. It was known as the oldest saloon in the city, a D.C. landmark. Ms. Lola dined there frequently with the Judge and would speak about all the affluent people she would see and the historic décor. I remembered her specifically talking about Odessa Madre making an entrance one night at the restaurant with an entourage of females following behind. Ms. Madre was known as "Lady Al Capone." She kept the peace amongst hustlers and was well respected. She owned several brothels throughout the city; there was even one on the corner where I grew up. She and Ms. Lola were associates.

O took my hand as we entered the front door. It was crowded, but we were seated right away. It seemed he was no stranger to the establishment.

"How are you tonight, Mr. Jones?" the waiter asked with a smile. "Would you like to see the wine list?"

"No, thank you," O replied. "You can bring me a Hennessy on the rocks and a ginger ale for the lady."

"Do you need a few more minutes to look over the menu?" the waiter asked.

"Amber, are you ready to order?" O asked.

"I'll have the salmon with broccoli and yellow rice please," I responded in a soft voice.

"I'll have the crab cakes, a baked potato with just butter and spinach, please," O said to the waiter while handing him the menus.

I sat and looked around the restaurant, soaking up the ambiance. There was a couple at the bar sipping on fruity drinks and enjoying each other's company. A group of older men were seated at a corner table, absent of smiles, all business. The waiters and waitresses moved swiftly and purposefully, all orders memorized. Our food arrived and there was something small wrapped in gauze on my plate. "Is this for me?" I asked O pointing to it.

O laughed quietly, closing his eyes briefly, lowering his head in disbelief, "That's a lemon wrapped in gauze to keep the seeds out while you squeeze the juice on your seafood."

I sat uncomfortably looking dumbfounded at the plate, not knowing what to say.

"You thought it was another gift?" he asked, smiling. "I take it you don't eat out a lot?"

"I frequent the Chesapeake Bay Seafood House, all you can eat for a set price. I take my workers there, they love it!" I said looking around. "But no place like this," I added.

"No worries; all that is about to change. Enjoy your food. There'll be more gifts to come. Let's get this money." We both smiled.

3

The sun was glaring, and I could feel the warmth of the rays on my face as I looked out the window watching a butterfly land on the windowsill as if to say hello, and then fly away over the wooden fence. I had breakfast waiting for him every morning, and he served me dick every night. O was grooming me to be his personal ho. I spent a good amount of time sunning at the pool, totally nude, reading books from his library. After all, I needed a dark tan when I returned home. I wanted to look legit.

I watched O finish up breakfast through the glass patio door. I wondered if he could feel me as I watched his every bite. A sudden chill came over me, as if someone was watching me from afar. I shook my head and closed my eyes and dismissed the thought. I needed to enjoy the heat of the sun lingering on the horizon before the predicted storm. I must've dozed off awakened by a clap of thunder in the distance.

O was sitting right next to me.

"How was breakfast?" I asked, waiting for his praise.

"I'm still a little hungry," he replied.

"I can fix you something else to eat," I said.

"I got everything I need right here," he said. He got to his feet and returned with the blind-fold in hand.

"Are we going for a ride?" I asked inquisitively.

"I'm not, but you are," he said in a low voice.

I sat up to gather my things.

"Stay right there."

I dropped everything that I was holding. He placed the black cotton napkin over my eyes and tied it tight.

"Lay back," he said almost in a growl.

Tiny raindrops began to speckle my body at a slow steady pace. O was opening my legs and licking my inner thighs. I started to squirm because it tickled. "Be still and relax," he said, more of a command. He raised both of my legs to a bent position up toward my tummy. He was circling my box with his tongue. The rain was more persistent, the drops hitting my body with an intense pounding as the storm made its presence known. He'd now found the "little man in the boat." A gasp, replaced by a moan.

I held on to his head, not wanting him to stop. I came simultaneously with a crash of thunder, closer this time. This was more than a ride, I was floating. It was more like an outer body experience. I couldn't get enough.

＊　　＊　　＊

There was a misty haze just above the trees as I glanced out of the window. I'd just finished cleaning up the kitchen after breakfast. I found myself wanting to venture. I climbed up the stairs to the bedroom, threw on a pair of dark blue bell bottom jeans and a burnt orange tie-dyed shirt. I descended the stairs and walked onto the patio where O sat sipping a cup of coffee.

"O, can I go for a walk outside the fence?"

"Why?" he asked with an inquisitive look. "You trying to run away?"

"No. I'm actually enjoying your company. I'd like to see where the butterflies go! I used to catch the most beautiful butterflies when I was a little girl. I would scoop them up in a mason jar and put holes in the top so they could breathe. Daddy said they would die and I should set them free. Two days later, they would be dead, just as he said. I would cry and say I would never do it again. Two weeks later, I would come home with another captured butterfly in that same mason jar. It takes me a while to learn my lesson."

"Don't go too far beyond the fence," he replied with a stern face. "You heard that fox the other night."

My eyes widened and my jaw slackened. "They come out in the daytime?"

"They come out when they're hungry no matter what time, day or night. They're usually more scared of you than you are of them, unless they're rabid," he said, grasping his cup, now on his feet, as he turned and walked back inside the house.

I quietly unlocked the gate and slipped through the opening, placing my hands behind me so it wouldn't slam. There was an earthy smell in the air from last night's rain. Right before my eyes was a sea of wildflowers, violets, black-eyed Susan, goldenrods, and asters. Those were the ones I recognized from my walks with Mommy as a child. Just beyond the fence was a butterfly habitat— every size and color imaginable, dancing from one flower to the next. I was in awe. I'd found my happy place. I was a child all over again.

Suddenly, I heard the sound of hoofs trampling dried leaves. Deer were migrating and coming in my direction. I ran to a huge oak tree with a large open cavity and stood still as the night. The deer enveloped me on both sides, kicking wet dirt on my jeans as they ran by. I wanted to close my eyes but I couldn't. I stayed there for several minutes after they were gone.

I looked up and there was O on the balcony holding a 12-guage shotgun pointed in my direction.

"Can you please bring your half white ass back inside now that you've bonded with nature?"

"On my way!" I said running toward the fence. I looked back, and the butterflies were gone.

Later that night, I awoke from sleep, and looked at O resting peacefully. I climbed out of bed, walked out on the wooden balcony and looked through the telescope facing north. It was a Cave Astrola, a popular brand according to O. I was no expert, as I aimed the telescope toward the sky and searched for the "Big Dipper." "Wow!" "A falling star," I said to myself.

O walked up behind me asking, "What are you looking for, Baby?" He placed both of my hands on the telescope and entered me from behind.

"I'm looking for the Big Dipper," I said with bated breath.

"Keep your eyes on the sky," he whispered in my ear. "Can you see it, Baby?"

"No, but I damn sure can feel it."

*   *   *

I awoke thirty minutes before O, listening to the mourning dove cooing on the roof. For days on end, I'd mistaken the sound for that of an owl until I opened the curtains one morning and saw the dove on the windowsill making the sound. I leaned on my elbow, resting my face against the palm of my hand, watching him sleep and wondering if I should pinch myself to make sure I wasn't dreaming. I ran my hand across his chest smoothing the hair, and then rubbed his beard ever so lightly with the back of my hand. He began to stir. He opened his eyes with a smile. It was just a glimmer, but I saw the love in his eyes smiling back at me. I don't know when it happened for him, but I was just where I wanted to be. Falling in love.

"You're exceptionally handsome," I said, my eyes traveling up and down his body, slowly, appreciating every inch of his physique.

He started to wake up, stretched and wiped the crust from the corners of his eyes.

"Thank you, Baby. What did I do to deserve that compliment?" he asked.

"I just felt like telling you," I said, leaning in and kissing him on the lips.

"It smells like jasmine in here," he said.

"I was burning candles last night. I like to read by candlelight," I said, still rubbing his chest as I spoke.

"What were you reading?" he asked, taking my hand and placing it to his lips, kissing it ever so gently.

"*I Know Why the Caged Bird Sings* by Maya Angelou," I said, laying my head on his chest.

"I haven't read it yet. We have something else in common; we both like to read books," he said, opening his mouth trying to stifle a yawn with no success.

"I love reading books. I get to travel without going anywhere through an author's words. Pretend to be the character, gently let the sand run through my hands as I sit by the ocean, watch the waves if only in my mind," I said with a smile.

"Too bad you don't have a passport," he said. "We could catch a flight to the Bahamas so you could see what a real beach looks like."

"I've got a passport!" I replied excitedly as I lifted my head from his chest and sat up in bed. I know this may sound crazy but that was one of the first things I got when I started making money. I knew one day I would be going on a trip to some faraway island with blue water and palm trees, I just didn't know when. If you take me into the city, I can get Chloe to get it for me," I said.

"I'll book the flight, and then we can get in the shower," he said as he played with my breasts. "Call Chloe and tell her we should be there by 3:00 p.m. She should meet us at the entrance to the alley near 9th and Webster Street."

It was hard for me to concentrate but I dialed the number, hoping Chloe would be at my parents' and answer the phone; after all, it was her home away from home. "Hello. . .Hey, Chloe. I need you to get the key to the apartment out of the pantry. Go there and get my passport. It's in a metal box on the top shelf in the bedroom. My friend is going to bring me into the city. Meet us with the passport at 3:00 p.m. at the entrance to the alley near 9th and Webster Street.

"No problem. I'll be there," Chloe said.

I knocked his hand away and jumped out the bed. "Book the flight now, and then I'll come back to bed," I said as he looked at me and wagged his finger negatively.

"Sex is not negotiable. I'll make the arrangements after. Now come here."

O was quickly realizing he had a goldmine that he loved dipping his dick in, he liked to hear my pussy talk, listening for that snap, crackle, and pop. He was rock hard with my legs in the air so long I caught a cramp in my big toe and a Charley horse in my right calf. I suffered through the pain because he bought me so much pleasure.

To my surprise, Chloe was actually on time. She was hesitant as she walked toward the car as we pulled up, not recognizing the vehicle and not able to see inside because of the dark tint. I rolled the window down and she saw my face.

"Hey, girl!" she said with a smile as she handed me the passport through the passenger window.

"Chloe, this is O," I said, smiling right back, happy to see her.

"Nice to meet you," she said, peering into the car making sure to get a good look.

"You probably should get out of the neighborhood. Your dad was just pulling up to the house for a break. I'll talk to you when you get back," Chloe said.

"Cool," I responded. She turned to walk away and I called out her name.

"Chloe, please stay out of trouble."

"Yes, Mommy," she said in her usual flippant manner.

We both smiled as O put the car in drive and we headed back to the house. The traffic was flowing on Georgia Avenue. We rode right past the Shell Gasoline station at Georgia and Upshur with the standard red and yellow border. I watched a truck driver making a delivery bend over exposing his crack with no drawers, smiling to myself at the image until two teenagers ran up on him with guns pointed at his head.

"O, look they're robbing that guy!" I said in a high pitch voice.

"Not our business," he said and kept it moving. "Drivers for those companies get robbed all the time. They need to stop letting them carry money," he said.

"I guess you're right," I said.

I stared out the window, trying to forget what I'd just seen while I rolled the window all the way down, a warm breeze danced lightly on my cheeks. That helped. O continued down the avenue, right past the Wonder Bread Bakery. The smell of freshly baked bread was drawing me in as it always did since I was a child. Nothing like hot buttered toast with sprinkles of cinnamon and sugar on top. As he drove further down the Avenue I found myself watching a group of kids ranging in age from seven to twelve playing tag, darting into the street, mindless of danger, just not wanting to get caught, remembering those days as if it was yesterday. I giggled to myself as I watched an inexperienced dog walker entangled in the leash as barking dogs spun around her in confusion. A group of Howard University students with large afros and African print dashiki shirts were making a mad dash back to campus after grabbing a snack in between classes. O made a left at 7th and T and parked right in front of the Golden Que pool hall.

"Lock the doors. Don't get out of the car. I'll be right back," he said unbuckling his seat belt, opening the car door and stepping onto the curb.

The junkies were deep like frenzied ants on a chicken bone. There was no discrimination amongst the masses; everybody's money spent the same. A gentleman in a three piece suit coped his dope and kept it moving, disappearing off the block. To my right, I could see addicts lining the wall of an alleyway with their bodies slumped to the side; their heads would drop to their shoulder and then back up again in slow repeated movements, oblivious to any and everything around them, even the pool of vomit at the entrance of the alley stinking to high heaven. A disheveled man walked past the car, a little too close, I leaned to the left and moved my purse from my lap to the floor. His hands were swollen like catcher's mitts, with red watery eyes. He wiped the mucous from his nose with the back of his shirt sleeve smelling like day-old pee, tearing at his skin trying to find comfort for a never ending itch. Others were moving fast with hurried steps and broken conversation, trying to cop. A police squad car was parked in the distance, watching.

O exited the pool hall, walking briskly, holding a bag close under his arm.

"What's up, O?" I turned my head as I heard an older guy with mixed gray hair speak to O in passing.

"Hey, Moose," O said, acknowledging the gentleman.

He opened the car door, sat in the driver's seat, and buckled his seat belt while checking out his surroundings. We were back in traffic on our way to his house.

O pulled up the driveway and parked. He unlocked the front door and disarmed the alarm as we went inside. I put my Chanel bag down on the chair, another gift from O, as I followed him up the stairs. "Pack light. Only a few outfits for dinner. You'll be in a bathing suit, maybe a cover up, but the majority of the time your ass will be naked. What you don't have I can buy after we get there," O said as he left me in the second bedroom to go pack his own luggage.

The next morning, we were at the airport, our bags checked and waiting to board the plane. I was nervous as hell. Once we were seated, I fumbled with the seat belt, trying to exude a look of confidence where there was absolutely none to be had.

"You need some help, baby?" O asked with a smile.

"No, I'm good," I replied as I heard the buckle finally fasten and I tightened the strap. I lifted the window shade, sitting up in my seat, peering out. When the plane started to move down the runway, I quickly sat back, closed my eyes and said a prayer.

"Are you nervous? You seem a little edgy," O said.

I opened my eyes and replied, "No. . .Yes."

"Which one is it, baby?"

"Yes. I'm scared as shit!" I said squeezing his hand in mine and chewing even harder on the piece of spearmint gum in my mouth, so hard my jaws were beginning to hurt.

He held out his hand with his palm upturned without saying a word and waited for me to take the gum from my mouth and place it in his hand.

"You were working overtime on that gum," he said. "Didn't I see you fold some tissue and put it in your pocket earlier?" he asked.

I dug in the right pocket of my jeans and peeled off a single sheet, handing it to O while I stuffed the remaining tissue back inside of my pocket. O put the gum in the tissue and placed it in the back compartment of the seat in front of him.

"I decided to tell you the truth because I think we shouldn't lie to each other," I said as I looked into his eyes.

"Are you really going to be able to handle the truth? Women in general are such emotional creatures," he said as if he'd had this conversation before, just not with me.

"I think you should tell me the truth, and let me decide if I want to deal with the situation, whatever it may be. Give me the option," I said, really wanting to discuss this further.

"Would you like something to drink?" the flight attendant asked before O could respond.

"I'd like a rum and coke, and a ginger ale for the lady, please," he said, then turned his head toward me and pointed out the window.

"Look at those clouds," O said.

I turned not wanting to miss a single thing. I was taking snapshots with my eyes. We never got back around to that conversation.

I dozed off to sleep with my head on O's shoulder, awakened by sudden instability. I grabbed O's arm and held on for dear life. The captain came over the loudspeaker stating, "This is your captain. We hit some rough turbulence. I changed altitude; it took several attempts to get out of it. It's behind us now; my apologies," he said as if this was a normal mishap on a regular work day.

I was relieved to put my feet on solid ground and to know that I had a few days to put my first flight jitters behind me, take in the beautiful weather, walk barefoot in the sand and most of all enjoy being with O. I'd had him all to myself for almost a month and I wasn't ready to give him back to the streets.

O had a car waiting for us outside the airport. The gentleman looked to be around fifty with a beer belly and kind eyes. "Amber, this is Jonathan. He'll be our driver on this trip," O said as Jonathan tipped his hat at me and then placed our luggage in the trunk.

Our suite wasn't quite ready yet, so we walked to a café to eat lunch. The sun hit differently. Much hotter than back home. The sky began to turn dark right before we finished our meal.

"It's about to storm," I said, gathering my bag, nervously watching the sky.

"It's hurricane season. You're always taking a chance when you travel to the Caribbean during the summer and fall months. Hopefully, this will be a quick shower and dry up as if it never rained," he said while laying a tip on the table, placing the water glass on top of the money so it wouldn't blow away.

"Why didn't you tell me? We didn't have to take this trip now," I said, sounding a bit agitated.

"Calm your little ass down. This is what we do. Take chances. I've never been caught in a hurricane, at least not here in the Bahamas," he said nonchalantly.

We got to our feet and walked back to the front desk to check on our room with me watching the sky like a meteorologist. The woman behind the desk directed her welcome and all other conversation to O, looking deeply into his eyes as she handed him the key cards. I'm sure he received that type of behavior from the opposite sex a lot. I never even received a glance or a warm smile. We walked to the elevator with the porter dressed in a white polo shirt and blue khaki pants, a uniform seen throughout the resort, trailing behind with our luggage. I looked back and he winked with a mischievous smile. Now I understood; the women on the island didn't care for women from the States and the men were overly flirtatious. Once in the room, O tipped the young man, and I proceeded to walk out on the balcony; the sun was already erasing any sign of rain. I pulled my bathing suit from the carry-on bag while O stripped and laid across the bed, he obviously had other plans in mind other than taking me to the beach.

"Relax, baby. We've got plenty of time to go to the beach. Take off your clothes," he said once again as a demand not an 'ask'.

I glared in his direction as I disrobed, but became a willing participant. We christened every corner of the suite from the bathroom to the balcony, from the walls to the floor, the furniture in the sitting area including the closet which we left wide open and got busted by the maid, trying to slip in and lay chocolates on the bed. We neglected to place the "Do Not Disturb Sign" on the door. I was embarrassed. I could feel my cheeks begin to blush as she quickly glanced at the two of us twisted like a pretzel, dropping the chocolate on the floor, hurriedly leaving the room.

"Fuck!" I screamed, trying to push O off of me.

"Why are you so upset? I promise you she's seen worse. Besides, she doesn't know us. We'll probably never cross paths again, unless we see her tomorrow morning," O said laughing loudly. "I'll leave her a nice tip if that makes you feel better," O added, still laughing and shaking his head at my reaction.

"I'm getting in the shower; you can join me if you'd like, and then we're going to the beach! I want to see the sun set over the water," I said knowing I had given him all of me and now I just wanted to gaze out upon the blue water and feel a little piece of sun on my belly button.

The next morning, I left O sleeping in bed, while I showered, put on a black bikini and cover up, grabbed my bag off the chair along with a bottle of water and headed for the beach. I spoke to all the men along the walkway just for the sake of not being rude. I found a spot under a straw beach umbrella with a small white plastic table and two blue lounge chairs. I knew O didn't like to sunbathe as long as I did, so I wanted to get an early start.

I stared out at the blue water. It was as calming as the butterfly habitat back home. I watched a cruise liner heading into port, an older fishing boat advertising for a private cruise around the island, a small wooden pier a few yards away with a honeymoon couple walking hand in hand, the occasional splash as pelicans dive bombed for fish.

O finally found his way to the beach with a drink in hand. I looked up and said, "Baby, let's get something to eat. I'm starving. I was waiting for you; I didn't want to eat alone." I rose to my feet, pulled my black cover up over my head and grabbed my beach bag. I wasn't that hungry, but I knew he needed to eat before he was on to the next drink, especially in this hot sun. He was a grown man, but it was times like this that he needed me to think for the both of us.

We dined in a different restaurant, on the other side of the resort with a view of the water. The birds were pretty aggressive. Swooping down on a table next to ours before the dishes could be cleared, feasting on whatever snippet of food was left on the plates, then sitting back and watching our table. They would hop down to the cement floor and walk underneath searching for crumbs. I felt like I was being rushed to finish my meal. They knew exactly what they were doing. I ate quickly trying to shoo them away so O could eat in peace. I hoped tonight we would be eating indoors.

O made reservations for dinner each night, without any input from me. He'd been to Paradise Island on various occasions so I trusted his taste. I wore a white strapless linen dress with slits on each side and white gladiator sandals that O purchased in a boutique at the airport. Thank God these big ass titties were perky. O made me leave all my expensive jewelry at home. He bought me some costume jewelry in a store in downtown Nassau. Looking in the mirror, smiling at the image staring back at me, the white dress complimenting my tan, along with a set of white bangles, I applied just a little lipstick to match my rosy cheeks. I walked into the sitting area and O stared at me as if I was going to be dinner, making me blush and my nipples hard. I looked down at my chest slightly annoyed.

"Look what you're doing! Can you please stop?" I said covering my nipples with my hands.

He paused before speaking as if he was tongue tied. "I didn't say a word," he said slowly rubbing his bottom lip, still staring, just like the first night we met.

"We'd better go before we miss our reservation," I said as I reached for my purse.

"That might not be a bad thing," he said walking toward me, undressing me with his eyes. I slipped right past him and quickly headed out the door.

O ordered lobster for the both of us. "I don't even know if I like lobster," I said looking down at my plate, not used to someone ordering food for me, much less something I didn't eat. I stared at the white meat on top of a bright red tail with a piece of green garnish solely for decoration. It didn't look appetizing to me at all.

"Here, taste it," he said, dipping a small piece in melted butter. "Open your mouth," he said cupping the lobster with his hand underneath, bringing it closer to my lips. I was used to hearing those words; it usually didn't include food, at least not the kind you could eat. I opened my mouth, chewed for a few seconds then swallowed.

"Hmmm."

"This is good!" I said cutting a piece for myself and taking another bite.

"A long time ago, lobster was considered the poor man's meal. Referred to as the cockroaches of the sea. They would wash up on the shoreline and pile up for days. Lobster was so abundant that even the poor could buy it. They used it to feed the prisoners and slaves. During World War II, lobster's popularity drove up the price, reduced the abundance and is now considered a delicacy," he said.

"Really! Thanks for the history lesson. Why did I ever think that I wouldn't love this?" I said taking yet another bite.

This time, it was O sitting back and watching my every bite. His Rolex gleamed underneath the light of the moon. His persona exuded money. I knew his reputation but now I was seeing it up close and personal. Goosebumps ran rapidly along my arm. An anxiety attack was upon me. I wanted to run. But where was I going? I was in another country, far away from home. I shook my head to dismiss the thought, closed my eyes, and took slow breaths out of my nose.

"You okay, baby?" O asked as he reached for my hand.

I played that shit off like a pro. "I've never been better," I said as I looked into his eyes as he took another sip of champagne and sat back once again in his chair.

"What are you thinking about?" I asked.

"How pretty your eyes are under the candlelight," O said.

"Thank you," I said, still trying to get used to accepting compliments from him.

"You should eat before your food gets cold," I said as I looked away from his stare and back down at my plate.

"Would you like to try some champagne with that? Nothing like good champagne and lobster," he said, while removing the bottle from the ice bucket, pouring half a glass and handing it to me.

"I don't want to waste your money. I know that bottle is expensive. No thanks," I said, handing the glass back to him.

"Have it your way, baby. You're missing out on some good shit!" he said, sipping the bubbly and savoring his meal.

After finishing dinner, we walked outside the restaurant. Jonathan was waiting patiently outside to take us to our next destination. We drove for a few miles and then up into the hills to a glass house tucked away at the very top of the mountain with an astonishing view overlooking the island for a private gambling party. I looked at O thinking he had a lot of prestige not just at home but here as well. I wondered how far his reach extended. He won $5,000 on the craps table, handing it to me saying, "This is for you. Thanks for being my good luck charm."

O drank and gambled until well after midnight, barely escaping laying hands on a gentleman that looked my way more than once and for a few seconds too long. We left with a little nudging on my behalf. "No drama. We're on vacation. Please, baby," I said as I pulled him toward the car. This was the first time I saw a hint of jealousy.

We returned to the resort. While exiting the car O said, "Let's go for a walk on the beach." It was pitch black. I could only hear the waves roll in and slam against the beach, carrying the sand back out to sea. I removed my sandals and took his hand following him into the darkness. At this point, I would've followed him anywhere. He unzipped my dress, letting it fall to the sand as I stepped out of my panties. We made love using my dress as a blanket. He ravished my lips and punished my pussy. I felt so uninhibited as we switched positions under the stars until just before dawn. Our chemistry was undeniable; I never wanted to leave.

Our last day on the island was spent shopping in Nassau. We passed a jewelry store and O doubled back with me straggling behind. I was like a child in an ice cream parlor. Walking from case to case staring at the goodies inside.

"What's your birthstone, baby?" O asked.

"Sapphire," I said in response, still admiring the shiny objects in the glass cases.

"I'd like to see your diamond and sapphire necklaces please," O said to the saleswoman who had been eyeing him from the very moment we entered the store.

I looked at her and gave her a phony smile with my head cocked to the side, "Like yeah, Bitch, I'm with him." She returned with several necklaces on a navy-blue velvet cushion.

"Do you see one you like?" he asked, motioning to the cushion with his hand on the small of my back. His touch sent a shiver down my spine.

"May I try this one, please?"

I looked at the price tag, trying not to flinch. It was a beautiful blue sapphire and diamond eternity necklace. Looking in the mirror I held back my gasp. It was a statement piece.

O told the sales woman, "We'll take this one." He paid with a credit card. "I'll take the box, the paperwork and the receipt please. She'll wear the necklace."

"Thank you, baby," I said standing on my tiptoes, kissing him on the lips while reaching up, touching the necklace making sure it was safely draped around my neck. "You've been showering me with extravagant gifts; please allow me to buy you something," I said. I really wanted to show him how much I appreciated everything.

"Baby, I've got a rack of material shit I've acquired over the years. I don't want you to buy me anything. All I need is your love and your loyalty," he said as he touched my face and gently rubbed the bottom of my chin.

"So does that mean we're. . . ."

"Shhhhh," he motioned with his finger to his lips. I did just that.

When we returned to the hotel, he unclasped the necklace, removed it from around my neck, placed it back in the box, and asked the manager at the front desk if he would put it in the hotel safe. We got on the elevator and walked to the room, undressed, and put on our beach gear trying to soak up that last little bit of sun.

Later that night, after a candlelight dinner on the beach, we danced the night away at a local club in the city.

"Can you teach me how to salsa?" I asked when I heard that beat.

"Now?" he asked, looking confused and just a little tipsy.

"Yeah now," I said as I pulled him out on the dance floor.

"Follow my lead," he said.

The dance was so sexy, it was easy for me to go with the flow.

"You catch on quickly," O said as he turned me around and watched as I fell right back in step. He pulled me in close. Now it was me staring upward into his eyes with that look of wanting, needing to feel him inside me. He stopped dancing, took my hand, and led me off the dance floor saying in a low voice, "Let's go. We've got a plane to catch in a few hours and I doubt if we'll get any sleep.

4

Wake up, sleepy head. I'm taking you home today. I've got some business to take care of out of town. The honeymoon is over!" O said as he smacked me on my ass. I couldn't believe a month had gone by so quickly.

"You can pack those clothes and take them with you," he said while adding toiletries to his leather overnight bag.

"You putting me out?" I asked as a wisecrack, but was dead serious on the inside.

"I'll buy you some new outfits when I get back. Get in the shower, please; we need to leave soon," he said, glancing at his watch, moving about swiftly, but organized, as if he was checking off a list in his head.

I showered longer than usual trying to prolong our departure. By the time I got downstairs, O had the Jaguar sitting in the driveway outside the front door.

"Okay, Ms. A, you know the routine," he said as he walked toward me with the blind-fold in hand.

"You can't be serious!" I asked in utter dismay, throwing my hands in the air.

"I don't need you giving me a hard way to go. I don't have time for drama. I got a plane to catch! Get in the car and let me put this on you. We don't need you stepping on any more rocks," he said, trying to lighten the negativity in the air.

I got in on the passenger side while O put the suitcases in the trunk. He climbed in and proceeded to tie the blind-fold tightly in a knot. We drove in silence. I turned toward the window, closed my eyes and hoped for sleep.

He turned up the volume tapping his fingers on the steering wheel just to annoy me. War was singing the hell out of "Slippin into Darkness." Once again, I could hear the gravel under the tires as he pulled off to the side of the road. He leaned in to remove the blindfold placing it in the glove compartment next to the Luger. I stared out the window until we were back in the city.

"You can drop me right here on the corner at Webster. I'll walk from here," I said with a pinch of attitude.

"I don't get a kiss?" he asked, shaking his head.

"I'll catch you on the flip side. Be safe."

I switched up my demeanor and he took that thing a step further. I reached for the car door when I felt him grab my left arm squeezing hard.

"I need to share something with you before you get out of the car," he said.

"You need to let go of my arm. I bruise easy," I said with nothing but attitude.

He held on tighter. "You belong to me. I didn't realize that you were a diamond in the rough. I'm just beginning to mold you into that bad ass bitch that you think you are. I've opened up those holes, just for me. You're giving and receiving to my liking, but we're going to take this thing to another level. I've invested time in you. I'm not sharing you with anybody. Do you understand?" He spoke in a threatening manner. I was too mad to be scared.

"So, do you belong to me?" I asked sarcastically, knowing the answer.

"You ask too many fucking questions!" he barked with a disapproving look.

"Don't you need to catch a plane?" I said, pulling away from his grasp.

"You a feisty little thing; I like that about you, but don't overstep. I'll call you when I get back. I'll have my folks drop off that package. Let me be a gentleman and get the suitcase for you."

He opened the car door and removed the suitcase from the trunk and placed it on the curb. I watched him pull into traffic and disappear from sight. I was angry with myself, realizing that I may have fucked up my chances with O by displaying my immaturity.

I grabbed the suitcase and began to walk up the street when I saw Ms. Lola pull up to the curb.

"Get in," she said. Her tone was funky. I knew this wasn't going to be good. I opened the car door, placed the suitcase in the back, and climbed in the front seat.

"You've lost your motherfucking mind putting me in a trick bag with your father. You were at the beach with me? This right here is all about a man; you got that freshly fucked look, I can tell by your walk. I know I'm the last person to preach, but I've tried my best to keep you out of trouble. This man is going to break your heart forty-five ways going north! I know you think you're grown, but you're only fourteen!"

"I'll be fifteen soon," I said as if I was turning twenty-one and legal.

Ms. Lola shot me an icy glare. I realized that I better shut my mouth before she slapped the shit out of me like I'd seen her do the boys countless times over the years.

"You're not mature enough to handle what he'll do with your body and your mind. You've been playing house for an entire month! That dick is a motherfucker, ain't it? Have you speaking in tongues. By the way, nice tan," she said, as she pulled my top off my shoulder, laughing as she spoke. "I'm the wrong bitch for you to think you can pull the wool over my eyes. You're handling things for Fats and Desi, aren't you?"

I remained quiet.

"Look at me, Amber. I need an answer," she said.

"Yes," I responded with a sigh.

"I got eyes and ears in these streets. I'll try to keep you safe. All I can do beyond that is be here for you when this man fucks you around because it's going to happen," she said.

She paused from her rant to massage her temples, trying to fight off an oncoming headache.

"Don't ever make the mistake of using me in a lie to your father. That I won't tolerate. You need to tell this man your age, sooner than later. If your father finds out, he'll have his ass locked up for statutory rape. The other thing I won't do for you is tell Fats. I'm leaving that one all up to you. Get out. You can walk."

I opened the car door and retrieved the suitcase. Ms. Lola looped a u-turn and disappeared over the hill. I stood on the sidewalk trembling. "I'm not going to cry. I'm not going to cry." I repeated those words several times out loud, looking toward the sky and willing the tears back into my eyes.

"Hey, Mommy. I'm home," I said as I walked up the front steps.

"Who gives a fuck?" she said while sweeping the bushes with a broom and dustpan, wearing a green plaid wool dress, white long johns, a black and white striped blouse buttoned to the neck, a black beaded hat with a veil and white usher gloves. It was close to ninety-degrees; she was sweating bullets as if she was still working in the cotton fields. Her words cut today. I could feel myself going down that dark hole. I took a deep breath, looked around to see if anyone was watching, thinking to myself, *I'm going to take a bath, style my hair, dress, and hit the streets. The Young Senators are playing at the Knights of Columbus tonight. I'm going to the Go-Go so I can dance all these fucked up feelings away.*

I took a short bath; there was no relaxing today. Mommy was in rare form, having a heated argument with the voices in her head. I shampooed and blow dried my hair, applied lotion, and then put on a robe to get something to drink from the refrigerator. To my surprise, Daddy had unfrozen a quart of eggnog. I slowly poured the liquid into a red Styrofoam cup and returned to the bathroom.

It was taking me longer to style my hair. I wasn't quite satisfied with that one curl in the front; it just didn't lie right. Mommy kept coming to the bathroom door, now minus the long johns, but still layered, with a garbage bag over her head, fucking with me.

"You little bitch! You're such a whore! Fucking everything in the neighborhood with a dick!" she screamed. "I don't want to look at you!" she said as she slammed the bathroom door so hard the mirror shook and the red douchebag hit the floor.

I locked the door. She stood right outside hurling obscenities, banging on the door with full force. I took a sip of eggnog, trying to stay calm. I'd just got the front of my hair to lie perfectly. The banging stopped. I opened the door, peeped out, and moved quickly to my room where I dressed in record time. Mommy was in her bedroom, howling at the moon.

"I wish you would close that back door. Why do you always want the neighbors to hear you talking crazy?" I said flustered. "You need to take off some of those clothes before you have a heat stroke," I said, knowing it would set her off, but I said it anyway.

She jumped out of the bed, flew across the room and out the bedroom door, ripping the garbage bag from her face, exposing macerated skin, hollow eyes with dark circles, a contorted mouth, uncombed curls with a film on her teeth.

"You'll never find a man to love you like your father!" she said vehemently, pointing her finger in my face. It was like she put a spell on me.

"Mommy, I wish you would just leave me alone! I get so sick and tired of you berating me! I can't wait until I'm old enough to get my own place! I'm done with your lies!"

I turned the cup up to take a sip of the eggnog and Mommy hit the cup from the bottom. The eggnog splashed all over my face and traveled throughout the front of my hair dripping on my eyelids.

"Why did you do that? Do you know how long it took me to do my hair? Fuck!" I screamed, now irate.

Mommy ran back into her bedroom and came out swinging a pair of hedge shears high above her head coming straight for me.

"You won't disrespect me, bitch! Come here and let me see if I can cut that tongue out!" she yelled as she lunged toward me.

I let out a piercing scream, jumped the stairs two at a time, as I ran straight for Ms. Lola's house. Mommy stood on the porch laughing. This time, she didn't follow.

5

I'd finally decided to take that ride with Ms. Lola to tell Fats about O. It took a few days for me to get my nerves together. My leg shook as I waited for Fats to enter the visiting room. He walked straight toward me, paused to give Ms. Lola a hug and kiss, took a seat, and focused his attention on me.

"Hi, Fats. How are you? You look good! I just wanted to let you know that business is great!" I said nervously, letting the words quickly spill out my mouth, while ringing my hands in my lap.

"Ma, do you mind if I have a word with Amber? It won't take long," he said, not waiting for a response.

"Tell me about the business," he said while inching his chair closer with cold eyes.

"I worked out a deal with O and it turned out to be a very profitable one for us," I said, trying to avoid eye contact.

"Did you give up the pussy before or after the deal? I heard you were fucking the nigga. I get the news in here most times before it hits the street. I hope you're happy. Keep my money straight," he said while turning his chair to face his mother, ignoring me for the rest of the visit.

I sat quietly as I looked around the room at other inmates with their families, laughing, talking, and enjoying their time together.

My leg was jumping uncontrollably; I kept trying to keep it still with both hands. I finally gave up. I picked specks of lint off my clothing, investigated the polish on my nails for the fifth time, and made a mental note to point out to my nail tech that one of my designs was a little off center. I went from staring at the floor to watching the clock as Fats and Ms. Lola continued on with their visit as if I had disappeared into the paint on the walls. I felt worse than shit on the bottom of a shoe.

The visit finally came to an end. Fats hugged his Mom real tight, kissed her, and said, "See you later." He never said goodbye to me, exiting the visiting room without glancing in my direction. I was hurt, but what else could I expect? What I did know is that I would stay on top of his money. I couldn't help but wonder who gave him the news about O before me. Not sure I would ever know that piece of information.

"I was happy to see you smile, Ms. Lola," I said on the walk to the car.

"I don't like seeing you sad, Amber, but you brought this on yourself. I'm proud of you though! You put on your *Big Girl* panties and dealt with the situation. Now you can drive us home," Ms. Lola said, throwing me the keys.

"Gladly," I said, smiling, loving the feel of being behind the wheel of the sedan.

The day was getting away quickly. Sunset was arriving much faster than the day before. Fall was just around the corner. The last boat ride of the season was tonight on the Wilson Line to Marshall Hall Amusement Park. I purchased tickets for Chloe and myself months ago. If you were anybody in the know in DC, this is where you wanted to be. I got Ms. Lola to drop us off on Maine Avenue.

It was a social gathering waiting at the dock to board the cruise liner. I bought a special outfit, a white jacket and shorts, with tiny clusters of daisies and a white midriff top underneath, which showed off my abs. The finishing touch was the white platform sandals with thin spaghetti straps that neatly wrapped around my ankles and tied in a bow. My accessories were large white hoop earrings and bangles on my wrist. Chloe had on lime green hot pants with a lime green and white off the shoulder crop top and mule platform shoes. Our style and looks were very similar. People would often mistake Chloe for me or vice versa. Small groups of individuals began to tighten as more partiers arrived. The swell of the crowd became quite dense. I took Chloe by the hand and worked my way through the multitude of bodies, pretending to party as we moved closer to the boat.

Once on board, I bought Chloe a cocktail and a ginger ale for me. The loud and intrusive blast of the horn signaled our departure. An unknown band was the opening act for Chuck Brown. We found our way to the outside deck to watch the dock slowly fade from view. The brisk wind was harsh on our hairstyles so we went back inside. Chloe made a beeline to the ladies' room. I followed to get my hair in check. I could hear her snorting some sort of drug from outside the stall. She stepped out, sidestepping me, looking in the mirror, adjusting her top. I stepped right up beside her as other ladies entered, whispering in her ear, "Make sure you clean your nose." She went back into the stall, came out with toilet paper, wet it slightly and then circled the inside of her nostril. She crumpled the paper into a ball and then jumped into the air, from a bent knee position, saying, "swoosh," as if she just made a three-pointer. "Chloe looked back over her shoulder in my direction and said, "I'm ready." I just shook my head as I followed her out the door.

I saw many familiar faces from the Go-Go; in fact, that's what the crowd reminded me of, just a larger version on the water. I noticed three chics staring, pointing and having a lot of conversation while looking our way. I thought they might've been admiring our outfits, until the three started to approach. *Aww, Hell! Can't a bitch be cute without no drama?* I said in my head as I rolled my eyes, removed my earrings and placed them in my pocket.

"You that slut that's been fucking my man," the short woman with wide hips said shooting daggers in Chloe's direction. By now, the smack had kicked in. Chloe's knees were bent, her eyes were closed and she was beginning to nod. "I fuck a lot of men. What's his name?" she said slowly with that drug-induced drawl. "This bitch right here," I mumbled under my breath before laughing out loud, her honesty was like a double-edged sword. Her comment and my laughter only infuriated the women. I could see this wasn't going to be a fair fight, so I swung first. Chris always said, "Swing while they're selling wolf tickets." That's all it took. Complete pandemonium broke out! It was an all-out brawl. I'm waxing shorty; her wig was on the floor revealing crooked braids on her head and a ripped blouse exposing her bra. I looked up and some ladies from uptown were barefoot and wrecking right next to me. That's what I'm talking about! That Northwest solidarity. I didn't know their names, only their faces from the Go-Go. This right here was real sisterhood!

Security began to separate bodies; the band was forced to take a break. DJ found his way to us from the upper deck.

"You two okay?" DJ asked, surrounded by Fats' soldiers.

I looked around and said, "Damn! Ya'll deep! Wait a minute. Is anybody working?" I asked, thinking about my money.

DJ got close with his head down next to mine and mumbled, "We're working now."

"I should've known," I responded, smiling at his response.

The band started playing again and it was like nothing ever happened. We would be on high alert when the boat docked. Normally, I would ride at least one ride at Marshall Hall, but I decided to sit back and people watch after the events on the boat. Didn't want anyone walking up on us.

"DJ, do me a solid and keep an eye on Chloe. I'm going to get some funnel cake. You want some?" I asked as I walked away.

"No. I'm good." DJ responded following a big ass with his eyes, headed toward the line for the roller coaster.

I've tried hard as hell, time after time, to master eating funnel cake without getting the powder all over my hands and face, but was unsuccessful once again. It was so damn good, it was worth the mess as I wiped my hands and face with a paper napkin.

"Chloe, you want some?" I asked, shoving the cake under her nose.

"Girl, you know I do," she said.

I broke off a piece and handed it to Chloe. She chewed slowly in between nods. The horn began to blow. The three of us headed back to board the boat.

Chuck Brown didn't disappoint again. We partied all the way back to DC. DJ had a line of security front and back as we disembarked from the boat. It was like Moses parting the red sea. The three young ladies that started the ruckus were nowhere to be found. On the ride home, DJ lit a joint; we smoked a little, talked a lot, and Chloe, at last, could enjoy her high.

I got home to a letter from Chris, lying on my pillow. I read it out loud, four times, through teary eyes.

> August, 1, 1970
>
> Hey, kid!
>
> This letter is going to be short and sweet. Never thought I would miss your loud mouth and big head. This place is no joke! I find myself in the middle of a real war, still wondering why me? This shit is intense, always got to be on alert. Nothing like that bullshit on television.
>
> It's hot as fuck over here! I watched one of my friends slowly become unhinged under the pressure of war. He ran off under the dark of night. Disappeared. We found him the next day hanging upside down, gutted and burned. Enough of that shit.
>
> Mail from home could take as long as twenty-one days. You've got my address now, so no excuses about

writing. You know I've got to love your ass to do this shit! I hate writing, but I know you would worry if I didn't. You got your own war going on at home dealing with Ma. Stay strong. Stop worrying Daddy. He doesn't deserve that shit! Write back!

Love,

Chris

I decided to put pen to paper and write Chris back before it got too late. I wrote by candlelight.

August 31, 1970

Hey, Big Bro!

I was so happy to receive your letter today. I hope you are in survival mode over there in Vietnam and staying out of harm's way. Sorry to hear about your friend. Mommy and Daddy are as well as can be expected. Your mother is off her meds; need I say more? Every day is a new adventure. Daddy works until the wee hours of the morning. I know he needs the overtime to maintain with Mommy being sick and not able to work, but sometimes I think he would rather work than be home. I guess that's his way of escaping, like you and me with the streets.

Those fast ass women are hunting me down to get info on you. You have to tell me who I can give the real skinni to. I'll write again soon. Sorry for the delay. I got caught up. Stay safe.

Love you,

Amber

The following morning Chloe and I went shopping for outfits for the first day of school. We caught the DC Transit bus on Georgia Avenue and got off at 7th and F Street downtown.

Those were some pretty long blocks walking from 7th Street to Garfinckel's Department Store at 14th and F. Thank God for the breeze. This particular store catered to an upscale clientele. Mommy hated Garfinckel's, and refused to shop there because she said they were racist.

We entered the store and casually browsed, stopping at the fragrance counter, sniffing several perfumes. Then, we rode the elevator exiting on the 3rd floor. Chloe didn't waste any time walking straight to an outfit she saw on a mannequin, finding the pieces, ducking down behind a concrete pole and stashing an outfit in her oversized bag. I took at least six outfits to the dressing room to try on, even stepped out looking for Chloe for her opinion, but she'd left the floor. Returning to the fitting room, I rolled one of the outfits real tight and stuck it in my panties under a cotton tent shirt. I observed myself in the mirror making sure everything was copacetic. I returned the unwanted items to the rack and walked toward the elevator. I was gliding as I strolled down the aisle on the first floor, past the fragrances, looking down my nose at anyone who cared to look back as I exited the store.

Chloe was sitting outside on a bench, waiting. We walked together up G Street, talking about anything and nothing. I wanted a piece of strawberry shortcake from the Blue Mirror. Who in their right mind could walk past that window with a display full of nothing but strawberry shortcakes adorned with the biggest strawberries I've ever seen, just beckoning us to come inside? It was too tempting to resist.

We sat down at a table near the back of the restaurant and placed our order.

"Let me borrow your bag, Chloe," I said already on my feet. I went to the ladies' room to remove my outfit from under my clothing and placed it in Chloe's bag. She'd made out like a bandit. Her ass was good at boosting; that's how she supported her habit in-between random men getting her high.

We couldn't eat all the cake. I stopped our waitress as she walked by, "Excuse me. Could we have the check and take out boxes please?"

"You sure can, young lady! I'll be right back!" she said as she headed to the kitchen with an arm full of dirty dishes.

We walked toward the cashier, a friendly woman with silver hair and ruby red lips, sitting on a stool behind the cash register, talking with a customer. I pulled out a wad of money to pay the check. I had more than enough to pay for the outfit that I stole plus the ones that Chloe took as well, but why should I? Apparently someone in that store had mistreated my mommy. This was the best way I knew how to get them back—hit them in their pockets; besides, it was a hell of a rush.

We walked back up F Street, past Rich's Shoe Store and Woodward & Lothrop Department Store. We passed by a small storefront with a purple neon sign that read "Fortune Teller" with a hand in the middle, a star on the right and a moon on the left. "Psychic Readings" was displayed underneath in red writing. It looked as if it didn't belong on the block.

"Chloe, I think I want to go inside and have my palm read," I said, peering inside the glass door.

"Why do you want to do that shit? You know that gypsy is going to tell you lies, and take your five dollars. You can give that to me if you're just trying to give your money away," Chloe said, still walking.

"No seriously, Chloe; I'm going inside," I said.

"I'll wait for you out here," Chloe turned and walked toward a wooden bench, took a seat, crossed her leg, and rolled her eyes in my direction.

I opened the door and stepped inside, as a bell rang above the door, of a dimly lit room. A thin woman in her early fifties with long dark hair and large dark eyes opened the curtains wide and stepped into the room.

"How can I help you?" she asked as she looked me up and down.

"I'd like to get my palm read please," I said watching the woman go around the room lighting candles one by one, leaving the four candles on the table for last. She wore a coin head scarf that outlined her forehead down past her cheek bones, a black baggy shirt with a skirt that dragged on the floor as she walked, large gold hoop earrings, a snake bracelet that wrapped up her arm to her elbow, and rings with stones on each finger.

"You can have a seat," she said with a slight accent, waving her hand like a magician.

I sat at the round table, covered with an old faded tablecloth. I stared into the crystal ball as if I could see into the future and fought off the urge to touch the tarot cards. I looked around the room at the burgundy and gold décor. There was an antique wall clock that had stopped running. The wall paper clashed with the Persian rug, which sat on top of a dark hardwood floor scarred from time, and the curtains were busy but in the same color scheme. Everything clashed. There was a strong smell of sage. I found myself wondering why I was here.

She took a seat across from me, lifting the crystal ball gently in the air so as not to disturb the burning candles and set it down to her left. "Give me your hand," she said with her hand outstretched. I placed the five-dollar bill on the table. She slid the money across the table and placed it in her pocket and then ran her thumb across the lines of my palm.

"This long line here represents success and money. You will receive a large amount of money in the near future. You are with child and you will marry your child's father. The marriage will end badly," she said, holding my hand tightly and staring into my eyes, wanting to reveal more. My blood ran cold. I pulled away from her grasp, jumped to my feet, knocking the chair to the floor as I fled the room.

"Come on, Chloe," I said, walking fast in spite of the extreme heat.

"So what did she tell you about your future?" Chloe asked, trying to catch up.

"Some bullshit! You were right. I could've saved my money," I said, still feeling a little shaken.

By the time we arrived at 7th Street, I was hot, tired, and reliving the fortune teller's words in my head, trying to focus on anything else but that. I looked down and spotted a nice shiny penny face up on the ground. I thought of the old rhyme Mommy would say quite frequently, "See a penny, pick it up, and all the day, you'll have good luck." I picked it up and put it in my pocket. The bus was taking forever as if it were running on a Sunday schedule. Chloe spotted a victim. A woman trying to hail a cab. When the driver pulled to the curb, Chloe stepped right up next to her and opened the door for the woman. As she turned her back to place her shopping bags in the backseat of the cab, Chloe reached into the woman's shoulder bag and slipped her wallet out stealthy and proficient. I took my eyes off Chloe just as I saw a bus driver in my peripheral vision, step off the bus, leaving it running, while he took a smoke break.

"Chloe, he left that bus running," I said as she walked back toward the bus stop with a devilish smile. I knew what to do. I'd watched the bus operators while sitting in the seat right across from the driver out of complete boredom. We jumped on the bus, closed the door, Chloe dove on the floor, and I took off up the Avenue slumped down in the seat, with the bus operator running behind us, screaming and waving his hands, "Stop! Somebody stole my bus!"

I knew I needed to get off the Avenue. An angry group of teenagers threw rocks and bottles at the bus as we rode right past the bus stop. I made a left at the next light and headed to 11th Street, hoping that there would be less traffic and I could maneuver a little faster. We cut through the neighborhood and made it to 14th and Upshur with me barely avoiding hitting several side view mirrors. I pulled over to the curb and jumped off the bus before the police rolled up on us. We cut through the alleys, staying off the grid until we made it to the house. Once there, we changed clothes and hairstyles, just to be safe.

Daddy was watching the evening news, eating a half-burnt meal prepared by Mommy. I sat in his face, waiting for him to lift the fork.

"Are you really going to eat that?" I asked, thinking this was way too much of a sacrifice for love. I didn't know what was worse—the burnt meal at dinner or the runny eggs for breakfast. He never answered as he scooped the food in his mouth and began to chew. When Mommy was sick, she burned everything she cooked. She was always annoyed by the voices and the distraction would cause her to burn the food.

I had fond memories of Mommy being an excellent cook, just not to Chris' and my liking. She would prepare roast beef with the blood drowning the platter as Daddy carved the meat. It looked as if it could just grow legs and get up and walk away from the table. Chris and I would hurriedly push each other out the way to get to the kitchen and throw the meat in a frying pan to brown on both sides until there was no sign of blood.

"You children have no idea how this roast should be eaten," Mommy would say irritated with our behavior.

"That might be true, but you can save this roast for those rich folks you work for; they must like it this way, but not us," Chris would say responding to her outrage.

Daddy turned his attention back to the news and away from me. "Well, will you look at this? Someone stole a D.C. Transit bus from downtown today and left it up here in this neighborhood. Folks got a lot of nerve!" He went right back to eating the burnt food. My eyes darted from the news back to Daddy. I didn't utter a word.

6

It was well after sunset when I called DJ to pick me up from the house to collect money from several locations, with money still in circulation.

"You awfully quiet," I said, noticing DJ's demeanor was serious, as if he had a lot on his mind.

"Amber, you know I've become very attached to you since Fats and Desi went in. You're like a sister to me, although I respect the fact that you're my boss," he said solemnly.

"DJ, say what's on your mind. Are you trying to work for somebody else? Do you need more money? You're valuable to me. Name your price," I looked in his direction waiting for his demands.

"Amber, it's nothing like that. You pay me real good. The bonuses are nice. I've been holding on to this for a week now. I'm just going to say it and get it out there. I saw O with an older woman. They didn't look like casual acquaintances. They were having a heated argument. He was pissed. Can't tell you much more than that because I didn't want to be seen. I got a feeling in my gut. I want you to be careful," DJ said, with concern.

"What do you mean be careful?" I asked, starting to feel butterflies in my stomach.

"Not business wise. He's been solid with that. I know you have feelings for the man. Think with your head and not your heart. That's all I'm asking," DJ said, looking briefly in my direction and then back at the road.

"Thanks, DJ. Good looking out. You always got my back," I said feeling hurt and confused, trying to mask my feelings with an upbeat response.

I hadn't heard a word from O since the day he'd dropped me on the corner. I thought he was still out of town. This mother-fucker is back in DC and seeing another woman. I belong to him. Guess I'm going to have to show his ass. Now I was the one who was quiet for the rest of the ride.

"Pull over. I'm not feeling good," I said, opening the car door while still in motion, emptying my stomach on the pavement with what was left of the strawberry shortcake.

Upon arriving home, I went straight in the house, moved the chair and area rug and put Fats and Desi's share in the safe underneath the floor. I needed to go to bed. I had a full day of school the next day and I felt really tired.

*　　*　　*

Chloe knocked on the door at 8:00 a.m. sharp.

"You ready?" she asked, looking real cute in her yellow sundress and white sandals, admiring herself in the full length mirror and checking me out at the same time.

"You look cute! When did you get that outfit?" I asked, thinking I knew everything in her wardrobe.

"I bought this with some of the cash that I found in the wallet I lifted yesterday," she said nonchalantly while still modeling in the mirror.

"You look a little pale. Put on some blush and lipstick," she said, looking back, giving me the side eye.

"I didn't sleep well last night," I answered, knowing that wasn't my only dilemma.

I went upstairs to fix my face. I came back down with my books in hand.

"Let's go!" I said, trying to sound enthusiastic.

"There you go!" she said with a wide grin as we headed out the door and down the street to school.

Chloe and I had different schedules, so we'd make sure to hook up at lunch. There was a new guy in my class, a transfer from Western. He kept looking my way. He was tall, slim with pretty hair and keen features. We kept flirting from across the room.

"Ms. Hayden. Could you turn to page twenty-eight and join the rest of the class?" Ms. White, my new English teacher, asked sternly, looking over her glasses directly at me.

"My apologies, Ms. White. I'm turning now!" I said looking back at the cute guy with a smile.

The 3:00 p.m. bell sounded. I was so ready to leave the building. Chloe left school early, hooking already. No sooner had I walked down the steps than I could feel his presence. O was parked in a white convertible Mercedes. I recognized the car. He parked just far enough away from the school so that he could sit and observe. I walked right up to the car, thinking inwardly, *I might as well get this shit over with.* I opened the car door and sat in the passenger seat.

"Look at you! Got on a *Big Boy* suit. Very impressive," I said, wanting to feel the material, but Mommy taught me that was rude, so I held back on my impulses.

He looked at me suspiciously from behind his dark glasses. He reached up and removed his shades so that I could see his eyes as he spoke while laying them on the console.

"Why didn't you tell me that you're still in High School? How old are you?" he asked with a confused look.

"I'm fourteen!" I said, overly confident.

He stared at me with skepticism before speaking. "When were you going to tell me? Do you know I can get locked up for fucking with your ass?" he asked, more of a statement than a question, sounding quite agitated. O had a way of talking with his hands. I tried not to get caught up in his hand gestures and follow the conversation; he was on the verge of his temper flaring.

"I was going to tell you when you got back in town and called. I heard you were back and had to go see your woman. So here I am and I'm telling you now! My age has nothing to do with the business. We won't be fucking anymore, so you don't have to worry about getting locked up behind me. You got some other pussy, so we can call this a wrap!" I said with a hard cutting motion against my neck. "No worries."

I reached for the car door and once again O grabbed my left arm, holding on real tight.

"Somehow, this right here seems real familiar," I said pointing to my arm with my index finger, giving him a nasty look. "Isn't this how we left off the last time I saw you? Let go of my arm!" I screamed as I pulled away. I was furious and could feel my ears begin to redden. I could see his eyes darken.

"Amber, I caught a case. My attorney thinks that it will look better to the judge if I have a wife," he said.

"And you're saying that to me to say what?" I responded sarcastically.

"We need to get married," he said with a straight face. I started laughing hysterically.

"I knew you weren't woman enough to do this bid with me," he said, shaking his head and staring out the car window.

"What the fuck does that have to do with anything you're asking right now? Are you facing jail time?" I asked in a questioning manner.

"It looks that way. Amber, I need you," he said, almost pleading.

"We don't even know each other," I said.

"I know that I love the way you make me feel. Tell me that you don't feel the same way?" he said, staring into my eyes.

I sat there, chewing on my bottom lip, stopping just short of drawing blood. "How do we make this happen? I'm too young," I said, not believing the words that were spilling out of my mouth.

"Can you ask your mom to sign at the courthouse?" he asked with a glimmer of hope in his eyes.

"Why aren't you asking your woman to marry you? That would be a hell of a lot easier, wouldn't you say?" I couldn't stop with the sarcasm, nor did I want to.

His mouth started to open but he stopped himself before answering, not that he had to get his thoughts together, but to refrain from losing his temper.

"First, she's not my woman. Second, she's a business associate with benefits. Third, I don't love that bitch. I love you! Are you going to do this or what?" he said, sounding perturbed.

"I need time to think about this," I said, rubbing the back of my neck and staring off into the distance.

"I don't have time! This shit needs to happen like yesterday!" he said, raising his voice, loud enough to make several students walking by take notice and look back toward the car. I sat quietly playing back the conversation in my head, hypnotized by the murmuration of hundreds of starlings gliding through the sky, bobbing and weaving in formation with such grace. A few birds broke off from the phenomenon landing on a telephone wire. There was a hierarchy taking place. I watched as the birds moved over or traded places. Four together, two apart. Then there was the General perched at a distance, watching over his soldiers.

"Amber. What are you going to do?" he asked.

I turned and looked at him, long and hard before answering. "Are you going with me to ask Mommy?" I asked.

"That's my girl," he started the car and we headed toward the avenue.

O found a parking space in the middle of the block. Lucky for us, it was early afternoon and most of my neighbors were still at work. Everyone on the block was very territorial about their parking spaces that didn't even belong to them for real. It was a matter of respecting one another to keep the peace.

I could hear Mommy's voice as soon as we stepped out of the car. She was sitting in the swing, singing "Nobody Knows the Trouble I've Seen" an old spiritual hymn, as if she was singing lead in the church choir. She was wearing a teal blue top and was naked as a jay bird from the waist down.

"O, I need you to hold up for a few minutes!" I said turning to face him, extending my arms out in front of me, fingers spread wide. "Let me get her in the house and dressed. Do you mind facing the street? If you see all that ass, you'll never hit the number!" I said, trying to make light of the situation.

He smiled and turned toward the street as I requested.

"Mommy, come with me inside the house please. I have someone I want you to meet, but you've got to put on some clothes first. You want to show him how much of a lady you are, right?"

She got up from the swing, never missing a note, with me shielding her backside with my body.

Fifteen minutes later, we stepped out of the front door onto the porch. O was sitting on the swing, fidgeting and looking out of place. "Mommy, this is O. I've been spending a lot of time with him and have come to love him deeply. We would like your permission to get married. I need you to come with us to the courthouse and sign the paperwork please." I prayed she wouldn't say no.

"This your beau?" she asked checking O out from head to toe.

"Yes, Mommy; he's my boyfriend."

He rose from the swing and extended his hand to introduce himself.

"Hello, Mrs. Hayden. I'm Anjelo Jones," he said politely.

To my surprise, she shook his hand.

"Let's be on the way. Need to get you married before these nosey ass neighbors see that you're pregnant," she said.

"How did you know?" I asked, completely flabbergasted.

"You got that glow," Mommy said, now frantically searching in her purse.

"Amber, you're pregnant?" O said looking bewildered, slowly sitting back down on the swing.

"We'll talk about that later," I said, not prepared to deal with such a sensitive subject at this particular moment.

"Wait just one minute! I forgot my handkerchief," Mommy said, spinning around heading back into the house.

I walked to the swing and sat down next to O. He placed his hand on my stomach. We looked in each other's eyes acknowledging his baby growing inside me. "Let me go check on her, she'll change her mind at the drop of a hat." I went in the house and saw Mommy hang up the phone abruptly, looking like a naughty child caught in the act. She pushed past me heading for the front door with her black pillbox hat sitting dead center on the top of her head and her handkerchief in hand.

"Let's go before she stops cooperating," I said to O as he quickly rose to his feet.

"Mrs. Hayden. Please allow me to escort you to the car," O said, taking her arm in his. Mommy was all smiles as she switched those hips from side to side while walking down the steps. She looked back at me and said, "I like him, Amber. He's got manners."

"Baby, can you put the top up please? I don't want to look like I've been in a whirlwind by the time we get to the courthouse," I said feeling a little nauseous.

"No problem, baby," he said, looking at me through the rearview mirror, smiling, while he closed the top of the convertible.

We were just about done with the courthouse ceremony. I was repeating the vows, "I take you, O, to be my husband, to have and to hold, from this day forward; for better, for worse, for richer, for poorer, in sickness and in health, to love and to cherish, till death do us part."

"If anyone can show just cause why this couple cannot lawfully be joined together in matrimony, let them speak now or forever hold their peace."

"I object!" My father shouted loud enough to wake the dead. No sooner had he stood and objected, that Mommy pulled him by the coattail hard, making him fall awkwardly back down into the seat.

Mommy rose to her feet and said, "You can proceed with the ceremony. She's pregnant; they love each other. This will happen today!"

"No objections!"

The clerk waited a few minutes longer just to make sure there were no more interruptions. "I now pronounce you man and wife. You may kiss your bride."

We kissed briefly. I took O by the hand and led him to my parents.

"Daddy, I know you aren't happy with me, but I promise you that we love each other and we're going to raise this baby together. Anjelo, this is my father, Mr. Hayden," I said.

"Nice to meet you, Sir," O said with utmost respect.

Daddy ignored his remarks, taking Mommy by the arm and damn near dragging her out of the courthouse.

"Congratulations!" was heard by all before Mommy exited the building. "Welcome to the family!"

"Love on a Two-Way Street" by The Moments was playing on the radio as we headed uptown in the opposite direction from his house.

"I'm going to have to drop you off for a couple of hours. I got something that needs my attention pronto. I've got to find a pay phone," he said looking from one side of the street to the other. "I know you don't want to go to your parent's house."

"You can take me to DJ's mom's. She's always happy when I drop in and the kids love to see me too! She never turns down the ducketts I put in her hand when I leave. She talks two tons of shit and makes me laugh. I'll stay there until you're ready to swing back and get me," I said looking at him affectionately.

"I couldn't have asked for a better wife," O said with a slight smile.

"The jury is still out on that one," I said laughing mischievously.

"Make a left on Euclid. I'll get out on 14th," I said.

I scribbled the house number on the back of a vendor card. "Call me when you're ready. You can pick me up right here."

His look was one of concern. "No worries. I'll get the kids to walk me." I blew him a kiss as I got out of the car. "See you soon."

O picked me up about three hours later. I was gliding down the block on a skateboard, my hair blowing in the wind with the kids running beside me, trying to keep up, carrying rocks, sticks and bottles prepared to fight off the oversized rats darting in and out from between the cars. I assured them that their arsenal wouldn't be needed but I couldn't convince them to leave them in the yard. I guess they knew better than me, living in the neighborhood for most of their lives. O stared in disbelief as I jumped off the skateboard and gracefully walked to the car, smoothing my hair.

"Bye, Miss Amber!" all six kids said in unison.

"Bye, babies!" I said, opening the car door and sitting in the passenger seat.

"Please don't do that anymore. You're pregnant, I don't want you to fall," he said with a stern look, while driving up 16th Street making a left on Allison.

"You know I'm spontaneous with my thoughts and my actions. I went home with you didn't I? Didn't ask permission, didn't check your references, and you could've been a serial killer. I'll stay off the skateboard if that makes you feel better," I said teasingly.

We were now on Blagden Avenue heading into Rock Creek Park. I thought I knew the park, but he was making some unfamiliar turns as he pulled into the driveway of a house back up in the cut. A black cat crossed our path as he drove into the garage. I had a look of anxiety on my face.

"What's wrong?" O asked.

"You saw that black cat?" I asked with concern.

"Don't tell me you're superstitious?" he questioned with a laugh. "We're not letting anything ruin this day," he said, getting out of the car and opening the door for me. I tried to shake it off as best as I could, but it was a sign. There was a silver BMW and an army green Range Rover parked in the garage.

"I know you're going to let me push that Range!" I said with excitement and a gleam in my eyes.

"Let's work on getting you a driver's license first," O said. "Now, close your eyes and turn around and face the wall," he said.

"Damn, you got me feeling like the St. Valentine's Day Massacre up in this piece," I said jokingly.

"Woman, stop playing and do as I say," he said as he laughed out loud. I could hear him open a door.

"Keep your eyes closed and turn toward my voice." He then picked me up and carried me into the entrance and up the stairs. This time, I was really being carried over the threshold. "Kick off your shoes." I could hear them bounce on the hardwood floor. "Keep your eyes closed until I tell you that you can open them," he said as he put me down. My feet began to sink in the shag carpet. "This is for you, baby. You can open your eyes now," he said.

The lights were dim. There were votive candles with red rose petals lining the pathway to the bed neatly arranged on the gray comforter in the shape of a heart. Red balloons were in the corner. A tray with two glasses, a bottle of Hennessy, a ginger ale, a bowl of strawberries, and whipped cream sat next to the heart.

"Baby, this is so special. So, this is your house too?" I asked looking around the room at the contemporary furniture from Scan.

"Yes. I stay here when I'm too tired to take that drive," he said uncomfortably not used to answering questions.

"You're full of surprises," I said with a closed smile.

"I got you something I think you'll like."

O walked to the bed and retrieved the ring box from under the pillow then turned and walked back to me as he placed it in my hand. I stared at the unopened box. "Open it!" he said, wondering about my hesitation. I opened the box, which held the most unique marquise and round diamond cluster wedding ring. O took the ring out of the box and slipped it on my ring finger. I couldn't hold back the tears. He slowly kissed the tears away, finding my lips, we shared a passionate kiss.

"How did you pull this off in such short notice?" I asked.

"I know people," he said with a half-smile. "I'll be right back. I got one more wedding present."

O left the bedroom. I could hear his footsteps on the stairs. I sat on the bed holding my hand out at reach, admiring my ring, smiling at the thought of being "Mrs. Jones." O returned with a package under his blazer. I heard a whimper and rose from the bed and walked toward the sound. "This little one's for you, to keep you company when I'm away." O handed me the most precious gray puppy with a big red ribbon tied around his neck.

"I don't even know what to say. Thank you, baby," I said through quivering lips.

"I already named him Zeus," O proclaimed holding my gift high in the air.

"You love the stars and Greek mythology as much as I do. I thought it only fitting that he be named after the god of the sky."

"I love the name!" I said reaching for my puppy.

"He's a Cane Corso. I got him from an associate in Italy. Zeus is going to be a big dog. He'll have to be trained to listen to commands; otherwise, he'll run this house, and I can't have that. Only one alpha male resides here," O said in a serious tone.

"I'm going to get in the shower," I said, handing Zeus back to O. "Hold my other baby for me please."

Zeus snapped at O's finger.

"He's trying me already," O said as he smacked the crown of his head.

"He's my protector, just doing his job," I said just like a proud mama. We both laughed as I headed for the shower. "I won't be long."

I showered quickly, wanting and needing to get back to my husband to consummate our wedding night. I was singing in the shower although I couldn't carry a note, but I was on a natural high. I dried off with an oversized bath towel and applied lotion. I came out of the bathroom to find O sitting on the side of the bed with a glass of liquor poured next to him on the nightstand, nodding, with Zeus at his feet. My first inclination was that he was tired. Then I watched him lift his head with some effort to slowly begin to nod again. I'd seen Chloe do the exact same gesture night after night.

"O, are you high?" I asked with a confused look. He opened his eyes, while scratching his head.

"Amber, I just took a little hit to take the edge off. I got a lot on my plate," he said as his eyes closed; this time, his chin almost touched his chest.

"Is this something I should be worried about?" I asked with concern.

"Come lay down," he said while pulling back the covers. He was good at evading answers. I climbed in bed. "You smell good. I want to eat your pussy." He was already in motion, his head between my legs, all about his work until the motion abruptly stopped.

"Baby. Anjelo," I called his name as I touched the top of his head. Still no movement. "O, I know damn well you didn't nod out while eating my pussy! What the fuck!" I screamed while pushing his head back and rolling him over on the bed. Zeus was startled and ran underneath the bed. I got down on my knees and called his name. "Zeus. Come here boy. I didn't mean to scare you," I said as I grabbed him by his paws and pulled him out from under the bed. I carried him to the bathroom, looked at my image in the mirror, speaking out loud to Zeus, "Hell of a wedding night. I love that man so much, but what in God's name have I gotten myself into?" I said to Zeus, as I looked into his eyes as if he could answer back.

*   *   *

Zeus was growing like a weed. O had his ears cropped, the healing process went well; his tail was already docked when he got him. O said if he got in a fight with another dog, he wouldn't have those floppy ears to grab on to so easily. I took him to the vet to get all his shots. I walked him every day unless it was inclement weather. I took him to the shopping mall so he could get used to crowds. The sounds of loud trucks scared him; he would dive behind me and shiver. We would sit on my parents' porch and observe the cars and trucks as they went up and down the busy street. He stopped hiding from the loud noises and began to bark instead. He was finally responding to his name. O or I would call him from different sides of the room and he would look toward our voices. He learned the command to sit easier than stay. I would go up the stairs and make him wait at the bottom, and then give him a treat if he waited for me to come back down the stairs. Zeus stayed between our house, my parents, and DJ's mom's. I wanted him to socialize with the kids. That was important because I was going to be bringing a new addition home to the family soon. He would no longer be the baby.

Mommy was back to her deceptive ways, pretending to take her medication, holding it in the back of her mouth and spitting it out when no one was looking. I put the key in the front door and she was having a frantic argument with the voices in her head. She was sitting on the couch, with Zeus lying in her lap.

"I told you motherfuckers before. I've taken this trip around the world too many times to be fooled by you. No, you keep wanting to fuck with me. I'm smart! You can kiss my ass. That's what you can do! Don't come near me! I'll fuck you up! Stay right where you are!" I could see she was getting more agitated by the minute. "Stop right there!" Zeus looked up at Mommy as if she was talking to him and began to whimper. "I got something for you. I said stop!" Mommy threw Zeus from her lap to the floor as if she was discarding an old rag doll.

"Ma, don't throw my dog!" I said scooping Zeus into my arms.

"Bitch, you can take that little bastard out of here with you," she said as she rose to her feet and ran to the kitchen.

She returned with a butcher knife in hand, cutting through the air as she walked purposely stabbing at the hallucination right in front of her.

I got out of her way, but said as a plea, "Mommy, please put the knife down." I'd witnessed this behavior many times before but each and every time I never knew how it would play out. I always believed that she would never hurt me, but I knew not to get too close. She released the knife. I watched it slide across the hardwood floor as she abruptly turned and walked toward the couch, sitting down hard on the cushions.

"You lay down with dogs, you get up with flees," she said, staring in my direction.

"Are you talking to me or the voices?" I asked, not wanting to ignore her.

"You'd know if I was talking to you. I'd call you by your name, bitch!" she said through clenched teeth.

"My name is Amber. You don't have to keep calling me that." I was preparing myself for a verbal war with my mother.

"I know what the fuck your name is. I gave you that name. I like bitch better. Come, Zeus!" she said while hitting the palms of her hands on her lap. My dog jumped out of my arms and into

her lap. I'd call Daddy first and then make that dreaded call to
her doctor.

7

It was now December and the hawk was showing no mercy as we left school buttoning our coats and wrapping wool scarves around our necks. The sudden downpour made the air seem frigid. Chloe and I scrambled to get our umbrellas out of our bags.

I looked up as I heard a horn blow. "Hey, Amber! You and Chloe want a ride?" DJ asked, slowing down the black Dodge Charger he was driving.

"We'll pass," I said, answering for the both of us, not recognizing the car. DJ was prone to stealing cars when he couldn't borrow one from a friend or relative. He refused to spend his money on an automobile when he could just as easily steal one. I was hoping in the near future that I would be able to talk him into making a sound purchase with all that money he was making.

"Damn, Amber, why couldn't we catch a ride to get out of this rain? It's cold!" Chloe said, not happy with my decision.

"I don't know where he got that car. I've got more than myself to think about these days. I'm not just taking chances for no good reason," I said walking a little faster.

"I knew your ass was pregnant! We were coming on our period at the same time and then you just stopped. I had to buy my own tampons," Chloe said.

"You need to buy your own anyway!" I said.

"Well, it looks like I don't have a choice now," she said and we both laughed.

We continued to walk. "Amber, does O think he's your first?" Chloe asked, staring in my direction waiting for an answer.

"I don't know. The subject never came up," I said cool as a cucumber.

"I saw you and Fats on Halloween night."

"What do you mean you saw us?" I was shocked by her statement but was listening intently.

"I followed you two after Fats snatched your bag of candy and you went flying after him," she said.

I was quiet, allowing myself to think back to that night.

"Look at that shit! It's a full moon. Motherfuckers lose their mind every time it shows its face. Not a good sign," I said as we turned the corner at the top of the hill.

"You're always talking about that old folk's shit! It's Halloween! Lighten up! We're going to fill our bags to the brim. I know all the houses to hit first. Just follow me," Chloe said, already climbing the steps to old man Pritchard's house. For once, Chloe was right. We headed home with bags so heavy we could hardly carry them.

We were both in good spirits now. I had my head down deep in the bag looking for a 'Baby Ruth' when Fats ran up on me, snatched my bag and took off like a flash toward New Hampshire Avenue. "Fuck no! I worked too hard for that candy!" I screamed as I took off with a burst of speed, crossing the Avenue with my eyes on Fats, darting into the street without looking. A car slammed on brakes with tires skidding. I never broke stride. Fats ran into Rock Creek Cemetery hiding behind the Davidson headstone. I'm sure he thought I would never follow him into the resting place of the dead. I snuck up on him and bust him upside the head, making him choke on a piece of my candy, forcing him to spit the candy out of his mouth.

"That's what you get motherfucker!" I screamed. He tackled my ass and we fell to the ground with half the candy spilling out of the bag. He was now on top of me; the cowgirl skirt was around my waist. He saw this as the perfect opportunity to take the real goodies. He pulled down my panties with his right hand holding my wrists together high above my head with his left. Surprisingly, I surrendered. The presence of ghosts was all around. Fats was invading my body while the ghosts were penetrating me with hollow eyes. I came, shuddering uncontrollably.

"So are you a voyeur?" I asked Chloe. I was the one now waiting on an answer.

"What the hell is that?" Chloe asked with a confused look.

"It's a person that enjoys watching others having sex. Is that your MO?" I asked, knowing her freakish ass enjoyed it all.

"I don't mind, so I guess I'm a voyeur among other things," she said. We both laughed. "I'm going to tell Fats that you saw his family jewels," I said, not able to hold back the laughter.

"He ain't gonna care!" Chloe said with an animated look on her face.

"You got that right! He's proud of his junk. He'd probably whip it out and lay it on the table for you to get a good look, if they'd let him," I said.

We cracked up laughing and kept walking as the drops of rain water beat a melody on the top of the umbrellas.

"Did you tell O you tried to commit suicide?" Chloe asked. I stopped dead in my tracks. I shot Chloe a look of disgust that made her question why she brought that shit up at all.

"That was a dark time in my life. I was too young to work through the lies that were being told about me when I swallowed all those pills. You know what makes it so hurtful? I was really feeling that dude," I said, staring off into the distance, just for a moment until the wind blew the rain hard against the side of my face, I picked up the pace and resumed the conversation. "I was still a virgin; he could've got the pussy. Instead, he chose to tell all his boys that he fucked me and that anyone could get it. They started saying real slick shit to me and that lie spread through the entire school like wildfire. Everyone was looking at me, pointing and whispering. I couldn't take it anymore. Thanks to you for telling Daddy our secret, it didn't happen," I said with a feeling of relief.

"I know I promised not to tell, but I would've missed you too much," Chloe said, looking sorrowful.

"Well, they pumped my stomach and I'm still here to talk about it. And to answer your question, fuck no, I didn't tell him about that episode. What I learned from that experience was that nothing and I mean nothing is so detrimental that you would even consider taking your own life. I came out on the other side and I choose not to think about it anymore. I suggest you do the same. This is the last time we'll ever talk about this shit," I said. Chloe lingered a few steps behind me, as if she had to decipher every word that was spoken, take it in carefully and never mistakenly bring it up again.

"Chloe, I don't mean to be so mean. I'm not myself today. I'm worried about my Uncle Deke. You remember when he got robbed?" I asked.

"I remember, but that was a while ago. They caught the guys using his credit card at the gasoline station where your uncle bought his gas every week, right? The manager recognized the name on the card and knew it wasn't him and called the police. "He's just going to court for that shit?" Chloe asked.

"Yeah, he's got to testify against those niggas tomorrow. I just don't have a good feeling about this shit," I said nervously. "You know my uncle; he wouldn't hurt a fly. He talks a lot, likes to make people laugh and he flashes his money way too much, always walking around with a knot in his pocket. He's proud of how far he's come with little education. My father sent him to night school when he first came to D.C. so he could learn how to read. Now, he has the keys to the entire car dealership where he works, that alone lets you know he's a trusted and valued employee. He's been there now for about forty years."

"Amber, I'm sure everything will work out just fine," Chloe said, now walking ahead of me.

We hit the bottom of the block and I could see the police cars, the red and blue lights flashing. My heart began to thump. I was sure they were looking for me. No need to run. I had some friends that were on the run for about eight months. They came home penniless and wound up getting locked up as soon as they stepped back into the city with added time on their hands. If they were there for me, I might as well face the music. As we got closer, I could see my father was in tears.

"Daddy, what's wrong?" I asked.

"Your uncle never showed up to work this morning. You know he never misses work. His job called me and notified the police. They've found a body in Rock Creek Park. I have to go to the morgue to make sure it's not him," he said fighting back the tears.

"I'll go with you," I said with tears flowing.

"No. If it's your uncle, I don't want you to see him like that. Stay with your mother. She's distraught. I'll be back," saying so, he got into the unmarked car with the detective.

The news report came across the television. Man found dead in Rock Creek Park, shot six times in the head. Mommy screamed. "I know it's him. I can feel it. Why, God, why?" I held her close. "Chloe, stay with Mommy. I need to call O."

I dialed the number. He picked up on the first ring as if he could sense something was wrong. "O, something terrible has happened. I need you to come to my parents' house. I'll explain when I see you."

"You okay?" he asked with concern.

"Yes," I replied, "but hurry, please."

O walked into the house, looked at Chloe and me, and then went straight to Mommy. He had a way with her that I didn't understand but never questioned. I stood back and watched as he held her and just let her cry it out. At least he got her to stop screaming. My nerves were shot!

Daddy came through the door with swollen eyes. He walked over to Mommy and took her in his arms. I knew then that the body in Rock Creek Park belonged to my uncle. I was devastated, never giving up hope until this very moment. O held me tightly and I cried in disbelief. How could this be happening to our family?

Winter had finally set in but today was different, it was warm outside, it felt like summer. It was a pleasant change after the bitter cold we had been experiencing earlier in the month. Daddy turned on the air conditioner in the car as we headed down south to lay my uncle to rest where he was born in Virginia. Daddy was stepping on the gas going down the road, wanting it all to be over before it began. Two and a half hours later, we arrived just outside of Petersburg, pulled up to the church and parked near the front entrance.

"Amber, I want you to stay in the car," Daddy said sternly trying to avoid an argument with me.

"I want to say goodbye!" I said begging with my eyes.

"He knew you loved him. I can't have that baby coming early. Do you understand?" I could see that vein bulging on the side of his head. Chris and I both knew not to further engage when that occurred. I fell back into the seat sobbing loudly, holding my face in my hands. Mommy and Daddy exited the car and walked slowly to the church. I rolled all the windows down in hopes of hearing some portion of the eulogy. I put my hands over my ears as the choir and the entire congregation sang "Amazing Grace." I just couldn't bring myself to listen. I rolled the windows backup tight. I told myself that I never wanted to hear that hymn again in life.

Once we returned home from the funeral, O came to check on the family.

"Do you mind leaving Zeus with me?" I asked through bloodshot eyes.

"No problem, baby. I didn't know if you needed time to be alone. He seems to have missed you. He kept going inside your closet. He would sniff your shoes but nothing more. I think he still remembers that ass whipping you gave him when he chewed up your $500.00 heels," he said and we both laughed.

Zeus followed me everywhere I went. I think he could sense my grief. I couldn't even take a shit without him whimpering outside the bathroom door. "Okay, Zeus! You want to go outside for a walk?" I could see his tail wagging.

I trained him to walk without a lease. He was right by my side, never walked ahead or behind me. I could tell him to lie down and the kids at DJ's could run around him in circles with noise and banter and he wouldn't move. If I told him to sit, that's exactly what he did. I could cross the avenue and he wouldn't move until I came back across the street and said, "Let's go." We made a very stately presence on our walks. No one dared approach without my approval.

8

A few weeks later, O bought me a Volkswagen beetle to make my runs around town. That night, I had to meet his boy at a new spot around the beltway. There were two things that were unique about this joker; first, his name was Chili. He said the women loved him because he was hot like red pepper. Second, he never met me at the same location twice. I was cool with that for real and he was always on time. I exited the car, leaving Zeus behind. We exchanged drugs and money and went our separate ways. I'd be lying if I said this life didn't have its moments. I was never nervous during the transactions; it was the endless ride to the destination afterwards. It didn't matter if it was an hour away or a mere fifteen minutes. I was constantly checking the rearview mirror, where I spent a good portion of my life, thinking I saw the police or a car following too close. For just a few seconds, I could feel the hair stand on my arms. I only allowed that shit for a brief minute; then, I shook it off and prayed to see another day.

I noticed a raggedy Oldsmobile cutlass in front of me balling with the front bumper holding on by a string. I moved two lanes over and slowed down hoping to avoid that shit when it came off, but I was too late. The entire bumper came flying in my direction.

I swerved to the far-left lane to avoid the collision. I could hear Zeus let out a yelp as his body was bounced from one side of the car to the other. The guy behind me was not so lucky. He hit the bumper head on, spun out of control and hit the cement guard rail. The car burst into flames. Looking in the rearview mirror, I had flashbacks of the Picture Man's demise. My hands were shaking as I gripped the steering wheel at ten and two like an inexperienced driver. I stepped on the gas, needing to get away from the scene as quickly as possible, thinking how that could've been me. Thank God, there wasn't a car in the lane beside me. That's all I would've needed to have an accident with drugs in the trunk, a gun in the glove compartment and no driver's license. How would I explain that shit to Daddy?

I exhaled a long deep breath as I was coming up on the New Hampshire Avenue exit. Once I took the exit, I pulled up behind a blue Buick at the red light, making sure to keep my distance. I could hear O's voice in my head, "Never get too close to the vehicle in front of you at a stop. Always be on 'ready, set, go' in case you have to get away fast." One more life lesson. A police car approached from out of nowhere, with lights and sirens blasting. I quickly sped around the Buick and pulled over to the curb, praying they weren't after me. The police cruiser pulled right up behind the Buick. The two police officers jumped out of the car with guns drawn. I put the car in drive and kept it moving. I took another deep breath and said, "Thank you, Lord; not tonight."

I dropped the packages off to DJ and the crew and left them hard at work, cutting and bagging the drugs for immediate sale. I continued down the road to the house with Zeus keeping me company. I needed to check on O. His so-called recreational drug had turned into a daily habit. There were several cars parked in the driveway. I didn't recognize one. So much for not bringing anyone to where he laid his head. An intense craps game was being played right outside of the house with a bunch of dudes I'd never seen before, shivering from the cold rubbing their hands together for warmth. I motioned to put the key in the lock just as the front door opened. It was a woman.

"You must be O's wife, Amber," the redhead said as if she was welcoming me to my own home.

"Who the fuck are you?" I asked more as a demand. Zeus began to growl.

"I'm Coco. Just one of the boys. I'm no threat, sweetheart," she said unbothered with my tone.

I could see O walking to the front door with his forty-five in his hand.

"Is there a problem?" he asked as if everything was perfectly fine and I was disrupting the peace.

"I didn't expect to come home to company, especially not a woman!" I pushed past O heading to the bathroom, not stopping to speak to his guests. I could hear O tell Zeus to sit. "Ohhhh, Jesus," I exclaimed, locking the door, unzipping my jeans and sitting on the toilet, finally able to release the pee. I'd held that water much too long. I was already having a difficult pregnancy. I couldn't keep anything on my stomach. I was underweight and stayed nauseous.

I then removed my rings to wash my hands, laying them on the back of the toilet. I dried my hands off and left the bathroom. "Come, Zeus," I said, already heading for the steps.

"Zeus, stay!" O commanded. I looked back over my shoulder watching my dog look confused. I repeated O's command, "Stay, Zeus." I didn't feel like getting into it with his ass over this shit today. O was already in his feelings about Zeus being apprehensive of his commands. He never really put in the time with Zeus but expected him to always obey.

I removed my top and jeans, throwing them in the dirty clothes hamper, and then my bra and panties. I took a quick shower and then pulled a nightshirt with a teddy bear on the front from the top drawer of the dresser and crawled in bed, pulling the covers over my head.

My mouth was dry, I wanted some water. I had to get fully dressed to go downstairs to get a bottle out of the refrigerator. As soon as I hit the bottom of the stairway, the smell of burnt popcorn and pizza hit the bottom of my stomach, making me feel queasy. There was a group of strangers snorting smack in my living room. The central air was on and the windows were cracked. It was cold as shit outside. O was sitting on the silk chaise with his headphones on his ears, loudly singing Al Green's song "Tired of Being Alone." I was starting to hate that damn song. It seemed to be a go-to for him whenever he was high and put those damn headphones on. I loved Al Green's voice but O was fucking the song up something terrible. I opened the bottle of water, took a sip to try to calm my stomach and headed back up the stairs.

I'd just dozed off when O entered the room, cutting on the ceiling light.

"Wake up, Amber," he said with urgency.

"What, O! I was asleep!" I said annoyed.

"Don't leave your fucking rings in the bathroom for someone to take," he said sternly. I sat up and immediately started running my mouth.

"Who you got in this house that would steal my shit? Doesn't that mean that they would steal from you? I'm your fucking wife!" I said, reaching out with my palm upturned. He placed the rings in my hand. I slid them on my fingers before diving back under the covers.

"Amber, I have to make a run. CoCo is coming past to pick up a package," he said while taking his gun from the nightstand and reaching for his keys.

"I have to get up to give her that shit?" I asked in a whiney voice, wiping my eyes.

"Yes. I'm leaving it on the dresser," he said.

"Am I getting money from her ass?" I asked, hoping to make this deal short and sweet.

"No. I'll get that later. Turn the ringer up on the phone so you can get the door," he said before cutting off the light and shutting the bedroom door. Footsteps could be heard on the stairs, muffled conversation and laughter, the front door being locked, and the alarm set. At last, there was quiet.

The telephone rang about two hours later. The doorbell rang in less than thirty minutes after the call. I wasn't happy to leave my bed and go to the door. I started down the steps and realized that I'd left the package. I doubled back and descended the steps one at a time with one eye open. After disarming the alarm, I opened the front door and let CoCo inside.

"I was hoping you were in a better mood than earlier," CoCo said, sounding like she just got her second wind at 1:00 a.m. and was just about to get this party started. I stared with no response, handing her the package.

"Goodnight," I said as I opened the door and let her out and then went back to bed with hopes of uninterrupted sleep.

The phone was ringing off the hook. It took me a minute to realize that I wasn't dreaming. I reached for the phone with my eyes still shut, I answered, sounding half asleep.

"Hello."

"Is O there?" It was a man's voice on the other end. I glanced over to the other side of the bed. It was empty.

"Who is this?" I asked.

"It's Jeff. Can you tell O that I found Coco in the bathroom with a needle in her arm? She's dead," he was sniffling as he spoke.

"What are you saying?" I asked, sitting straight up in the bed, wide awake now.

"I just wanted him to know," the phone went dead.

O came through the front door just as I hit the landing. Zeus was wanting to play, bouncing around at my feet. "Stop, Zeus!" he lowered his head, quickly turned, headed back to the corner, and laid down with his head on his paws.

"Jeff just called to say that Coco was dead. She overdosed. I gave her that shit!" I said with emotions running rampant.

"She wasn't new to this thing. You know I stand behind my product. Come on now; she should've known better," he said as he walked to the kitchen, opened the cabinet just above the sink, turned on the faucet, rinsed the glass, and poured a drink.

"You don't care? I thought that was your friend," I said, with uncontrollable tears, the flood gates had opened.

"What do you want me to say?" he shrugged as if she was a stranger.

"I'm more upset than you! How can you be so cold?" I asked through trembling lips.

"You better get over that shit, quick. Don't say anything about this to anyone else. You got me?" he said lifting the glass from the counter, putting it to his lips and taking a sip. I saw another side of O that I didn't recognize. I turned and headed back up the stairs, climbed under the covers and cried unrestrained tears for the death of a woman that I didn't even know, delivered by my hands. Yet another secret.

9

I overslept the next morning, missing school for the day. I had no energy and no appetite. I could've stayed in bed for the rest of the day. I knew the signs. Depression had raised its ugly head. I had to do something to make myself feel better before it pulled me under. I'd been boosting for months and had become a pretty good thief. I decided to go shopping.

I put all my diamond studs in my ears, three on the left and four on the right. I would always get that same question. "Did you lose an earring?" Truth be told, I've lost those earrings on several occasions, not at the same time, but singularly. I would lose one and then find it at a later date after much worry and aggravation, forcing Daddy to finally add my jewelry to his homeowner insurance. I lost a diamond stud on my way to the airport on a trip to New York with O to see Ike and Tina Turner at the Fillmore East. I had a terrible habit of carrying the studs in my hand, thinking I could put them in my ears once I got in the car. We were well on our way to the airport when I realized I'd dropped one. It was raining for points that day, the kind of rain you couldn't dodge in between the drops. I was sad thinking I would never see that earring again. Surely it would wash down the sewer before we returned.

When we got back, several days later, I jumped out the car scanning the street for my earring and lo and behold there it was. It was a few feet away from where the car was parked before we left, the post was bent, but it was still there waiting for me. Maybe my luck was changing.

I put a diamond solitaire around my neck and a wide sterling silver bangle bracelet around my wrist. Simple but elegant. I applied just a dab of Rive Gauche at my pulse points. My long sleeve silk shirt and lined wool pants were complimented by my leather platform shoes and my Saint Laurent bag. I added a swing coat to make the outfit complete. It wasn't the warmest but I'd only be dashing from the car to the stores. I did a once over in the mirror before walking out the door, smiling at my reflection.

To be the perfect thief you not only have to look the part but you have to carry yourself with an air of confidence. It was as if I was playing a role in a movie. I'd pretend that I was as wealthy as the clientele that shopped in the exclusive stores. O showered me with hot clothes and jewelry. More than I could ever wear, but it was never enough. I too had an addiction—mine was designer clothing. I liked looking rich and I guess in a way I was, just "Hood Rich."

Today, I decided to go to a boutique at the Watergate. I saw the older woman sitting at the front as I entered the store. I assumed she was waiting for someone shopping. I looked through the clothing and found an ultra-suede skirt that wrapped and tied on the side. I loved the feel of the material and it was washable, no dry cleaner bill. The price tag was six hundred dollars. I wanted that skirt and when I wanted something badly enough, nothing got in my way. I quickly folded it and placed it under my arm beneath my coat and then calmly walked to the back of the store, browsing.

"Are you a member of the cast at the Kennedy Center?" the saleswoman asked with a pleasant smile.

"No. Just here from out of town. I decided to do a little shopping before leaving," I said before I found my way back to the front of the store, just shy of the exit.

A woman approached from my left. "Would you like to give me that skirt?" she said with a dirty look.

"What skirt are you speaking of?" I said knowing full well what she was asking.

"The skirt underneath your coat," she answered with a disapproving tone.

"Oh, this skirt?" I said snatching the skirt from under my arm and throwing it in her face.

I turned and left the store, mad as shit because I wanted that fucking skirt! I glanced behind me once I was halfway down the block. No one was following so I quickened my steps, jumped in the car and headed through Rock Creek Park to Chevy Chase.

I loved Saks Fifth Avenue. The window displays, the sales clerks, the whole vibe. I hit them up at least twice a week. I started making small purchases so as not to bring attention to myself. I tried on two out of the five outfits that I carried to the dressing room. One or two outfits were going home with me. I was still upset about that damn skirt, not as focused as I should've been on the job at hand. Or maybe I was just too damn comfortable. I stashed what I wanted on my body and was on my way out of the store when I was stopped by security. "Come with me!" I recognized her face. Mid-forties, with crows' feet under her eyes, wearing a blond wig. She'd probably been watching me for months. I knew I should've gone to school today.

Getting locked up for this bullshit wasn't in my plans. Her first mistake was trying not to make a scene. I elbowed that bitch hard! She bent over in pain holding her side as I bolted, pushing a few customers out the way, scattering a display. I heard glass shatter as it hit the floor but never once looked back as I burst through the front door, jumped into the beetle and pushed the pedal to the metal.

I drove uptown and went straight to find DJ.

"The car needs to disappear today," I said to DJ while reaching into the glove compartment and placing the 9mm in my purse.

"Damn, Amber! O just bought that shit for you. You still got paper tags!" DJ said, nodding toward the tags. "Won't he be mad?"

"It's not like it was brand new! Hell, if he's that mad I'll give him his fucking money back. I almost got locked up in Saks. I hit the security lady and ran like shit! It needs to go!" I said with an exaggerated head movement.

"Your ass was stealing! That's what the fuck O is going to be mad about, not the car." DJ said laughing like shit.

"Shut up!" I screamed. "You think everything is a joke!"

DJ was cracking up.

"I'm going to Ms. Lola's. Call me when it's done," I said, handing him the keys.

"No problem," he said, shaking his head as he walked toward the car, still laughing.

He opened the driver's door and got in, adjusting the seat, the mirrors and then he partially rolled down the window. "Hey, Amber! I'd like to be a flower on the wall when you tell O that shit!" This time, DJ quickly rolled up the window and drove off before I could make a comment. I managed to give him the middle finger as he pulled off.

I walked up the street to Ms. Lola's, stuck my key in the lock and opened the front door.

"Hey, Ms. Lola! What you doing?" I said walking in the front door taking a seat at the dining room table as if I didn't have a care in the world.

"Getting these numbers together," she replied, looking up over her reading glasses, reaching for a Kleenex to cover her mouth as she coughed.

"You okay?" I asked as I watched her stand and walk to the kitchen to discard the used tissue and come right back to take a seat.

"I'm good," she said, never once looking in my direction.

"That cough didn't sound good," I said.

"I said I'm good," she gave me a hard stare and changed the subject.

"Your daddy hit the number the other day," she said, still writing down bets.

"Really? He never mentioned it to me, but he never does," I said, a casual comment.

"You shouldn't care. You've gotten everything your heart desires from that man. He deserves to have a little pocket change," she said smiling, still looking at the slips of paper.

"Elena cooked dinner early? Something sure smells good!" I said standing up and walking toward the kitchen. I washed and dried my hands before opening the lid to the big pot on the stove, looking inside. "String beans," I said out loud.

"Amber, I hear you rambling through those pots. Come out of that kitchen. You are more than welcome to come by later for dinner," she said.

I walked out of the kitchen and sat back down with a piece of smoked turkey neck on a paper plate.

"You and them damn bones. You're going to mess around and that baby is gonna come out wanting to eat bones too!" She said with a smirk.

"Ms. Lola, don't say that! O would not be happy," I said laughing at the thought.

"Where's Elena?" I asked, chewing on the turkey neck.

"She said she wanted to go visit Desi. I told her she could wait and go with me on Thursday, but she acted like she had to see him today. I'm sure she'll come back with stories about her experience riding to Lorton on that jail bus." We both laughed.

"Have you seen Chloe lately?" I asked as I took a tangerine from the weave basket on the table, peeled it, and popped a slice in my mouth.

Ms. Lola looked at me oddly and said, "You got some strange cravings going on."

I just laughed.

"She came by the other day, high as Cootie Brown. Talking about how much she misses Desi. You know that boy ain't thinking about her! I told her she needed to get a life. Pretty girl; such a waste. You can't talk no sense into her ass?" Ms. Lola asked never once looking up from the number slips.

"I don't know what's going on with her. She's been ducking me lately," I said.

"I heard she's been hanging at the strip club down the street," she said, taking a slice of tangerine out of my hand and throwing it in her mouth.

"Really?" I said, pondering on that information. I glanced at my watch; it was close to 5:30 p.m.

"Ms. Lola, let me borrow your car for about half an hour, please," I asked.

"The keys are next to my purse on the credenza," she said, answering the phone and jotting down a new bet.

I grabbed the keys and went out the back door, started the car, and backed down the driveway. As an afterthought, I put the car in park, got out, opened the trunk and took a cleaning rag out of the bag and tucked it over the back tag. I got back in the car and headed down the Avenue.

I pulled in a space three doors down from Foxy Playground and walked around the side to the back of the club with my gun drawn, just in time to see the bouncer throwing Chloe out the back door. She landed on her knees, scantily dressed with smeared mascara as well as a runny nose.

"Don't come back here, slut! Ain't nobody going to get shut down because you lied about your age. I should kick your ass to teach you a lesson!" he said as he proceeded down the steps toward Chloe. "Better still, I'm going to let you suck my dick before I deliver this ass whipping. He started to unzip his pants as

Chloe was slowly trying to get up off the ground. I creeped up on his ass and pointed the Luger at the back of his head.

"I suggest that you don't take not one more motherfucking step. Get up, Chloe!" I shouted.

"I need to get my coat, and where is my check?" she asked with a froggy voice, folding her arms and rubbing both with the palms of her hands, shaking from the cold.

"Fuck that coat and that check! You won't be coming back!" I yelled. The temperature had dropped and I could see my breath as I spoke.

"Get on your knees and empty your pockets," I said as a demand, pushing the bouncer's head forward with the gun. He laid about eight hundred fifty dollars in cash with some loose change on the ground.

"Spread that shit out so I can see exactly what you got there," I said.

"Chloe, pick up the money. He owes you for a coat," I said. She quickly grabbed the money and threw it in her purse.

I walked around the side of his body, slowly dragging the gun with pressure along the side of his face, over his ear, across his temple, now staring him in the eye, face to face.

"You're not so macho now, are you? Open your mouth," I said with the barrel of the gun pursed against his lips. I pushed the gun into his mouth, moving it slowly in and out, watching his eyes widen with fear.

Once I'd had enough fun, I removed the gun, grabbed Chloe by the hand and ran toward the car.

"It's been real, but I don't want her to catch her death from pneumonia," I screamed back at the man over the sound of our footsteps echoing on the sidewalk, laughing as we made our escape.

"Bitch, you better hope I don't see you again," he said with a snort. Once we reached the Avenue, I unlocked the car, Chloe jumped in on the passenger side, and I pulled into traffic, barely avoiding being sideswiped by a trash truck.

I made a right on Columbia Road and parked near 13th Street. I got out of the car and removed the rag from the plate and returned it to the trunk. I got back inside and took Chloe's chin in my hand as I looked her straight in the eyes.

"Don't let the streets beat you up. That's a hard cold death."

The tears began to flood from her eyes.

"I miss Desi. I know that sounds crazy, but you can't help who you love, even if they don't love you back," she said.

"I understand," I replied with a sigh, trying to show some compassion for her, although I still hated his ass. "If you keep going hard like you're doing, Desi will come home and walk right past you. Although I think that nothing motherfucker is going to do that shit anyway, but if you take care of yourself, at least you got a shot," I said trying to make her feel better. "What the fuck were you doing dancing in the Foxy Playground anyway? I heard they treat their dancers really bad. Letting customers stick liquor bottles up the dancer's pussy and feeding them drugs to fuck in that dirty ass backroom...." I stopped in mid-sentence.

"Was this about a free high?" I asked in disbelief. "You've never cared about fucking strangers, so it's got to be about the drugs. Chloe, you've got to pull it together," I said with a sigh, shaking my head. It's time for a change. Promise me you'll do better," I said.

"I don't like to make promises. I feel bad when I let you down. I'll try to do better. Is that good enough?" she asked, as she wiped at the tears.

"That works for now. I better take Ms. Lola's car back. You want to go to the Go-Go tonight? That always makes me feel better."

"Yeah, I've missed that," she responded with a smile.

It was 10 p.m. Mother Nature was playing tag with the wind against our faces as we walked to the avenue, hoping to see somebody to catch a ride. We stopped to dance to the music, spilling out of the Holiness Church as we'd done since we were kids. The door opened suddenly. The pastor was scolding us about mocking the church. Startled, we took off running and didn't stop until we reached the next block.

"We've been standing out here for a while. Everyone is probably already in route. Let's hitchhike," I said with no hesitation.

"Cool," Chloe responded by putting her thumb in the air.

An older guy in his sixties with silver hair, driving an El Dorado Cadillac, pulled over to the curb, rolled down the window and asked, "Where are you two pretty ladies heading?"

"We're going to S.E., Byrne Manor," I said.

He unlocked the car doors and said, "I'm not going quite that far, but I'll give you a ride part of the way."

Chloe jumped in the back and I got in the passenger seat.

"What are your names? he asked.

"I'm Nancy and my friend's name is Jessica," I said, happy to be in a warm car, glancing back at Chloe with a wink.

"I'm Jersey. I was born and raised in Newark. Been here for the last ten years," he said, his accent sounding just a little like my cousins who live in East Orange. Jersey was listening to oldies, which was just fine with me, not so much Chloe's choice.

"Do you mind if I turn the station?" Chloe asked, pushing her body across the console with her hand already on the radio dial. "Ring my Bell'" by Anita Ward came on the radio and she almost lost her mind.

"Pull over! Stop the car!" Chloe shouted. "That's my motherfucking jam! Open the door and let me out!" she said even though we'd just got a little heat, not even enough to warm our toes.

I got out, lifted the seat to let Chloe out the back; she turned the music up on her way out the car. She was on the sidewalk, in front of the corner store, dancing like her life depended on it! I had to join her; she was having way too much fun! We partied like shit, with cars on the Avenue honking their horns as they rode by.

We danced all the way to the end of the song before we climbed back into the car.

"Okay, Jersey, we're ready now," Chloe said.

"Well damn! You two got a lot of energy!" he said laughing like we'd made his night.

We talked and flirted until before you knew it we were pulling up in front of Byrne Manor.

"Jersey, we really want to thank you for the ride," I said as we climbed out of the car.

"You want to give me a number where I can reach you at a later date or maybe later on tonight?" Chloe asked, leaning in showing her cleavage.

"Sorry, baby, but I'm married. If only you'd caught me a few years back. Just trying to do a good deed today," he said as we jumped out of the car and he drove down the driveway, past the bushes and disappeared from sight.

Walking toward the entrance, I realized I still had the Luger in my purse. "Damn, I'm going to have to stash this gun until we come out of the Go-Go. Watch my back," I said to Chloe as I walked toward the bushes. I bent down and quickly placed the gun on the ground underneath a holly.

"I'm good. Let's party," I said with new enthusiasm and plenty of energy.

"How are we getting home?" Chloe asked with her face all screwed up.

"You're just thinking about that now?" I asked, shaking my head. "Girl, DJ is more than likely inside the building. That's the least of our worries."

The Young Senators were groovin! A smooth sexy beat. Chloe and I were dancing opposite each other—the joint was filled to capacity. There was hardly room to breathe but no one cared. Go-Go music is like a drug, a euphoria that you crave day after day. It never gets old. We were already sweating, when the crowd stopped dancing and circled around someone in the middle that was unseen. Chloe and I squeezed through the crowd for an upfront view. Cutty, a regular at every Go-Go, started coming out of his clothes, high on Angel Dust. He was giving us a show, dancing hard and fast until he came out of every stitch of clothing. The water poured off his body as if he was in a sauna. He danced to the rhythm in his head, no longer on beat with the band. His dick swung heavy as he jerked every inch of his double-jointed ass like a contortionist, at the circus. Chloe and I burst into laughter as he was finally escorted from the dance floor by security and taken outside.

It felt good to see Chloe enjoying herself without being high. I had no idea how long this was going to last.

"I need some water! It's hot as shit in here," I said to Chloe, making my way to the bar. I caught a glimpse of DJ with a young thing pressed against the wall. I walked in his direction.

"Hey, DJ! I don't mean to interrupt, but Chloe and I need a ride home," I said, still bouncing to the beat.

"Who is she?" the young girl asked with a roll of her eyes.

"What! We starting this thing off real wrong! I'm going to find some pussy that don't talk!" DJ said leaving her with her back against the wall as he walked away and grabbed another little cutie and took her out on the dance floor to get his freak on.

I looked back at the girl who looked like she was really in her feelings, mouthing, "Sorry," with both hands outstretched, palms in the air.

When 2:00 a.m. arrived, I laid back, waiting for the crowd to disperse. "Ya'll ready to leave?" DJ said getting some digits from yet another young lady.

"I have to get my gun from under a bush outside. Trying to wait for the crowd to die down," I said, speaking to some guys from S.E. that I knew in passing.

"Let's go now before the police be watching our every move," DJ proceeded toward the door. Chloe and I followed.

I ducked down, quickly grabbed my heat and placed it back in my purse.

"Where are you parked?" I asked, sounding just a little tired.

"I'm on the street," he answered, picking up the pace.

"I really had a good time, Amber!" Chloe said while skipping behind DJ to the car.

"See, you don't have to be high to get your party on. I had a ball!" I said.

I opened the car door, letting Chloe get in the backseat. I jumped in the passenger seat, with my hand on the dial searching for some music on the radio. We'd missed most of the traffic but were only a few blocks away from the venue when I said, "Pull over." DJ was used to the routine by now. I got out of the car and vomited bile. It left an awful taste in my mouth. I returned to the car and DJ handed me a mint.

"You okay?" he asked with a look of concern.

"I feel a little better now," I said with my hand on my stomach.

"Amber, I've watched my mom go through this pregnancy shit a half dozen times and it was never like this. I think you need to see a doctor. This ain't good," he said with concern.

"I'll make an appointment," I said as I closed my eyes and rubbed my stomach in a circular motion.

We drove to the suburbs with little conversation. The heaviness of exhaustion hit me like a weight. The rain drops started slow but picked up speed quickly, drumming against the car roof. Chloe snored in the backseat while the rain came down harder turning to hail, crashing against the windshield. I sat straight up, fully awake now.

"DJ, you okay?" I asked, concerned with how quickly the storm had turned violent.

"I'm good, but I think after we drop you off, Chloe and I are going to get a room. Not driving back across town in this shit!" he said.

"I hear you. Sounds like a sound decision to me. I'm going to give you a word of advice. Don't stick your dick in Chloe. And if you do, don't come to me complaining," I said, speaking facts.

"I heard my name," Chloe said awakened by the thunder.

DJ and I looked at each other and burst out laughing. He proceeded up the driveway with caution, it was looking quite ominous. He pulled right up to the front door to let me out. I wasn't feeling well and the house was pitch black. The wind and torrential rain had knocked the power out. Chloe remained in the back seat and blew me a kiss as I exited the car, soaked to the bone before I closed the door.

I unlocked the front door, kicked off my rain-soaked shoes and coat. I walked to the left toward the kitchen in search of a flashlight in the drawer. The lightning lit the room for a brief moment and there was O sitting in the dark, with a 45 Magnum in his lap, drunk, with a menacing frown. He took a shot of Hennessy straight to the head from the bottle. I ran to the bathroom with the flashlight in hand and held my head over the toilet. Once again, nothing came up but bile. I rinsed my mouth with water, dabbing at the corners with a tissue, grabbed a towel from the perfectly arranged set and started to dry my hair.

I turned to walk out the bathroom and O was in the entryway blocking my exit.

"Where the fuck you been?" he asked with a snarl.

"I went to the Go-Go with Chloe," I said nonchalantly. "I got caught boosting earlier today. I ran so I wouldn't catch a charge. I had DJ get rid of the VW. I'll need another car for business," I said, still looking in the mirror as I spoke, continuing to dry my hair.

The lights flickered on and off, but still no power. There was an unsettling quiet. An intense fear began to rise from within.

"Where is Zeus?" I asked, feeling uneasy.

"All you worried about is that fucking dog?" his words slurred just a little. Amber, you're married now. You need to stop going to the Go-Go. What the fuck are you stealing? You got so much shit upstairs you're taking up two closets and then some. That's some sick shit! Do I need to remind you that you're pregnant with my child?" he said in a menacing tone of voice.

I squirmed past him calling for my dog, "Zeus, come here, boy." I ran up the stairs, going in every room calling his name, leaving tiny puddles of water wherever I walked. "Zeus!" "Zeus!" Running back down the stairway, I ran to the kitchen, pushing past O and continued to run out the patio door. "Zeus, come here, boy!" I walked the length of the pool with the beam of the flashlight leading the way, heading toward the fence.

The wind and rain were hammering my body. I stopped, bending over to catch my breath, fighting an oncoming panic attack, then swung the fence open wide. I pointed the flashlight toward the butterfly habitat. There was Zeus lying on the ground. His short coat glistened in the rain with a gunshot wound to the head. My heart sank. I walked over and sat down beside him, placing his head in my lap. The blood stained my top a strange hue of pink. "I'm so sorry, baby. You didn't deserve this. I never should've left you here with him." The tears flowed down my face mixed with rain and were now coupled as one. Zeus' breathing was labored; he held on long enough to see me for the last time. I removed his head from my lap and left him lying where I found him. I couldn't feel the cold because I was numb. The rain had stopped; a dense fog set in quickly covering my footprints as I walked toward the fence, secured the latch, and proceeded through the patio door and went inside. O was getting up from the chair stumbling toward the stairs.

"Why did you kill my dog?" I spoke with ill will.

He never turned to give me eye contact as he answered, "I don't tolerate bitches that can't follow directions. He kept going out that damn gate. I wasn't going to keep chasing his ass," he said unsteadily as he took the next step.

"He was probably looking for me, you bastard!" I screamed, the rage overflowing. "I would. . . take him. . . to the habitat and he would. . . lay beside me. . . while I. . . read my book." I spoke in between sobs, my words jumbled, barely recognizable.

I took off running, jumping on his back, pummeling his head with my fists screaming, "You're the bitch!"

"Get off me, Amber!" he yelled, swinging his body hard. I lost my balance. I could feel myself free-falling, but it felt like it was in slow motion. The last thing I remembered were sharp pains, and then everything went black.

I woke up shivering in a hospital bed. I couldn't get the vision of Zeus dying in my lap out of my head. I blinked a few times and realized Mommy, Daddy, and O were at my bedside.

"Is the baby okay?" I asked, just above a whisper. Silence was my answer.

"I'd really like to be alone. Mommy and Daddy, thank you for coming to see me. I'll call you tomorrow," I said, turning my head, feeling a tear roll down my cheek.

"Amber, what happened?" Daddy asked, unable to remain quiet for another minute. It was like the question had been burning a hole in his soul. I looked at O who for once looked shaken.

"I slipped on something wet on the marble floor. It was an accident."

The tears began slowly and then before I knew it I was wailing. I hated to cry, but I needed to mourn the death of my baby. Loud uncontrollable sobs began to escape through my mouth. I beat on the mattress with clenched fists. O left the room and came back with the nurse.

"She needs to be sedated. Visits are over for the day!" she said as she prepared the needle.

I didn't feel the needle pierce my arm. I don't know how long I sobbed. I welcomed sleep. I wanted to close my eyes and wake up the next day from this terrible nightmare and everything would be okay.

10

I awoke to find the room filled with flowers, lilies, carnations, daffodils, and birds of paradise. Each arrangement had baby breaths nestled inconspicuously throughout. The detail was extraordinary; each arrangement was unique. A lot of time and money was spent. I hit the call button.

"I'd like the flowers removed please. Give them to the other patients. I'm allergic," I said with little emotion.

"No problem, Mrs. Jones. We'll have them removed right away." The young girl at the nurses' station came with a string of nurses and quickly took the flowers from the room. O was asleep right next to my bed. His hand holding mine. I watched his body flinch in his sleep while snoring through an open mouth. He finally opened his eyes and sat up straight in the chair, looking around the room, trying to get his bearings, now focusing on me.

"What happened to the flowers?" he asked.

"I gave them away. I can't look at flowers right now. I just can't," I said as my hands began to tremble and the tears began to well up in my eyes. "What happened was not your fault or mine; it was ours. We both have to take blame for this loss. I don't even know how to find my way back, to not just loving you, but loving myself. I'm going to need some space," I said, trying to fight back the tears.

"Amber, if I give you space, you'll end up hating me. We have to figure this out together." I tried to pull my hand away and he held on tighter. I finally gave up the struggle, crying myself back to sleep.

O only went home to shower and return to what looked like an uncomfortable hospital chair with a straight back. I was released at the end of the week. The drive home was filled with short snippets of conversation with no purpose. He wanted to carry me up the stairs but I didn't want to be that close to him. I couldn't eat or sleep. I kept popping pain pills like candy on an empty stomach.

O opened the bedroom door carrying a tray with hot chicken noodle soup. I could smell the aroma from the bed, but it made me feel nauseated. He pulled the chair up next to the bed.

"I'm not leaving. Open your mouth. Damn if I'm going to watch the woman I love die right in front of me," he said as he scooped a spoonful of soup out of the bowl, blew on it to cool it down, and then placed it near my lips. I could tell by the determined look on his face that he wasn't going to leave until I ate, so I opened my mouth. The hurt that I felt in my heart was like a death sentence. I ate a few spoonfuls and then turned my head, but he wouldn't leave, so I ate a few more so that he would finally leave me alone.

"Close the blinds. I just want to sleep," I said, shutting my eyes tight. We repeated the same ritual every day for three weeks. The only thing that changed was the soup.

The Monday of the fourth week I finally got the energy to ask with a look of disdain, "Did you bury Zeus?" I asked, waiting for his answer.

"Amber, I was out of my mind that night with worry. Please forgive me," he said apologetically.

"I lost both my babies that night. I don't know how to feel whole again," I said as the tears began to flow.

"We'll get through this, I promise," he said as he rubbed my face with the back of his hand, the same way I used to rub his beard. He never answered my question.

At least the company, the drugs, and the liquor had dissipated. When he came up to bed, I would fake sleep so I wouldn't have to talk to him. I knew that in time I would stop blaming him. He was my life line. We needed each other to heal from this devastating loss. I just didn't know where to begin.

Winter came and went. The leaves changing color, the snow drifts in the backyard melting, and birds singing from the rooftop were all a blur. It's like three months of my life just didn't exist, as if I'd been in a coma and was just waking up.

O's court date was approaching. He was temperamental as shit from the door, but this had him in a whole mood. I found myself tip-toeing around his ass. The least little thing would set him off.

Mommy was back in St. Elizabeths Hospital. I'm sure the loss of her grandchild and my depression helped put her back there. I had to see her. O paid a guy to detail all the vehicles. He pulled the Benz out the garage and parked it right out front. It looked shiny and bright as I came out the front door. I was greeted by a red robin landing on the hood, leaving me a gift of shit before flying away. I damn sure hoped this wasn't a sign as to how my day was going to go.

The drive to DC was pleasant. I rode past a work crew removing dead branches and fallen trees, remnants of winter's end, from the parkway. I rolled down the windows so I could feel the breeze on my face and stuck my hand out as if I was a child, so I could feel alive again. Marvin Gaye's new album "*What's Going On*" was being featured on the radio. "Inner City Blues (Make You Wanna Holler)" had a vibe that I was feeling. I reached down and turned up the sound, passing a church with a unique steeple that reminded me of the Empire State building. I turned my head as I drove by, thinking that I hadn't been inside a church for worship in years. I was a sinner and when I did enter those doors all I did was cry. I felt as if I didn't belong. I wasn't ready to give up street life so I stayed away. The money was too good.

I drove through the metal gates, past security, and parked. I gave my identification card to the front desk clerk; she was new—twenty something, with a short haircut, large round eyes, and long slender fingers. She handed me my ID and pointed toward the elevators.

Mommy was sitting near the window, rocking from side to side. She had bed head on the left; I couldn't wait to hug her and fix those curls like I did on every visit. She spotted me and flashed a wide smile, showing the gap in the front of her mouth. I walked toward her, but she brought me to a standstill with her words. "Don't just walk past your husband! I know you're mad with him, but go back and speak!" she said pointing at the young guy standing next to the entrance, looking like a zombie.

"Mommy, that's not O," I said, looking confused.

"Go speak to your husband!" she said louder this time.

I turned and walked toward the young man quickly waving hello, spun around, and walked back toward Mommy, who seemed relieved.

"Look out that window. I'm going to buy you a new car! I know how much you love cars. That should make you happy! Just pick the one you want!" she said pointing to the street. I looked out the window. Down below was a parking lot filled with new and old automobiles in an abundance of colors, belonging to the hospital staff.

"I think I want the blue sports car, parked next to the tree. You see it? Right over there!" I said with excitement.

"I'm going to put that order in today," she said with a wide grin.

At this point, I would do or say anything to appease her. I just wanted this visit to go well. I needed her, even in this state; she was still my mommy. I fluffed her curls, massaged her shoulders and back and she rewarded me with a song.

Her expression took a sullen turn from out of nowhere. I looked behind me and a woman was approaching, slowed by the medication but strong-willed.

"You know her, Mommy?" I asked, feeling uncomfortable.

"No," her look and her response made me that much more uneasy.

"You can stop right there," I said as I scanned the floor for an attendant. She was a pretty girl, but the light was gone from her eyes.

"You're with Anjelo. He's Satan, you know. You better run as fast as you can. He's evil! I tell you he's evil! You have to get away! You have to leave now!" Her voice was high pitched as she began to scream and flail her arms as if she was fighting an invisible enemy. The attendants in white coats grabbed her from both sides and whisked her away with her feet dragging the floor. This upset the patients; some began to cry, others moaned loudly. Mommy sat quietly, rocking harder and faster, staring into the distance.

"Mommy, I'm going to leave now. I'll see you again soon," I said as I kissed her on her forehead. There was no response. It was as if she no longer knew I was there. The walk across the room seemed endless. I looked down and my hands were trembling as I waited for the door to be unlocked.

I was in deep thought as I drove to the house, barely avoiding a pothole that I saw on the ride to S.E. I didn't want to fuck up a rim today. I didn't feel like hearing O bitch and complain. Sometimes, I felt like he loved his cars more than me.

Why did she say that O was the devil? Who was she? How did she know me? I was thinking a little too hard as the car drifted across the white line. The oncoming driver laid on the horn. I turned the wheel hard to the right, steering the car back into my lane just as I remembered who she was. The widow's peak and the gash in her eyebrow, it all came back. She was in this exact car with O. She threw the trash at my feet.

I pulled off to the side of the road, cut off the engine, closed my eyes and focused on my breathing. I inhaled and exhaled slowly while counting to five between each breath. My heart finally stopped racing. I started the car and pulled back onto the road and continued my drive to the house. I had questions that needed answers.

I pulled up to the front door, parked and went inside. O was back to his old habits. Liquor and heroin were his sustenance. I was the icing on the cake. The one thing that tied it all together and completed his set of weaknesses.

"How was your visit with Mom?" he said while pouring more Hennessy into an iceless glass.

"It was great until your ex walked up. Why didn't you tell me she had a nervous breakdown?" I asked through narrowed eyes. He stood and gave me his back, as he walked away with no response. "She said you were the devil. Those were her clothes upstairs. How did she get that gash in her eyebrow? Did you do it?" I said with my voice reaching a higher pitch with each word. I was damn near on his heels, determined to get answers.

"You know, you got asshole in your DNA!" I screamed angrily at his silence. He turned and back handed me with such force that I fell to the floor.

Standing over me, looking down through bloodshot eyes, he spoke through clenched teeth. "Don't ever mention that bitch to me again. As far as I'm concerned, she's dead. Stop asking me so many fucking questions! I don't answer to you or anyone else. Get your ass up off the floor! I don't want to put my hands on you. Don't make me do it again!" he said, infuriated with my questioning.

The dam broke as I ran past him, tripping up the stairs several times, on my way to the bedroom, slamming the door behind me. I stripped down to my bra and panties, sat in the middle of the bed with my hands interlocked around my knees, close to my chest, rocking and crying, rubbing the soles of my feet against the silk sheets seeking comfort, at the same time rubbing the snot from my nose with the back of my hand on his pillow. My fuck-you gift to him. I must've slumped down into a fetal position as I cried myself to sleep. When I awoke he was removing my panties and apologizing for hitting me, trying to get some ass.

"I don't want to," I said through instant tears.

"It's not about what you want. It never was."

This was the beginning of a new chapter in our lives. If I ran my mouth to much, which I often did, I got punched in the face and then fucked. He was trying to break my spirit, so he could be in control of his pretty little bird with a broken wing.

11

I put a load of clothes in the washing machine, my panties were getting low. Eddie Kendricks' song "Girl, You Need a Change of Mind" was playing loudly in the background. One of my favorite Go-Go bands, The Young Senators left DC to be the backup band for Eddie Kendricks after he began his solo career after leaving the Temptations. I had the bass turned all the way up! The speakers were thumping! The song had this hard driving beat that made you stop whatever you were doing and bounce your head. I played this one often; somehow it kept the memory of those Monday nights at Bryne Manor, dancing and sweating to The Young Senators, fresh in my mind.

The machine stopped in the midst of the spin cycle. "I can't believe this is happening!" I went to retrieve the warranty book from the kitchen drawer and dialed the number.

"I'd like to make an appointment for service please. My washing machine stopped midway through the spin cycle," I said as I spoke to a customer service representative on the other end.

"Could I have your name and the serial number please?"

"Amber Jones. The serial number is ABW0015."

"Would Friday at 11:00 a.m. be okay?"

"Friday at 11:00 a.m. will be great. Thank you."

I got a trash bag from the pantry and filled it with the wet clothing. I might as well drive into the city and go to a laundromat in the old neighborhood; it helped me stay grounded. I loaded the bag into the trunk and headed into the city.

"Amber, how you been? Long time no see," Doc said with garbled words while trying to keep his balance, still drunk from the night before.

"Hey, Doc," I said, realizing that some things never change.

Doc was the neighborhood drunk. He entertained the shit out of me every time I saw his ass. He'd dance for a few dollars, coming out of that drunken stupor just long enough to make me smile. I always bought him a meal and asked about the family. His wife let him stay in the basement. He was lucky she didn't throw his ass out. I made a mental note to drop some money off to her before I left the city. Doc was more than happy to carry the bag of wet clothes into the laundromat for me. I looked down at my feet as I closed the trunk realizing that I had on two different tennis shoes. I hadn't been myself lately, coming home from the grocery store just the day before I put the aluminum foil in the refrigerator and the fresh cut fruit on the pantry shelf. Stress was gnawing away at me slowly.

Sonny ran the laundromat. He was a cool OG, with salt and pepper hair, a slight bulge around the gut who always wore a button-down shirt, slacks and dress shoes, like he had somewhere to be every evening after work.

"Hey, Mr. Sonny. Could I have some quarters for this ten-dollar bill please?" I asked while keeping an eye on Doc as he struggled putting the bag on the table.

"Girl, you can get all my money if you act right!" he said holding a half-smoked cigar between his fingers and giving me a wink.

"Now, Mr. Sonny, you know if I was going to cheat on my husband, it would definitely be with you, but I can't; you're not trying to see me in a pine box or better yet floating down the Potomac River, are you?"

We'd laugh and talk shit for whatever time it took for me to dry the bag of clothes.

"Amber, you trying to create a new style?" he asked pointing to my tennis shoes. I was embarrassed to say the least, but I think quick on my feet. "That's exactly what I'm doing! Next time I come uptown, I'll see who's copying my style. Good seeing you, Mr. Sonny. I always enjoy our time together," I said with sincerity.

"Amber, I'm not going to wait forever. I got women lined up. You must know that. I'm just willing to put you up front," he said as he walked me to the entrance, stepped outside, and lit his cigar. I smiled as I waved goodbye.

I could hear Doc stumbling up from the rear, "Amber, I got you! Let me put that bag in the trunk," he said expecting money.

"No problem, Doc. I appreciate you," I said, opening the trunk. Doc placed the bag inside the trunk—it was loosely tied, but I didn't touch the bag. I wanted Doc to feel good about himself and that one task. I made a left at the corner, drove to Doc's house and knocked on the front door. His wife opened the door wide with a welcoming smile.

"This is for Doc. You use it however you see fit," I said handing her the money.

"Thanks, Amber. You got a good heart. You be safe in them streets. See you next time," she said as she closed the door. I walked down the steps and got in the car and headed home.

The traffic was a little snarled on South Capital. I turned the music up and checked my patience. Once it started moving, I tried to make up time. I was doing about eighty miles an hour when a large buck leaped from a hill on the right and ran out in front of the car. I slammed on brakes, with no time to even look in the rearview mirror. I could hear the traffic screech to a halt, just before hitting my bumper. The buck casually walked across Suitland Parkway and disappeared into the trees. I sat there stunned, knowing that if I hit a deer of that size, at that speed, I more than likely would've been killed. Car horns began to blow behind me. I stepped on the gas and continued down the road.

It took about thirty minutes before I arrived back at the house. The sun was beginning to set as I drove up the driveway. I opened the trunk and saw that half the bag of clothes had spilled out, probably when I slammed on brakes for the deer. I gathered the clothing stuffing it back inside the trash bag, distracted by wings flapping on a low flying bird. I quickly closed the trunk and ran inside the house.

*   *   *

"Evil" by Earth Wind and Fire was blasting on the stereo. I was grooving to Maurice White singing lead and playing the Kalimba as I folded clothes into neat piles on the living room couch. O came through the front door and headed straight to the bathroom without as much as a hello.

"Give me your keys to the Benz," he said while drying his hands. "I have to make a run; then I'll be down 9th Street."

"Okay," I said, as I reached in my back pocket and handed him the keys, still dancing. He went right back out the door.

I looked up when I heard the front door open again. O came back through the door and walked toward me with something balled up in his hand. I could see he was mad as all get out!

"I knew you was fucking somebody!" he said as he threw a pair of black bikini underwear in my face followed by a hard right hook to my left eye.

I grabbed my eye, screaming, "Stupid motherfucker, I just came from the laundromat! I can't believe you just hit me again! Get the fuck on where you were going!" I screamed with the rage slowly bubbling up from deep inside.

I was applying ice to my eye and pacing the floor talking out loud to myself, "The next time he hits me, I'm going to fuck him up! I'm tired of being scared!" Just then, the phone rang. I answered.

"Hello."

There was silence on the other end.

"Is O there?" It was a woman's voice.

"Who the fuck is this?"

Dead silence once again.

"Disrespectful bitch, don't call my house no more!" I screamed as I slammed the phone down on the receiver. I snatched the keys to the jaguar from the pantry closet and headed for the city, straight to 9th Street. While driving, I reached up lightly touching my eye with my index finger, wincing at the pain. I needed to feel every bit of that pain so when I rolled up on his ass I was going for blood. I spotted him having a conversation with three other guys in front of Chez Maurice. I double parked, jumped out the car and crept up on his ass. I could faintly hear someone say, "Here comes O's crazy wife!" I took off running, jumped on his back, putting him in a choke hold as I pounded on his head.

"Amber, get off of me!" he said, jerking his body trying to get me off, but I held on tight this time. I landed a few good blows to the side of his face before the three guys intervened, pulling me off his back.

"That bitch called the house! You better get her in check. Don't let that shit happen again, motherfucker!" I yelled as I snatched away from their grasps, turned, and walked back to the car, peeling rubber as I drove down the street.

Two weeks had passed. We were barely speaking. Thank God my black eye was nearly gone. I would apply makeup to hide the bruising for my trips to the grocery store. I'd become somewhat of a pro, playing with different techniques to cover my misfortune. At least I knew I could get a job in a department store as a makeup artist if I ever needed one. I damn sure had experience.

Chloe had been checking on me every day, but this call was different.

"Hey, girl," she said with glee, I could feel her smiling through the phone.

"Hi, Chloe. What's up?" I said while I waited for her to tell me some juicy gossip about her life.

"'Lil Man' is throwing a house party on Friday. You know he always hits it out of the park with his affairs. It's been a long time since we've hung out. Tell me you'll go. It will be like old times. You, me, and DJ," she said, trying to convince me to go. I was quiet as I contemplated going.

"Amber, you there?" she asked, thinking we got disconnected.

"I'm here. I want to go," I said, trying not to show too much excitement. O was listening to my every word.

"Cool. DJ and I will pick you up around 10:30 p.m. See you on Friday," she said.

"Talk to you later," I said, ending the call, thinking about Friday already.

"Who was that on the phone?" O asked, knowing damn well he was listening to the call.

"It was Chloe. She wants me to go to a party with her and DJ on Friday," I said as I hummed a tune, dried the dishes, and put them neatly away in the cabinet.

"You need my permission. Next time, give me two weeks' notice, no more of this last minute shit," he said with a superior tone.

"I didn't marry my father. I didn't even give him a two-week notice to go anywhere! Besides, I didn't ask if I could go!"

His jaw tightened and his look was intense.

I took a deep breath, lowered my voice and asked, "O, I would really like to go to the party if it's not a problem. Do I have your permission?" I said. That shit was killing me.

"That's better. See, we won't have any problems if you learn your place," he said as he looked me right in the face, waiting for me to buck. I kept drying the dishes, while I cussed underneath my breath.

I awoke early Friday morning. I cleaned, cooked, and fucked the shit out of O just so everything would go smoothly. I decided to wear a little makeup, nothing too much, a little eyeliner, mascara and lipstick. By 10:15 p.m. I was dressed and sitting by the door.

"Baby come here and let me see what you're wearing," he asked.

I rolled my eyes, but kept my mouth shut, got up, and walked into the living room and modeled my outfit for O knowing I was cute!

"You look good, baby. Come here and give me a kiss before you leave." I walked over, bent down, closed my eyes and moved in toward those lips. I felt his hand grip my face, opening my eyes to only close them shut again as he smeared my makeup with his free hand.

"Go wash that shit off! You're not going out of here looking like a hooker!" His eyes burned as he spoke.

I backed away from him in disbelief, turned, and went up the stairs to the bathroom. I quickly removed the makeup and washed my face. I slipped the lipstick in my purse. The phone rang. I answered.

"Hey, girl! We're outside!" Chloe said, all pumped and ready to party.

"I'll be out in a second."

I descended the steps with my head held high.

"See you later," I said from the foyer.

"Can I get a kiss?" I let out a sigh as I walked to the other room.

I walked into the room, gave him a quick peck on the lips, turned, and walked in a lively manner to the front door, grabbed my umbrella out of the stand, closed the front door behind me, raising the umbrella before I stepped into the driveway. It had been raining all week. Usually, I hated going out in the rain but tonight, it didn't matter. I was free.

Lil Man had really outdone himself with this party. He rented a house that was walking distance from the water, ten minutes away from downtown Annapolis. I could only imagine the sunrise while sitting on that front deck. There was a statue of an African warrior in the entryway. It commanded your attention as you entered the home. The guests were confined to the inside because of the inclement weather but no one cared. There were half-naked women serving hors d'oeuvres on silver platers, a fully stocked bar and two bartenders with a DJ who was pumping the music. The African art on the walls was breathtaking. We hadn't been at the party for more than thirty minutes and Chloe was trying to get into some devilment.

"I'll be back," she said as she walked up the stairs hand in hand with some guy.

I kept my mouth shut. I didn't feel like playing "Mommy" tonight. I wanted to dance, eat a little something, maybe smoke a joint, and just breathe. I was enjoying the music while I scanned the room. I thought I saw the young man from English class. Our eyes met. He walked toward me smiling.

"I thought I'd never see you again and now here you are. You never came back to class. What happened? You transferred to another school?" His eyes gleamed as he posed the question.

"No, I got married," I said reluctantly.

"Damn. That's a blower! Well at least hit this joint with me."

"Cool," I said, eager to get my high on and continue to enjoy the party.

I think it was the second or third pull when the room began to spin—I can't remember. I felt nauseated. People, plants, and paintings were all out of focus. I could feel my body begin to sway; I was lightheaded and hot at the same time. I walked toward the window, to try to pry it open; I needed some fresh air. I could feel someone's hands on mine trying to stop me. The next thing I knew everything went black.

When I opened my eyes, DJ was carrying me to the car dazed and lethargic. Chloe was damn near running beside us trying to hold the umbrella over us both. I was soaked by the time we pulled out of the parking spot. Chloe was in the back seat with me applying a wet washcloth to my forehead.

"What the fuck are we going to tell O?" DJ asked in a panic.

"Hell if I know. O is mean as a rattlesnake. I still don't know if he likes me or not!" Chloe said. The fear was ever present in her voice. "I guess we can tell him the truth," Chloe said, not really believing her own words.

"Tell him the truth! Chloe, are you bat-shit crazy? Were you there with her? Cause I damn sure wasn't. How do you explain some shit you didn't witness to that motherfucker?" The panic had set in. I closed my eyes wishing that I had said no to coming out to the party. I didn't know what to expect when I got home.

The twenty-minute ride seemed to drag out for hours. DJ hit a pothole and I swear I thought my head was going to explode. I was still tripping but tried to pull it together. We were riding up the driveway; I recognized the bushes even from my horizontal position on the back seat. My heart beat loudly as it pushed against my chest in an erratic pattern. DJ put the car in park. He and Chloe walked me to the door, rang the doorbell, and ran like shit to the car and were in the wind.

As O opened the door, I tried my best to quickly walk past him heading for the stairs. He grabbed my shoulder from behind and spun me around.

"What the fuck happened to you?"

He stared at me with those cold eyes and waited for an explanation.

"I was at the party. . . and I was smoking a joint and. . . I got dizzy and. . . I passed out," I said, explaining in short clipped words.

His fist connected with my eye so fast I didn't have time to duck. He threw me over his shoulder, walked up the stairs, and went straight to the master bathroom. He turned the cold water on in the shower full force and pushed me in fully dressed, shoes and all.

"Stay there until I tell your ass you can come out." His eyebrows alone made me afraid.

My eye was beginning to swell shut, I was shivering violently from the cold water plummeting on my head but I was too terrified to move, but I was so weak and so cold that I slowly sank to the floor of the tub. O finally came back to the bathroom, after what seemed like forever and cut off the water.

"Take that wet shit off. Dry off and go to bed," he said with a look of disappointment. I think I was no longer the best wife he would have wished for.

I lay in bed but sleep wouldn't come. I could hear his footsteps coming toward the bedroom.

"Here. Put this on your eye," he said with little compassion.

I took the ice bag from his hand and placed it on my eye, pained by the touch. He undressed and climbed in bed next to me. I could feel him staring at me with both eyes closed.

"Amber, why do you keep doing crazy shit?" he asked with that unsettling gaze.

"I honestly didn't mean for this to happen. You have to believe me. I thought it was just weed," I said truthfully.

"Do you know how embarrassing it is to have my wife getting high and pass out at a party?" he asked as if I didn't know. I was the one it happened to and I was totally embarrassed. It was one of those things that I wished I could erase from my life. I reached for his hand, wanting his forgiveness. Instead, he opened my legs and started finger fucking my pussy before he climbed on top of me for a revenge fuck. I just laid there with my arms to the side and let him have his way with me as I stared at the ceiling through one eye.

I made myself get out of bed around noon. I showered and brushed my teeth. The bristles on the toothbrush were worn. I needed to pick up a new one, surprised I even noticed; I was in a bad head space. I jumped in a pair of old jeans, a midriff top, and tennis shoes, looking at my feet to make sure I had on a matching pair. I avoided looking in the mirror, but glanced anyway. My eye was fucked. The bruises would disappear after going through the metamorphosis of colors, black, purple, green, sometimes yellow, but I would forever remain mentally scarred.

I walked down the steps to the kitchen, opened the cardboard box on the counter and took out a croissant. I turned to get a napkin from the cabinet. O was sitting on the stool, reading the paper, just like it was any other ordinary day. I was fuming inside, but tried to remain calm, just looking at him was infuriating me.

"Amber, I can't have you embarrassing me in the street. I have a reputation to uphold," he said, very business-like, never looking in my direction. I dropped the croissant just as I was about to take a bite, nauseous at the sound of his voice. Suddenly, I didn't have a taste for it anymore, letting it fall to the kitchen counter.

"I passed out at a party, you snorting dope! That brings your stock way down," I said, waiting for his response. He lowered the paper. I saw his eyes darken. "What the fuck about my reputation? I got a closet junkie for a husband. This has all been a facade," I said as I waved my hands widely and looked around the room.

"The night we first met and you asked if I wanted to go for a ride to discuss business, you knew what your intentions were then. You wanted me, but you got caught up. That wasn't part of the plan. Now you think the only way you can keep me is to hit me so that I'll be too afraid to leave. I bet you did that with your ex. What was she, a model? A college chick from a prominent family on the gold coast? Whatever she was, you broke her. I'm young and maybe somewhat naïve, but I was raised by a schizophrenic mother, I've been fighting a war all my life and aside from that I'm street, you'll never break me, motherfucker! You might want to try a different strategy if that's your end game. I grabbed the Hennessy bottle, slammed it against the island. The liquor splattered on the wall, my clothing and then dripped on the floor as I ran toward him with the bottle raised.

"You want to keep hitting me? Oh we can fight; it just won't be a fair fight. I'm no longer scared. Stop putting your fucking hands on me!" I threw the bottle to the floor. It shattered in tiny pieces as it hit the marble. I snatched my purse and ran out the house, jumped into the 450 SL and gunned it down the driveway.

I stayed out late; I had to get my mind right. Then I stopped past Mommy's, she was finally home from St. Elizabeths, to get one of Daddy's fishing knives. If he came anywhere near me, I was going to gut his ass. I put my key in the door, and disarmed the alarm. Hitting the light switch, I was on guard, prepared for a fight, but O wasn't home. I went upstairs, showered, and went to bed. I awoke the next morning and realized that he never came home.

O had a hard time apologizing. Every time he tried, the words were swallowed somewhere deep in his throat. Instead, he left me gifts on the bed, new trinkets, and designer outfits or added cash to my bank account. This shit was getting old.

12

Ifound myself looking forward to doing runs. O bought me another used car for business, a Ford Focus. Anything to get out the house and away from his ass. I'd simply slip on my Chanel sun shades and drag that shit out as long as I could without being questioned.

The following Thursday, Daddy called, sounding frantic.

"Amber, you need to come home. Your mother is missing." I heard him sniffle as if he had been crying, his voice sounded distraught.

"Daddy, what do you mean she's missing?" I said, not able to hide the anxiety in my voice.

"I came home from work tonight and she's not here. I'm worried."

"I'm on my way," I said as I hung up the phone.

I knew in my heart the reason Mommy had disappeared. She came home from St. Elizabeths assigned to a new doctor and new medications. It was never a good combination for her. She didn't handle change well at all.

"O, Mommy's missing. I have to go to the city to look for her." I spun around in circles not able to remember where I'd laid my purse.

"Hold up. I'm coming with you." He turned off the television and grabbed his keys. We had been like strangers living under the same roof, barely speaking, but to be honest I needed him tonight. He pulled the Range out of the garage. I opened the door and could hear Miles Davis' "Bitches Brew" coming from the speakers. My mind was wandering trying to think where Mommy would go, alone at night. When she was off her meds, she wasn't scared of shit. In fact, anyone that came in contact with her might want to turn and run in the opposite direction to avoid a physical altercation or at least a verbal cussing out that they wouldn't easily forget.

"You okay?" O asked with genuine concern.

"I'll be fine once we find her," I said.

He took my hand, pulled it toward his lips, and kissed it softly. I turned and looked in his direction for a sweeping moment and then back out the window.

"O, I need to say this to you while I'm not cursing or being disrespectful and you are sober and really listening to what I'm saying. This right here is the man that I fell in love with. You turn into a monster when you're high. I want this man back," I said, wringing my hands together nervously.

"I'm going to try to stop getting high. I don't want to lose you. Amber, I love you more than anything," he said convincingly. I took in a deep breath and let out a long sigh, staring back out the window.

We arrived in the city and drove straight to my parent's house. Daddy's eyes were bloodshot and swollen. Lord knows he loved that woman. I often thought how lucky she was to have a man that loved her unconditionally, mental illness and all. I thought about the time she was outside in front of the house, leaning against the cement bricks, her curls uncombed, her outfit thrown together, nothing matched, the soles of her feet were black as coal from walking on the sidewalk with no shoes.

I said to her, "You keep coming outside looking like that and Daddy's going to leave you for another woman."

She looked back at me with a crooked smile and said in that slow southern drawl, "Your father ain't never going nowhere. You can put money on that," I giggled out loud at the memory.

"What's funny, baby?" O asked wanting in on the joke.

"I just had a pleasant thought about Mommy, that's all," I said and then looking at my dad, I added, "Daddy, O and I are going to drive around to see if we can find her. You stay here in case the police call back."

He just stared into space with no response.

We turned to walk out the door and Daddy spoke, "Amber, take your mother's inhaler. Her asthma has been bothering her lately." I walked back to take the inhaler from his hand.

"So where to, baby?" O asked.

"Maybe we can start at 14th Street. She used to take me to shop there when I was a little girl, before the riots. Next, we can try U Street, and if no luck there, downtown to the department stores. My last resort would be Georgetown. She and my dad worked for a rich family there. She was the cook, the maid, and the babysitter. He was the butler and the driver. She used to take Chris with her to work sometimes; the family adored his bad ass. They had a pond out front with ducks. Chris took each duck one by one and broke their necks just like he'd seen my uncle twist the necks on the chickens in the country."

"Damn! I know he got his ass whipped," O said.

"I doubt it! He was only two," I said. "Mommy said Chris would wander away from the house and out onto the highway, when they worked at the house in McClean, Va. Some stranger would pull up and knock on the front door to safely return him. They knew which house to go to; he was the only little black boy in the neighborhood. She finally bought a toddler harness for his ass," I said thinking back on family memories, hoping Mommy was okay.

We slowly rode down 14th Street with me scanning both sides of the street. O made a left on Irving and a right on 11th Street. It wasn't long before we came up on the pimps and prostitutes. I was always amused by the performance they displayed, almost circus like, for any and all onlookers. You never knew what you might see. Tonight, they were boisterous and talking big shit to each other.

One pimp was standing on top of his hot pink El Caballero Cadillac, with white wall tires, excess chrome, and a naked lady painted on the side. He was dressed in hot pink with his shirt unbuttoned to his waist, showing off his washboard abs, flashing hundred-dollar bills at the others. O blew the horn, acknowledging "Big Tony" as one of his good paying customers, getting out of his tricked-out Rolls Royce, in his money-green-and-gold custom-made striped suit with matching hat and platform boots. His permed ponytail hung down his back while in the front, ten gold and diamond necklaces draped around his neck— one was a diamond encrusted cross that hung from midway of his chest to his waist, bold and gaudy were the diamond rings proudly displayed on each finger. Tony's face was adorned with oversized sun shades, even though it was nighttime. The frames were drenched in diamonds of various sizes. His ladies of the night were dime pieces walking the block, strutting like peacocks, leaving very little to the imagination, getting that money.

"Hey, Honey!" I yelled out the window.

"Amber! Where have you been, girl?" Honey said with excitement. She was one of "Big Tony's" top money makers.

"I see you still with that fine specimen of a man," she said, batting her eyes with a flirtatious smile. "You need to let me slip up in that bedroom with the two of you. I could show you some tricks so he'll never leave. As good as he looks I might do that shit for free!"

"The hell you will, bitch! Get back to work!" "Big Tony" shut that shit down real quick.

O and I laughed out loud. Car after car pulled over to the curb; the women were ambitious and competitive in providing a service. One down on to the next.

Once we reached U Street, O drove slowly past the Lincoln Theater.

"Stop! Can you back up please? I thought I glimpsed a shadow in the alley," I said as I turned to look back.

O parked halfway down the block. We walked to the theater, stopping at the entrance of the alley. There was Mommy, sitting on the ground with her back against the building, one shoe on, one shoe off.

"See, that's where you're wrong, I'm a child of Christ," she was having a debate with the voices in her head, wheezing in-between each breath.

I ran to her, wanting to wrap my arms around her, but she wasn't having it tonight.

"Don't touch me, whore!" she screamed. I looked back at O for help, shaking my head.

He took the inhaler out of my hand and walked right up to her and asked, "Mom, what are you doing out here?"

"I'm waiting for the movie theater to open. I tried to get. . . my hair done at. . . the beauty parlor. . . but they were closed too," she said as she wheezed heavily.

"Come on, Mom, take a couple of puffs, and then I'm taking you home." She took the inhaler from his hand, shook it, and put it to her lips.

"We can come back later when everything is open for business," he said and then helped her get up off the ground. She walked right past me. Tonight, I was a stranger, again.

Daddy didn't want to take her back to St. Elizabeths Hospital. The very thought tore at his heart. He was afraid that the other patients were a danger to her. I found some of her old medication in the kitchen cabinet.

"O, please get her to take these pills. It will help her sleep. I'll make an appointment in the morning to meet with this new doctor," I said as I handed him the pills.

"Okay, Mom," he said as he handed her the pills with a cup of water from her China tea set. "I need you to swallow these." She took the medication with no resistance. Daddy and I stood back and watched, shaking our heads.

Next morning, Mommy and I sat in the psychiatrist's office waiting for her arrival from an unscheduled meeting. I stared at her name tag on the heavy wooden desk, as if that would reveal something about the woman. She had a wall dedicated to certificates and diplomas, nicely framed. Everything on the desk was perfectly arranged, nothing out of place.

She walked into the room, stern faced with oval glasses and coffee in hand.

"Good Morning, Ladies. I'm Dr. Simon. Mrs. Hayden has been assigned to me for treatment. Mrs. Jones, you seem to have a problem with the new medication that I've prescribed for your mother? I'm the psychiatrist. I've been practicing for many years, as you can see on that wall." She pointed to the wall, and Mommy and I both followed her finger, as we turned to look in that direction.

"You have to give these things time," she said. "You have to give the medication a chance to work."

But I interrupted before she could continue with her practiced spiel.

"Time is up, Dr. Simon. Change my mom's medication back to what she was taking before your arrival. We've been down this road since I was a little girl. No more playing guinea pig with my mother. She's had everything from shock treatment to Thorazine, and now this, which I can't even pronounce! Find a new test dummy! You prescribe these new drugs without a care and go home to your family for a nice dinner, while we go home to chaos! Put her back on the previous medication or I'll sue the shit out of St. Elizabeths Hospital and you personally for not listening to what the fuck I'm saying. You have a nice day, Dr. Simon. Come on, Mommy; let's go!" I took Mommy by the arm pulling her up out of the chair, walking toward the door, looking back at Dr. Simon.

"I'll be waiting at the pharmacy. Make it happen!"

13

O and I decided to stay at the house in Rock Creek Park so I could keep a check on Mommy. He didn't make it two days before I found him high on the living room couch, singing his heart out to Jimi Hendrix's "Purple Haze." Our constant arguments became routine. We would go days, if not weeks, without speaking. He started going out a little more often. I became withdrawn without the Go-Go and escaped into my books.

This particular night he spoke before leaving, "Be back later. I have some business to handle."

I looked over the top of the pages and watched him adjust his belt, and take his keys off the dresser, smelling and looking real good. He quickly glanced in the full-length mirror, before closing the bedroom door. That's when I knew he was fucking with that bitch.

He had no idea that under the covers, I was wearing a sexy red lace teddy. I was finally going to seduce his ass and call a truce to this war. Now, I was pacing the floor like a raging bull. I went down the stairs to the kitchen, opened the refrigerator and spotted the bottle of Dom Pérignon. No time like the present to take that first drink. I popped the cork and took it to the head, drinking half the bottle. I sat down on the chaise still clutching the bottle in my hand, feeling a little foolish.

"Here's to the end of a marriage," I said, too angry to cry.

I put the bottle to my lips and punished the rest of the bubbles.

"I think I have an idea where that bitch lives. Let me get my purse," I continued to speak out loud, as I headed to the garage, wobbling, in just the teddy and heels. I saw the cobra nestled in the corner, O's favorite car. I stumbled back into the house to get the keys and my heat.

"I'm coming for you, O," I said as I made my way to the car.

I started her up, opened the garage door, and pulled down the driveway. I loved the sound of the engine. It was like being back at the race track. I pulled down the hill, drove through the neighborhood and onto Beach Drive.

"So, this is what it feels like to be tipsy as I weaved over and back across the white line. I think I'm closer to being drunk," I said out loud followed by a hearty laugh.

"It's Too Late" by Carole King came on the radio.

"The DJ couldn't have picked a better song for tonight. Too bad I can't hit repeat," I said as I glanced in the rearview mirror and saw two men with ski masks following.

"Of all times for this shit to happen. You got the right girl tonight because I don't give a fuck! Drunk or not, I know these curves like the back of my hand," I said out loud.

The adrenaline kicked in and I went from 0 to 100 in a matter of seconds, blew through the three way stop sign at Beach Drive and Piney Branch Parkway with the tail on my ass. I reached for the Luger, held on to the steering wheel with my left hand, looked back, pointed the gun and emptied the clip, hitting both men. Their car veered off to the right with the driver slumped over the wheel, hit the curb going airborne and plunged into the creek just shy of the 25 mile an hour speed limit sign as I rounded the first curve before the Zoo. I continued on toward the tunnel, the brick entrance begging for my attention, buried deep in the crevices the graffiti sang out loud refusing to be ignored. I exited the tunnel, made a right and another right on Connecticut Avenue. I felt a few raindrops hit my face.

"I've got to get this damn car back in the garage," I said as I continued to have a conversation with myself out loud.

I was more afraid of the cobra getting wet and having to face O than what just took place. I pulled up the driveway, opened the garage door, turned around and backed in slowly. In my intoxication, I thought it was straight. As I exited the car, I stumbled twice on the way to the house and decided it might be easier to just crawl up the stairs. I climbed into bed, falling fast asleep, while hugging my favorite pillow.

I was having a recurring nightmare. I couldn't wake up. There was an eighth of cocaine on the dresser, which transformed right before my eyes into the "Pillsbury Dough Boy." He jumped from the dresser onto my chest where he grew to four-hundred-pounds in a matter of seconds with a sinister laugh. He began feeding me all my favorite desserts, one after another. I couldn't breathe. I was drowning in sweets.

I knew exactly why I kept having this nightmare. Subconsciously I feared getting fat. I watched my mother's weight fluctuate year after year. She was too heavy for her small frame when on her medication and would hastily drop the pounds when she stopped taking it. I was damn near anorexic. Daddy worried.

I was struggling to wake up. Unbeknownst to me, O had propped me up in the bed with several pillows behind my back. He held a 45 to my temple. I opened my eyes once I felt the cold metal against my skin. He pulled the trigger. I heard the gun click, but it didn't fire. I think my heart stopped beating for a moment. He was playing Russian Roulette with my life.

"You do a lot of shit that I let your ass get away with. Don't you ever and I mean ever drive that car again! Am I making myself perfectly clear?"

He was hostile in his delivery.

The tears streamed down my face and I had to pee. My head was throbbing, but I was crippled by fear. He pivoted and left the room.

I ran to the bathroom, not having time to remove the teddy, sat on the toilet, peeing through the material, my leg shaking uncontrollably. I sat there and sobbed loudly as if someone had died; maybe it was me that I was mourning. I think I was dead inside.

I struggled out of the teddy, tossing it in the trash. Turned on the shower and stepped in, still sobbing as I slowly washed my body. As I dried off, I caught a glimpse of my reflection in the mirror. I stared, letting the towel fall to the floor, wiping the tears away. I could hear Neil Young's song, "Down by the River," but it was Buddy Miles' gut wrenching rendition. The song was about a man shooting the woman he loved. He was playing the song to clearly bring the message home. I decided right then and there that no matter what he did to me from this day forward, he'd never see me cry again. I never mentioned the shooting. Another secret.

Our fights became more violent.

"Bitch, you really think you're rough! So you're not going to cry?" he yelled.

"Fuck no!" I screamed at the top of my lungs.

"The next time you swing, I'm breaking this motherfucking lamp over your head!" While smashing one of his favorite statues against the wall to get my point across. I'd pack my shit and leave him bloody, go to my parents, to only turn around and go back two weeks later. No one understood. Why should they? I had no answer except I loved him.

We packed up the house down the way and sold it to pay the high profile lawyer with promises of bringing the numbers down. We damn sure didn't need two houses with him going away. I liked the house in Rock Creek Park, not so many tragic memories.

I was dressed in black for his sentencing. US District Court, or as I referred to it as "Big Court," was no joke. The marshals were no nonsense, no smiles and downright intimidating. Chloe sat next to me on the wooden bench, fidgeting with her bracelet. I hit her hand to make her stop; it was annoying. As I looked around the courtroom; it seemed so much larger than the ones on the television.

The bailiff announced, "All rise for the Honorable Judge Nathan Hughes."

Chloe and I rose to our feet as the judge entered the courtroom. I felt queasiness in the bottom of my stomach. I listened intently as the judge stated all the reasons why O should be remanded into custody to serve a sentence of three to six years.

I waited until the marshals removed O from the courtroom before I cried. I really was going to have to step up now. My husband and my partners were incarcerated at the same time.

14

I circled the parking lot in search of a space several times before opting to find a park on the street. The central air was circulating like a whisper in the waiting area at the D.C. jail. I continuously wiped at the beads of sweat rolling down the side of my face. The perspiration ran down the middle of my spine to my lower back, finding a home in my cotton shirt. I crossed and uncrossed my legs and looked at my watch every fifteen minutes. Time was dragging.

"They must be doing count. Amber, you need to learn some patience," I said to myself agitated. Two hours passed before people started exiting the visiting area to my surprise. I saw a guy I knew from uptown. I smiled and said hello. His response threw me all the way to the left. "Your husband got a visitor in there," he said that shit in passing and kept it moving. I began to focus on every woman exiting the room. I knew my antenna would go up as soon as I saw her. There she was. Older, chic with an air of confidence. We were finally face to face. Her smile faded as soon as she saw me. We stared each other down, not saying a word. My beef wasn't with her; it was with him.

I glanced around the visiting area spotting him already seated behind the glass. I sat down and put the phone to my ear, the same one that she used to speak into, laugh, and share time with him. In my head, I kept repeating, "Keep your composure, Amber."

"Hi, baby." I said with a fake smile.

"You look sexy," he said, happy to see me. For a brief moment, when I looked into those eyes, he almost had me. But not today!

"I'm going to keep this brief, and say how I feel with a smile on my face, not trying to give the guards a show. I waited for two hours to see you. It was like a sauna out there. You want to put that bitch in front of me? This will be my first and last time coming to see you at this jail. You better hope I accept those collect phone calls. See you when I see you." I politely put the phone on the receiver, got to my feet, and put an extra little something in my walk as I left without looking back.

One of the guards had enough nerve to approach me on my exit.

"I can take care of all your needs while he's here. You want my number?" he asked as if I would really be interested. I just smiled and kept walking. Outside, I saw the jail bus pulling in from court. I waved as always, not knowing if someone I knew was on board.

The phone was ringing off the hook as soon as I walked through the door. I answered. It was a collect call from the jail.

"Damn O must've timed this shit!" I said out loud.

"Hello."

"Amber, what the fuck! You think because I'm in here you gonna treat me with disrespect?" he said spitting venom. I could feel his anger growing through the phone.

"Must I remind you that these phone calls are being recorded?" I said in a sing-song voice.

"I don't give a fuck! You bring your ass over here Wednesday!" he yelled.

"I'll accept your phone calls, but I won't be back. You don't deserve to see me. Peace." I simply put the phone on the receiver and ended the call.

The months passed quickly for me, mainly because I was back to what gave me life, the Go-Go. O's phone calls were frequent, as if he could cock block through the phone. This one was earlier than usual.

"I'm being transferred to Lorton. Please come see me, baby. I can hold you . . . stick my tongue down your throat. I know you miss that," he said, sounding all sexy making my pussy wet. I closed my eyes and got a chill.

"You not out there fucking, are you?" he asked boldly.

"Lucky for your ass I don't want no dick but yours. I've purchased a variety of sex toys and named each one after you. They get the job done. Sometimes, I come so hard I have to cut that bitch off!"

We both shared a laugh.

"That's one of the things I love about you because you make me laugh. I need that," he said. "Baby, I got to go! I'll see you soon!" he said. The call ended. I guess I'd punished him enough. I was looking forward to visiting him at Lorton.

Today was a special day; I was turning sixteen. With everything that I'd been through I felt as if I was turning twenty-five. I had some important business to take care of this morning. Daddy was taking me to Motor Vehicle to take my road test.

That man is always on time; in fact, we arrived fifteen minutes early. I was nervous as hell, which made no sense because I'd been driving for years. I just didn't like taking tests of any kind. Thank God, I passed with flying colors. I ran to Daddy jumping in the air and screaming with everyone staring. He hugged me and smiled. He knew how much this meant to me. He gave me a birthday card with two nice crisp hundred-dollar bills enclosed. I kissed him on the cheek as I jumped out of the car and went inside the house. I was finally going to see my husband today.

Any other normal teenager would be excited about their sixteenth birthday and having a big party with all their class-mates and friends, but here I was waiting to see my husband at the penitentiary. I had to admit I had butterflies in the pit of my stomach.

O sauntered into the visiting room looking all buff. I could see other inmates acknowledging his presence with head nods, some speaking; others stared as if they were in the presence of God as he made his way toward me. I wanted to run and jump in his arms but I knew better. I stood once he was close enough and let him wrap his arms around me. He stuck his tongue down my throat just like he said he would. We laughed, talked, took photos, and French kissed like two teenagers in the back room of a high school party. It was the best birthday I'd ever had.

Time passed way too fast. I was sad having to leave him. He could see my eyebrows lower and my smile disappear.

"I need you to be strong," O said while grabbing my chin and looking in my eyes. "I got this. I'll be home in no time. You still got your love affair going on with your sex toys?" he asked, trying to make me smile.

"Of course," I said putting my head down, feeling my cheeks begin to blush.

"Next time you come, bring a $10.00 bill. I got a surprise for you."

Just then, the guard announced, "Visiting time is over."

We stood and he kissed me as if no one else was watching. I didn't realize how much I missed him, until I had to leave him.

I left Lorton and drove straight to DJ's mom's house. I could hear Donny Hathaway's song "The Ghetto" blasting from the stereo inside. He was playing the hell out of the piano as the notes flowed out of an open window as I came up the walkway. I bounced in the front door dancing. Broke that thing all the way down as if I was at the Go-Go.

"You're celebrating a milestone today, baby girl! Look at you! Coming back from seeing your husband! Got you all pumped up!" she said, now dancing with me as she displayed that big wide grin.

DJ's mom was bagging up last minute orders for lunch and dinners sold throughout the day. There was an aroma in the air filled with a blend of fried catfish, chicken wings, macaroni and cheese and greens with her secret seasoning and sauces. I could smell the carrot cake baking in the oven. It was one of my favorite desserts. I'd secretly tried to watch her prepare the food over the years while carrying on a simple conversation, hoping she wouldn't notice. Once she looked up and realized I was watching a little too hard, she would back me up out of that kitchen with the quickness.

"I already packed up your plate, baby. Your dessert too! This is my third carrot cake today. Your little crew came back for seconds. Acting like they ain't never ate no good food before! DJ went to go get your presents. Are you going to hang out for a little while until he comes back? I know you ain't in no rush to get home," she said while hitting her hands together letting the flour fall to the counter.

"You know I like being here anyway, even if it wasn't my birthday. Where are the kids?" I asked inquisitively, looking around.

"They went with their dads. I needed a break. Didn't want them all up under foot while I was cooking," she answered with a sigh of relief. "This has been a good day, Amber. I tripled my money, not including the tips. Your crew look after me real good. I appreciate them and I appreciate you."

She spoke in a humbling manner. I accepted her words with a genuine smile.

DJ arrived with a professionally wrapped box and a bow on top. I caught a whiff of the seafood as he walked by.

"My man! Can I see what's in the bag?" I asked, getting excited because I loved me some seafood.

"Damn, Amber. You are worse than the kids. I was trying to surprise your ass, but you beat me here. Open this one first," he said, handing me the box.

I carefully removed the bow and then tore into the wrapping paper as if it was Christmas. I placed both hands on either side of the box and lifted. I could see the Gucci insignia. I pulled the purse out of the dust bag.

"You got me the purse I saw in Neiman Marcus when we were in Dallas! I can't believe you remembered! Thank you, DJ!" I said, jumping to my feet planting a kiss on his cheek as I wrapped around his waist and hugged him tight.

"Are we going out tonight to celebrate?" he asked, already in dance mode.

"No. I think I just want to go home tonight and eat my seafood," I said with a grin.

"Who said that bag was for you?" he joked.

"Don't play! Let me see!" I said doing my happy dance.

I opened the bag and removed the foil. There was a lobster tail stuffed with crabmeat, golden brown French fries, coleslaw, just the way I liked it, without a lot of mayonnaise and cornbread.

"I'm loving the purse, but you know for real nothing makes me happier than good food," I said as I gathered all my plates and put them in a shopping bag to devour later and for the next few days.

I decided to stop at a liquor store on 14th Street to see who I saw hanging outside that could purchase a good bottle of champagne for me; after all, it was my birthday! There were no parking spaces so I pulled up on the corner. I saw Pit jump out of his car and head for the entrance. I rolled down the window and called out his name.

"Hey, Pit. Come here for a minute, please," I said waving him over to my car. I looked at his face thinking, the craters weren't as noticeable, but the nickname still remained.

"What's up, Amber?" he said in a rushed tone as if he was in a hurry.

"Can you buy me a bottle of Dom, please? It's my birthday." My smile said it all.

"I got you," he said as I handed him several hundred-dollar bills.

He turned and headed toward the entrance and sidestepped a scruffy young woman with a black scarf, a purple and pink jumpsuit with a yellow hoodie, crusty feet, and flip flops as she was being kicked out of the store just as he approached the entrance.

"Fuck you! Ya'll ain't shit no way!" she screamed as she placed the wrinkled bills back in her pocket.

"Sir! Do you mind buying me a bottle of 'Cold Duck'?" Her words were slurred.

"Nah. I'm in a hurry," he said.

"Fuck you too!" she screamed mad at the world.

I watched the woman walk to the alley and take a seat, still cussing. Pit left the store, stopped momentarily, and looked around before he walked toward my car and handed me the bag and change.

"Here's a fifty for your trouble," I said, handing him the money.

"Thanks, Amber. Oh by the way, the Cold Duck is for the drunk lady, but I didn't see her and I got to run." He turned and ran back to his car and disappeared around the corner.

I climbed out of the car and walked toward the alley.

"Here's your drink," I said as I handed the brown paper bag to the woman sitting on the ground looking lost. She reached inside her pocket to hand me the bills.

"That's okay, sweetie. You can keep your money. This one's on me," I said with a smile and turned to walk back to the car.

"Hey, Miss! I can eat your pussy!" she said loudly, so all ears around could hear.

"No, I'm good. I'm straight and I got a husband. Enjoy your drink," I said and got in the car and headed to Suitland Parkway.

When I arrived home, I stripped down to my underwear, placed a champagne glass in the freezer to chill, put on my royal blue silk robe trimmed in satin and warmed up my lobster tail and fries in the oven. Food tastes so much better when warmed in the oven instead of the microwave. I popped the cork on the bottle of Dom Pérignon and poured a glass. I said a toast to myself out loud, "Here's to making it to sixteen."

The telephone rang. I knew it was Chloe I hadn't heard from her all day.

"Happy Birthday, Amber! Please forgive me for being late with this call. I had the craziest shit happen today."

"And today was different than any other day because . . ." I said, waiting for her answer.

"Hush!" she said as she continued with her story.

"You know I've been fucking with the married man for a minute," she said. I could tell this was going to be interesting.

"He still got the piranha?" I asked.

"Girl, hell yeah! You remember that day you came to help me feed it?

"Who could forget that shit?" I said laughing.

"You said we were going to open the top to the tank on the count of three. I was supposed to throw the food in the tank and that damn fish shot up in the air as soon as you opened the top as if it was waiting to escape. It landed on the floor and was flapping all around. We ran around the apartment screaming until I got the broom and the dust pan, swept it up and threw it back in the tank," Chloe said while laughing. "Girl, that was some funny shit! Now let me finish my story. You remember how I kept complaining about going back and forth to the clinic with yeast infections. I'd use the cream, get straight, and that shit would be right back! Well, he came by the spot today; you know I've been staying there off and on because he was paying the rent. I'd just showered, put on my robe, and was laying across the bed. We started kissing, juices were flowing, he pulled out his dick and it looked like somebody poured Clorox on that shit! We've been playing tag with yeast, but it looked like he got it the worst! Do you know this motherfucker still wanted to fuck?"

"Chloe stop! You making my stomach hurt," I laughed loud and hard as Chloe continued on with her story.

"I hurried up and snatched my purse and got the hell up out of dodge in just my robe. That shit freaked me out! But hold on; it gets better! He then proceeds to start throwing my clothes out the window, from the eleventh floor! I'm picking my shit up off the ground and cussing his ass out at the same time! This homeless lady walked up with her eyes sparkling like she just hit the jackpot, helping herself to my shit!" Chloe said still not done. "I told her, 'Drop my shit and don't make me cut your ass!'"

Luckily, I was able to hail a cab. The driver got out and helped me gather the rest of my shit and put my clothes in his trunk. It wasn't until I was safely in the cab and could take a breath that I realized I'd left my blow. Man, I'm done! I don't even want that dick no more!" We both burst out laughing.

"You know that's Karma biting you in the ass for fucking with somebody else's husband. Love triangles don't mean nobody no good," I said hoping my words hit home.

"Alright, Amber, with your lecturing ass! I'm out. Enjoy what's left of your birthday! We'll celebrate on another day real soon. I already got your present! Love you!"

15

I was pushing it down 95 South. Cumulus clouds were in abundance, like white cotton balls overhead. It was hard to keep my eyes on the road. I really enjoyed watching the sky. I had my driver's license so I pulled the Range out the garage, thinking to myself how O had his favorites. I checked my bag several times before leaving to make sure I had a ten-dollar bill.

O had been transferred behind the wall to maximum security. Once arriving at the complex, I had to catch a bus with noisy and energetic women, who just like me, were giddy with anticipation of seeing their men. I sat patiently waiting for O to enter the visiting area. My heart began to flutter as I watched him walk toward me. We kissed, long and deep.

O held me tight whispering in my ear, "Did you bring the ten-dollar bill?"

"Yes, baby, just as you asked," I said.

"Good."

I noticed O watching a door, not far from where we were sitting. An inmate exited and signaled O. He took me by the hand and walked toward the door with me fast walking behind him, handing the inmate the ten-dollar bill, as we crossed the door sill.

There was a sea of mattresses separated by white sheets. Some were already occupied with sounds of sexual gratification filling the room. O pulled a sheet back and stepped in with me following.

"Get naked," he said while unbuttoning his shirt, craving my body.

I was out of my dress and boots in record time, discarding my underwear haphazardly on the floor, too aroused to care. I lay on my back, watching him undress, anxiously waiting. He climbed on top of me, foreplay was not an option, grasped my wrists above my head, with his hard dick rubbing against my inner thigh before he hit the bullseye. My eyes were wide open, we were cheek to cheek, until he hit that spot, I almost lifted his ass off the mattress. He felt my body quiver underneath him and covered my mouth before I could scream. He pulled his dick out abruptly.

"Turn over," he commanded.

I got on my knees. He pounded harder and deeper, until I fell to my stomach, clutching the sheet with both hands. Once again, he pulled out and ordered me to "Turn over."

O placed my feet on his biceps and entered me again. My head was thrashing from side to side. I was cupping my breast, circling my nipple with my left hand and covering my mouth with the right, suppressing the scream lingering in the base of my throat. Just when I thought I couldn't take anymore, we both came simultaneously. He collapsed upon me, his weight heavy on my body, but I didn't complain. I heard the knock at the door.

"Times up," the inmate announced in a deep grown man voice.

"Put your clothes on, baby. That pussy was on the money."

I now understood what it meant to fall in and out of love in a marriage. I was all in—knee deep in quicksand and sinking fast, going down with a smile. We were back in our seats in the visiting room. I couldn't take my eyes off of him. He smiled because he knew he had me.

He leaned in close, whispering in my ear, "I'll let you know the next time we're having a conjugal visit. Bring a ten-dollar bill and some packets of heroin." I tried to sit back to look him in the eye but he held me close. "You can put them in a balloon and stick it up in your pussy. I know what you're thinking, but I'm not getting high. I'm doing some bartering," he said.

Our next visit was in a private area with several other couples. I was wearing a flowered wrap dress, a Diane von Furstenberg. It accentuated my shape. I could tell by his smile when he entered the room that he approved. The guards allowed music to be played; Edwin Starr's "Twenty-Five Miles" was the first song of the night. The entire room, including the guards, were singing the words in unison with conviction. I loved seeing O's million-dollar smile, which he rarely displayed, as we hand-danced and bopped the entire visit as if we were on a stage for the whole world to see.

Later that week, I got the phone call.

"Hey, baby. The next visit should be a good one. I can't wait to see you," he said, sounding quite cheerful. I knew what that meant.

After the next run, I stopped by one of the workhouses off Martin Luther King Avenue in S.E. It was empty. These niggas keep late hours, no need to be up this early in the morning. I sat down at the square table and set about my work. I wore a mask while I cut the heroin, just needed a one on it, before placing the substance in small plastic bags, running my fingers across the top to make sure each was closed properly. I cleaned up my mess, looked out the window to get a feel for the block, and then left unnoticed.

I was dressed in designer garb from head to toe and ready to take that ride. I stood in the mirror studying myself long and hard.

Speaking out loud, "This shit is like throwing rocks at the penitentiary. The things you do for love."

I scanned the visitor list upside down and saw two women's names that I didn't recognize. I remembered what Ms. Lola said that if a nigga can afford more than one house, and more than one car, than more than likely they can afford more than one woman. It doesn't matter how good your pussy is or how well you cook or how many times you put money on his books, there's always going to be someone else. She wanted to prepare me just in case because that's the life I signed up for.

I put that shit out of my mind. I was carrying contraband and didn't need the negative energy. I made sure I did a lot of flirting with the male guards as I walked through the metal detector. They got a charge out of squeezing my titties just a little too long, sliding their hands between my legs, up and down my inner thighs, feeling my coochie and cupping my ass like a stress reliever. I took that shit with no complaints and a smile, even though it was degrading as fuck to get felt up in front of others. The female guards were the worst. I just wanted to get to my husband with no problems.

This time, after greeting O with a kiss, I knew the drill. I was more than ready to go to the room designated for quenching desires.

O leaned in and whispered in my ear, "The dude that killed your uncle is in here, waiting to be shipped to the Feds," he said as he leaned back and looked into my eyes. We both were quiet. Nothing else needed to be said. I knew he wouldn't make it out of Lorton.

I saw the guy give him the signal. We stood and walked to the room. He handed the short thin guy with the braids the ten-dollar bill. We both undressed quickly as I reached up in my pussy and pulled out the balloon. Now it was my time to enjoy my man.

O investigated the packets, holding them up against the dimly lit light bulb, giving me a strange look.

"Amber. Are you coming on your period?" O asked a little perturbed.

"Not that I know of, I haven't had any cramps, which is a definite sign for me. Why?" I asked with concern.

"This shit ain't no good. It's a little pinkish coloring in the bags," he said as he cast them to the side.

"My apologies, baby. So we not fucking?" I asked nervously, thinking the worst.

"Hell yeah! When have you known me not to be a soldier? It might get a little messy," he said, holding his dick with a sly smile.

"I thought you were mad with me," I said, relieved that he wasn't angry.

"No worries. I know some dudes that shoot-up. They'll be happy with this. It's all good. Open your legs!" He said now on his knees and spreading my legs wide without waiting for any assistance on my behalf. He was focused on getting his nut off. I knew that look; this was all about him I was just his repository.

16

DJ had finally found him a love interest. Someone he truly cared about. She was a pretty little chocolate thing with Indian hair, no titties but with an ass big enough to sit a drink on, named Gina. I met her for the first time about a year ago while having dinner at the Market Inn. She was extremely quiet, borderline shy with an observant eye. The conversation remained on bullshit, in-between cracking open crab legs and ordering more champagne. DJ and I laughed, talked, and drank. He tried to pull her into the conversation, if only with a wink and a smile. It was something about her that I just couldn't put my finger on. I never wanted to be close to her nor did I want her around when we were doing business. I've never trusted women, had no real use for them. I didn't like the drama, cattiness, jealousy, or just wanting to be your friend because of your lifestyle. Chloe got a pass because she'd been there for most of my life. DJ was in love and I didn't want to fuck that up as long as it didn't interfere with the business. Lord knows he dealt with my shit with O. Always there to move me back and forth every time I'd pack up and leave and then go right back. He never once complained nor was he judgmental. I loved him for that.

The heat was relentless and it was way before noon. I dialed DJ's number. The phone rang several times before he answered.

"What's up," he said, sounding hungover, again.

"Meet me at Hogates by 1:00 p.m." He knew that when I kept the conversation short, it meant business. I saw him as I walked into the entrance of the restaurant. He was sitting at the bar nursing a drink with a clean shaven head.

"You shaved your head," I said.

"You saw those bald spots. The doctor said it came from stress. I couldn't keep walking around with that shit. I shaved it off last night," he said.

"Before or after you started drinking?" I asked while I scanned the menu at the bar.

"It don't really matter. I did okay," he said while running his hand over his head.

"I like the new look, but didn't you have enough to drink last night?" I asked with no sympathy and a scowl, as I looked into his eyes and then at the glass in his hands.

"This right here is my remedy for a hangover. You wanted to meet? I'm here and I was early. I'll drink plenty of water once I get back in the house," he said as he swirled his cognac, and then took another sip as he rose from the bar stool and followed me to the hostess stand to be seated.

"How are you both today? My name is Carol and I'll be your waitress. Can I get you anything to drink?" she asked with a plastic smile, looking as if she glued it on along with her uniform at the beginning of her shift.

"I'll have an Arnold Palmer. If you don't mind, can you take our food order now? I'm starving," I said.

"Of course. What would you like to order?"

"I'll have the seafood salad and can you bring him the salmon and asparagus, please? Thank you so very much," I said as I watched a tray of food being delivered to another table. Mommy always said it was rude to stare. I wonder if that included food. I smiled at the thought.

"My pleasure," she said as she collected the menus and turned and promptly walked toward the kitchen.

"Before you say anything, you need some protein. You'll feel better after you eat; trust me," I said looking away from his glare.

"DJ, you've been drinking a lot lately. What's going on?"

He rested his elbow on the table and rubbed his fingers across his forehead, took another sip of cognac before answering, "I keep having these nightmares that won't let me sleep. I see the faces of the people that I've killed. The liquor helps."

"You're going to have to get a handle on this. Take a vacation. Drive down to Myrtle Beach, just you and Gina. Come back with a clear head. I need you to be on point at all times." I reached for his hand and looked into his eyes with that sisterly love.

"I'm going to talk to Gina about getting away. Maybe that is what I need."

"I got a package I need you to take care of tonight. Are you going to be able to handle that?" I asked.

"I got you, Amber. No worries. I'm going to go home and get back in bed. I'll be straight by tonight."

*   *   *

I went to bed early, after swallowing a couple of pain pills; the menstrual cramps were kicking my ass. I was awakened from a deep sleep by a ringing phone, reaching blindly for the receiver with my eyes still closed.

"Amber, DJ's been shot." It was his mom on the other end. Her voice was barely audible.

"Please tell me he's still alive," I said, trying to keep it together.

"Just barely. He took several bullets. Someone was trying to kill him, Amber. They don't know my baby's a fighter." I could hear her voice crack as she spoke.

"What hospital?" I asked with my feet already hitting the floor.

"Howard," she replied.

"I'll throw on some clothes. I'll be there shortly," I told her.

I opened the garage and could see Cody pulling up the driveway. He got out of the car and walked toward me. I rolled down the window.

"Amber, you can't be alone right now. I'll drive you to the hospital. DJ always said that if something were to happen to him that I should step up. I got you. Park the Range and ride with me, please." I could tell by the look in his eyes that he wasn't taking no for an answer.

I didn't have the stamina to put up a fight and besides Cody was known to be especially dangerous and what I needed in an enforcer. We pulled up to the Emergency Room entrance. Cody double parked and escorted me into the hospital. I could hear DJ's mom sobbing as I came through the doors.

"Amber, he's dead. My baby is dead!" I ran toward her, wrapped around her, apparently not holding her tight enough, as she slipped through my arms and collapsed to the floor. Cody and I lifted her from the floor and sat her in a chair. I grabbed a magazine from the rack in the corner and began to fan her rapidly with the pages. The clerk, a thin older woman with a creased forehead, came from behind the glass asking, "Is she okay?"

"She just lost her son. No, she's not okay," I said matter-of-factly. I was numb.

"I'll get her some water," she said as she turned and walked with quick steps in the opposite direction toward the pantry.

The detectives were pressing for answers. I stared blankly as they asked one question after another. None of us had answers. No one witnessed what was now another homicide. I wouldn't have given up any information any way you sliced it, regardless of the situation. I didn't have nothing to say to the police.

"I want to take her home and get her in bed. You can finish your questioning on another day," I said to the detective, not waiting for a response. He silently watched us exit the hospital. I climbed in the back seat and Cody helped DJ's mom into the passenger seat up front.

"Cody, you know he's writing down the make, model, and tag number. Take care of that, okay?" I said.

"I got you," he replied and drove away from the hospital respecting the speed limit.

I had to damn near force DJ's mom to take the sedatives. I stayed with her until she fell asleep. A few close relatives that I'd met over the years began to trickle into the house. I gave each one a hug, a kiss, and my condolences.

"I'll be back later in the day. Here's a number where I can be reached," I said as I handed DJ's first cousin, Maureen, the slip of paper.

"Amber, how are you holding up? We know how close you two were," Maureen said as she pulled me in close for a hug.

"I've been more concerned about his mom. I haven't processed any of this yet," I said sadly with a sense of loss.

"Cody, I'm ready," I said as I walked out the front door. Several of my workers were posted on the front porch on alert. Cody opened the car door for me and walked around to the driver's side, got in and started the car. "Take me to Ms. Lola's, please."

We pulled up on the corner and I reached for the door handle to exit the car.

"I'll be right here waiting," he said with a different voice, assuming his new position. "Thanks. I know I don't have to tell you, but stay alert," I said.

"Will do."

I walked up the steps and entered Ms. Lola's home as I had done since I was a young child. Today, my heart was heavy. Ms. Lola could tell with just one glance.

"What's wrong?" she asked with that motherly instinct.

"DJ got shot. He's dead. I need to see Fats. Can you tell him when he calls that I need to see him, please?" I said.

"You need to see me for what?" I turned toward the voice. The voice I'd known all my life, just deeper. There he was standing on the landing, looking all ripped. He was always handsome, even with the extra pounds, but now he was eye candy and looking like a force to be reckoned with.

I walked toward him and fell into his arms. He held me tight and kissed the top of my head. He made me feel as if everything was going to be alright. I had someone to take some of the burden off my shoulders.

"Well, isn't this a touching scene? I thought your ass was married. You look like you're trying to give Fats some welcome home pussy," Desi said with his normal sarcasm.

"Fuck you!" I said with poison on the tip of my tongue.

"It's so nice to have all my babies back under one roof! I guess some things just don't change. I'm going to add a little extra to my prayers tonight. There's always hope," Ms. Lola said as she got up from the dining room table and walked to the kitchen, passing Elena as she walked out.

She leaned her head back out the archway and asked, "Can I get anything for anyone?"

"Ms. Lola, that's my job. I'm cooking a special meal for my boys!" Elena said with a big grin.

"Now that this is no longer a secret, Amber you're invited too! I'm so happy!" she said as she turned and disappeared back into the kitchen to finish preparing the meal.

"Come upstairs so we can talk, alone," Fats said to me, shaking his head while looking at Desi.

"What?" Desi asked as if he had no clue.

"I'll fill you in later," Fats said to Desi as I followed him up the stairs, carefully avoiding boxes of wood, paint cans and a ladder at the top—the second floor was being renovated. Now sitting in the boy's room, I looked around at how nothing much had changed. Thinking about all the nights I fell asleep in the bed next to Fats as a child when I didn't want to go home to Mommy.

"DJ was shot. He died at the hospital. The workhouse on P Street was turned upside down. The drugs and money are gone. I've been calling his girlfriend Gina but she's not answering her phone. She knows that if I'm calling her ass, it's important. They were inseparable. Something's not right," I said looking at Fats, still not believing he was standing right in front of me.

"Are you handling this okay?" Fats asked with concern.

"It's like I know I have to be strong, but at the same time I've lost a close friend. It hurts," I said, wringing my hands, looking downward, holding back the tears.

"You've done damn good. The men respect you. That says a lot for how you've held things down in our absence. DJ would've given his life for you. This you know. It was his time to go. He wouldn't want you to cry. We chose this life and what happened to DJ could happen to any one of us at any given time. Tomorrow is not promised," he said with certainty. "Tell me about this Gina," he said sitting next to me on the bed.

I looked into his eyes then back down to my hands. The chemistry was still there. *Get your emotions in check, Bitch,* I thought quietly in my head. I told Fats everything I knew about her, which wasn't much and brought him up to date on the business and the money.

About forty-five minutes later, we went downstairs to eat. Elena had laid out quite a spread. There were shrimp and chicken tacos, beef empanadas, chicken fajitas, rice and beans, Desi's favorites, salad along with golden batter fried chicken, beef brisket, mashed potatoes with gravy, corn on the cob and a mix of sweet tea and lemonade. There was so much to choose from but I wasn't hungry.

"Amber, you need a little meat on them bones. Fix your plate," Ms. Lola wasn't having it, not tonight. I fixed a small plate and sat at the table next to Fats. We talked and laughed about old times. Each one of us shared a memory about DJ. Remembering the good times would hopefully get me through the night.

"I'm going to go home and get some rest, Ms. Lola. Can I fix a plate for Cody? He's been sitting outside the entire time. I know he could use some food," I said as I ran my hand over my head smoothing out the curls.

"Of course you can fix a plate for Cody, but, Amber, I think it's best that you stay here tonight. Give this a little time. Let the chatter hit the streets," Ms. Lola said walking to the bar with an empty glass in hand to get a refill.

"Yeah, Amber; it will be like when we were kids." Desi said jokingly.

"She'll sleep with me tonight," Ms. Lola said without hesitation.

"I'm going to take Cody his plate. I'll have him pick me up in the morning. I have to help DJ's mom plan a funeral," I said still in disbelief that my friend was gone.

17

I dressed in a white linen suit, white leather heels and pearls for DJ's home-going service. No traditional black for me, except the Chanel shades; DJ liked those. O was being transferred to the Atlanta Federal Penitentiary today of all days. The news brought on an extra layer of sadness, no more rides down 95 South to Lorton. I would now be flying the friendly skies to see my husband.

I thought back to the day I made DJ purchase an expensive suit. He looked striking after the tailor made some adjustments. It fit him to a tee.

"Amber, tell me again why I need this shit?" DJ asked, done with the whole experience.

"Every man needs a good suit in their wardrobe. You'll thank me later," I said with a smile.

DJ's mom and I decided to bury him in the suit. The funeral home did an excellent job. The bullets ripped through his chest. Thank God, not one touched his face. I sat in the front row with his mom and the kids. She seemed to be in a daze, like none of this was really happening. Individuals walked up, one after another, giving her their condolences. She'd look up with a closed smile and take their hand, but no words escaped her mouth. I touched her shoulder every now and then, just to let her know that I was there, giving her all the support I could muster.

I watched each and every individual that walked by to pay their respects. Still no sign of Gina. It was as if she disappeared into thin air. The services were just about to begin. I neatly folded the "Fuck the Police" tee shirt while I ran my fingers across the "letter K" which was beginning to lift at the edge. DJ had given the tee shirt to his mom to hold, not trusting himself enough not to wear the shirt. It was just a homemade iron on tee shirt, but it meant a lot to him and he respected me enough not to wear it.

I walked to the casket, laid it inside and said my Goodbyes. I could feel all eyes on me, but they would never see me cry. I turned and stood with my back to the casket, removed my shades and looked out over the pews. There was only standing room in the church. I glimpsed Chloe sitting next to Ms. Lola. I was satisfied with the outpouring of love and respect for DJ. I knew there were some enemies in the mix, but they could do him no harm now. I returned to the pew to help DJ's mom walk to the casket. She held her head high but broke down once the casket was closed. Her screams sent a chill through the entire church. His brothers and sisters began to wail. I still refused to cry. The services began.

We exited the church as the DEA watched, got in the limousine, and headed across town to the cemetery. The repass was at DJ mom's house, just for family and a few close friends. DJ's mom had been quiet since the service. I went down to the basement to kiss all of the kids. I climbed up the stairs and let out a sigh when I reached the top. It was time to tell DJ's mom that I was leaving. I walked over to where she was sitting on the couch directly in front of the television. It was DJ's favorite spot where he sat and watched sports on down time.

"I'm leaving," I said.

"Amber, I want to thank you for everything. You have been so generous and . . . " I cut her off before she could say another word.

"We're family. You're not going to be able to get rid of me, okay, so let's not act like this is goodbye. I'll check on you tomorrow," I embraced her and kissed her on the cheek.

Fats and Desi were absent from the funeral and the repass. Still laying low. Fats told me to put the word out that there was a reward and I should be contacted if anyone got wind of Gina. The streets were watching in every corner of the city. One thing for sure, money made folks tell on their mama. If she was still in the city, I'd know real soon.

Cody drove me to Ms. Lola's house after the repass. I opened the locked door. The house was quiet. I walked to the dining room table, stepped out of my heels, and proceeded to open a box of Whitman's Sampler filled with assorted chocolates. I did as I'd always done with Daddy's sampler, bite into a chocolate without looking, only to discard it in the trash if it didn't make my taste buds happy. Ms. Lola and Chloe came through the front door just as I was going back in for another.

"Amber, if you don't close that damn box!" Ms. Lola said already annoyed knowing my routine.

"I only took two," I said as I twisted in my seat as if I was five telling a little white lie.

"I know if you're admitting to two, then you've thrown away four. Don't make me check the trash!"

We all laughed. All of it was so needed, the chocolate in the trash, the scolding, and the laughter. I was surrounded by what was familiar; I'd had enough of death for one day.

I walked up the stairs, down the hallway to what used to be a storage room. Fats had turned it into a studio for his paintings. I stood in the middle of the floor admiring his work, up close and then stepping back, tilting my head from left to right, trying to understand the meaning of this one particular abstract. I was intrigued.

Fats' had a God given talent. He walked up behind me and whispered in my ear, "You see something you like?" he asked.

"I do," I said, not moving an inch. "This one right here. What are you going to name it once you're done?" I asked curiously.

"What makes you think it's not finished?" he said moving closer to the painting, running his hand across the canvas.

"You haven't signed it, and sometimes you give your work a title."

"I didn't know you paid that much attention," he said with a closed smile.

"I love your art. It's thought-provoking," I said as I stared at the colors on the painting.

"You know how you read books to escape? I do the same thing with my paintings," Fats said, knowing we both needed to step away from time to time from what was our chosen reality.

"Fats, I need to talk to you," Desi said as he barged into the room before I could comment. I slipped right past him and out the door, back downstairs with Ms. Lola and Chloe.

"Have you heard anything about that girl yet?" Ms. Lola asked, lighting a Newport cigarette; she'd finally put those camels down.

"Not a word," I said, speaking between drinking sips of water out of a white plastic cup. "It was a very nice service, Amber," Chloe said with a seldom seen reserve.

"It really was. Thank you both for coming. It meant a lot," I replied.

"When are you going to see your husband? The coming weeks will probably be the perfect time to go. Ain't nothing moving right about now. Too much unwanted attention. The DEA was out in full force today," Ms. Lola said, turning on the television to the evening news.

"You're right. I do need to see my husband," I said, not looking forward to flying again, not being a fan of the turbulence, and I needed some space between me and Fats.

O reached out and gave me the telephone number and address to a lady down Sursum Corda, who had a first-class roundtrip airline ticket to Atlanta for half price. I made the call and purchased the ticket the same day.

The following Monday, I took the sapphire and diamond necklace out of the safe and ran my fingers across the stones. I closed my eyes and remembered my trip to the Bahamas with O. Nothing could ever replace those memories. I put the necklace back in the safe and walked outside to the car where Cody was waiting to drive me to National Airport.

I arrived an hour early. I got in line at American Airlines, checked my luggage, and then proceeded to the gate. I went in search of a gift shop to purchase some gum. I knew this would help even out the pressure in my ears, and I wouldn't have O next to me making me spit it out. I could chew as hard and as long as I wanted. I glanced at the magazines, but didn't make a purchase because I was trying to finish a new book I'd just started reading, "The Other Side of Midnight."

It was time to board the plane. I gave my ticket to the boarding agent, walked down the ramp, and stepped aboard, feeling apprehensive as I was greeted by the flight attendants with counterfeit smiles. I had a window seat in first class with two empty seats next to me. I was relieved that there was no one sitting beside me to watch me nervously fidgeting with the seat belt. I closed my eyes, said a prayer for a safe flight out loud, and hoped that God heard me.

The clouds looked magical from where I was sitting, as if I could just reach out the window and grab one. The sky was the bluest of blues. I couldn't have asked for a clearer day. The flight attendant offered me some champagne. *Maybe a glass or two would calm my nerves,* I thought. *I'd be straight by the time I picked up the rental car and checked in the hotel.* Excitement was flowing all the way to my toes. I was on my way to see my husband.

I followed O's directions from the hotel to the penitentiary. I parked on the street and walked several blocks. Atlanta Federal Penitentiary was a massive building; it looked as if it took up a few city blocks. I climbed the stairs to the entrance and just as I was proceeding down the hallway, I could hear my name being shouted from my right and my left. "Amber. It's Joe Green." "Hey, Amber. It's Dexter." "Amber. It's Sonny." I looked in both directions and waved, quickening my steps toward the guard, not wanting the attention, especially not here.

The sound of the metal gates as they slammed shut behind me made me feel as if I was locked up. I was escorted by a guard with other visitors to the visiting room. I took a seat at a table awaiting O's arrival. I was able to greet him with a kiss and that was all. We took seats across from each other. I reached out to hold his hand. A guard walked up, hitting his baton on the table. I jumped as he said in a no-nonsense manner, "No touching!" It was two total extremes. Lorton was a playground compared to the Feds. The visiting hours were twice a day on designated days. It was like torture being so close but yet so far. I kept the conversation real light.

"I hear Fats and Desi are home," he paused while he looked me square in the eyes as he waited for an answer.

"Yeah," I said showing very little emotion, changing the subject quickly. I wasn't going to waste my visit talking about them. I knew his temperament could turn ugly on the drop of a dime. I didn't want him to end up in the hole for some stupid shit.

I left O knowing that I'd be back for the next visit. We were both all smiles. My stomach was rumbling—I was a tad bit hungry, so I drove to the Phipps Plaza to get something to eat and kill some time. Window shopping was never my thing, but I found myself doing just that, until I saw a raw silk two-piece suit in a soft golden-brown hanging on the mannequin in the window. I looked at the stitching—the material, the color was so rich. Maybe I'll just go inside and try it on for fun. I knew the entire time I was going up the escalator, checking out my surroundings that it was going to find its way into my bag.

I usually didn't move recklessly, but the skirt and blouse I wore today left no room to stash anything on my body. I knew I was rusty. I'd hung up my boosting shoes or so I thought. I found that

I still had that confidence. I located the outfit and took several others in the dressing room with me.

A sales lady knocked on the door pleasantly saying, "Let me know if you need any assistance."

"No problem. I'm good for now," I said while rolling the outfit tightly as I placed it in my purse, speedily discarding the hanger in another fitting room.

I thanked the sales lady on my way out, handing her the outfits as I walked out of Saks Fifth Avenue with what I came for, knowing I would look fantastic for my husband on tomorrow's visit.

I drove back to the penitentiary and found a parking space a few blocks away. I looked in the mirror and reapplied my lipstick, before I exited the car. I opened the trunk, placed my purse inside, removed the suit and discarded the tags. I tucked the suit carefully in the corner of the trunk, and then walked toward the entrance. The second visit of the day went much smoother. I knew not to touch him and he seemed more relaxed. Once again, the time went by much too quickly.

"I'll see you tomorrow?" O asked, with his eyes devouring me.

"I'll be here with bells on."

"I'll be glad when I can see you with just bells on," he said while rubbing his chin as if he was contemplating that thought in his head.

I flashed him a wide smile as I left the visiting room. I walked three blocks to the car, still smiling, so happy to have seen my baby. I drove to the hotel, had a few glasses of champagne at the bar, went up to the room, showered, turned on the television, and climbed in bed. As I flipped through the channels, there was nothing that held my interest. I was having trouble falling asleep. I closed my eyes and imagined O's face, his hands. I circled my nipples until they were hard. Slowly, ran my fingers from my chest to my belly button, moving further south, in between my legs, leisurely stroking my clit until I came, shuddering; now I was finally able to drift off to sleep.

I checked out of the hotel wearing my newly acquired silk suit, feeling like a runway model as I tipped the bellman to place my luggage in the trunk. I drove to the penitentiary with the music thumping and in really good spirits. This time, I managed to make it down the hallway without hearing my name being shouted from both sides of the entrance. The visitors were once again escorted to the visiting room where I awaited O's arrival. I'd just seen him yesterday, but my heart still danced when he entered the room. The visit was never long enough, as we talked, stared into each other's eyes, and looked forward to the evening visit before the first was even over.

"Baby, I'm catching a flight tonight. I'm going to miss you so much," I said trying to hide the sadness that was about to overcome me.

"We're both going to have to live off the memories of those date nights down Lorton," he said, smiling. "Okay, baby, come give me a hug and a kiss," he said as we embraced. "Until the next time."

He turned and walked out of the visiting room. I stood there momentarily, wishing I could see him one more time. I was the last one to leave the room.

I headed to the airport, dropped off the rental car, found my way to American Airlines, and sat at the gate waiting to board the plane. Once on the plane, I buckled up, said my prayer and unwrapped a stick of spearmint gum and popped it in my mouth.

Dinner was served; it was the first time I'd ever tasted duck. It really wasn't bad. By the second glass of champagne, I was feeling relaxed as I stared out the window at the orange hue cast against the clouds, possibly the most amazing sunset I'd ever seen.

Cody was sitting outside when I exited the airport. He got out of the car and took my luggage.

"How was your trip?" he asked once I was seated inside the car and was making his way through traffic.

"It was really good," I said, still holding on to the vision of my husband's face in my head.

"I got some news for you. We found Gina trying to catch a Greyhound bus at 4:00 a.m. in the morning. She was covered in Muslim garb, but it's hard to hide that ass. I questioned her thoroughly; she never gave up a name. She was more afraid of him or her than dying. I slit her fucking throat and left her body deep in a hole in a construction zone out of the city," he spoke as if he was reliving the act with murder in his eyes. Then, after a pause, he added, "Gina asked me to deliver a message."

I could only stare as I waited for him to continue.

"She said you need to watch those close to you."

18

Daddy called almost as soon as I walked in the door.

"Hi, Daddy. I'm just getting back from Atlanta," I said, sounding just a little tired, as I rubbed the back of my neck.

"Amber, I need you to come to the house," he said in that serious do-what-I-say tone.

"Daddy, can it wait until tomorrow?" I asked hoping he would agree.

"No. I need you to come now," he said.

"Is it Mommy? Is she gone again?" I asked as I tried to conceal the apprehension in my voice.

"No, it's not your mother. I need to see you."

"Okay. I'm leaving now."

I picked up my purse from the table and walked toward the garage, as I stopped to get the keys to the Benz and my luger.

I drove to the avenue, wondering what Daddy could've heard about me. I found a spot across the street from the house, sat for a minute, and watched my surroundings before exiting the car. I put my key in the lock and turned, but the chain was on the front door. I banged. The door swung open as I looked back over my shoulder, to make sure no one was following.

"Hey, Big Head," Chris said, looking quite debonair in his army uniform. I jumped in his arms, with tears streaming down my face.

"When did you get home?" I was totally surprised, as I dabbed at the tears.

"I just got in a few hours ago. Daddy came and picked me up."

"You look so handsome and all grown up," I said and hugged him one more time.

"Thanks, Amber. We have a lot of catching up to do," he said with a funny stare.

"Yeah we do," I said, not looking forward to this conversation.

"So, Daddy, you wanted to surprise me, huh? I thought I was in trouble," I said with an inordinate amount of relief.

"I knew you would be upset if I didn't let you know your brother was home. I'll leave you two to catch up," he said as he walked toward the stairs, going up to his room for peace and solitude.

"I'm so happy you made it back from Vietnam. I kept you in my prayers," I said, putting my hand on his as we sat at the dining room table.

"You've been through a lot since I've been gone. Daddy has been filling me in, as much as he knows about. How's marriage?" he asked with a look I would've expected from Daddy.

I removed my hand from his and nervously rubbed the palms of my hands on my thighs.

"You're just getting home. Can we ease into this conversation a little later? When the word gets out that you're home, you're going to be too busy to have me under the microscope," I said quickly trying to change the subject.

"I'm focused on finding a good job and taking care of my daughter. No time for partying and running the street like I used to do," he said, sounding more mature.

"That girl has been real iffy with letting us see Jasmine. She's all good with me dropping off money and clothes. I knew you would handle the situation when you got back. I'm so happy to have you home, Chris," I said as I kissed him on the cheek. "I'm going home to get some sleep," I said as I reached for my purse.

"We're not done with this conversation, but we can talk later," he said, really sounding like he was my father.

I leaned in and whispered in his ear, "You might want to go get some pussy and let go of some of that pent up military frustration. I'm out!" I said laughing, as I walked to the front door, giving him the peace sign with two fingers, looking back over my shoulder, watching him shake his head, realizing that his little sister had grown up too.

Several months later, I rode with Chris to try to see Jasmine again. Luckily, we avoided the two-hour gas lines because of the gas shortage; Chris had a good friend who owned a gasoline station. We'd just fill up late at night after closing. Jasmine's mother wasn't having it; she had a new man and Chris was a problem for her. She no longer needed him. We sat outside Jasmine's school and watched her play tag with a group of little girls on the playground. She'd discarded her sweater on top of a pile of cardigans. It took me back a few years, remembering one night at the Go-Go.

Daddy bought me a fake fur coat with real fox fur trim from Garfinckel's Department Store at the Montgomery Mall earlier in the day. He saw me put the coat on to wear out the door that night. "Amber, don't wear that coat out of here to the GoGo," he said sternly with a hard stare.

"I'm not, Daddy; I was just trying it on again because it feels so good," I said as I continued to model in the mirror, lying through my teeth. I waited for him to go upstairs. I left out the front door wearing that coat, looking real cute if I had to say so myself. Chloe was waiting out front in her black 280Z that she purchased last spring after lifting eleven thousand dollars off a man at the Preakness horse race. It felt good not to have to drive all the time. I jumped in the car with Chloe and we were on our way.

The Go-Go was at the Masonic Temple on 16th Street. We walked in and all eyes were on us, some jealous, some wanting, and a few admirers. There were a few guys whom I danced with regularly. One came over and asked me to dance just as I slipped off my coat.

"Chloe, hold this for me while I dance," I said, handing her the coat.

Go-Go has a way of taking over your body like a holy roller at a Thursday night revival, totally out of your control. Erotic tendencies are set free as soon as you hear that beat. The cool flow of the rhythm, engulfing your spirit, your soul and your mind. Your fingers begin to snap while raising your arms high in the air. I could feel the percussion in my chest; I laid my hand across my breasts to keep it right there if only for a minute. My head began to rock, my hips began to sway; I had my own style, not to be copied. It was so relaxing but yet uninhibited, a safe haven from all the problems at home. If you wanted to bend over and shake your ass, it was cool—there was no judgment. I forgot who I was dancing with, losing myself totally in the music.

I opened my eyes and saw Chloe dancing too, one guy in the front all between her legs and one in the back all up on her ass. Then it hit me.

"Chloe, where is my coat?" I asked with anxiety. She pointed to a pile of coats on the floor while still dancing. She closed her eyes tight enjoying the feeling of skin on skin. I walked toward the pile with my heart about to jump out my chest, not from the percussion, but straight fear. The coat was gone. I was so ready to go! What the hell was I going to tell Daddy? *The coat you forbid me to wear to the Go-Go was stolen at the Go-Go.* I was mad as shit with Chloe.

"Why the fuck did you lay my coat down?" I screamed shivering on the walk to the car. "Amber, I'm sorry. I just wanted to dance," she said. She was caught up in that same trance as me. How could I be mad?

I arrived at home realizing too late that I'd left my house keys in Chloe's car and had to knock to get in the house. Daddy came to the front door, watching me shiver through the glass pane.

"Where is your coat?" he asked as if there were more questions to follow.

"I left it in Chloe's trunk. I'll get it tomorrow," I said as I scaled the steps to my bedroom. I called Fats and explained the entire ordeal. He took me downtown to Garfinckel's the very next day and bought me the exact coat. Lucky for me, they had one left in stock and it was my size. Fats always looked out for me.

"I love her so much," Chris said, bringing me out of my daydream, now focusing on Jasmine. I'd forgotten just how much she favored my brother.

"Amber, I'm going to take her," he said with a straight face.

"Take her as in kidnap?" I asked, needing clarity, uncertain about what he was saying. He never answered my question but kept talking.

"They can't keep me away from my daughter. I'll have to cut all ties with the family; that's going to be rough, but if I made it through Vietnam, I can make it through anything. I don't want any of you involved, so the less you know the better off you'll be. I just felt in my heart that I needed to give you a heads-up, just so you won't think I deserted you," he said, never once looking my way.

It was a quiet ride back to Mommy's house. He'd turned off the radio and never turned it back on. I just got my brother back and he was leaving again for good. There were so many mixed emotions swirling around in my head and my heart. There was no need in trying to talk him out of it; I'd never seen him look more determined than when we sat and watched my niece from a distance. I went inside the house and took some money out of the safe, placed it in a plastic bag, and took it outside and handed it to Chris. I turned around and went back in the house, never once looking back. There weren't enough tears to cry.

The family was brought in for questioning. I didn't know any details. Mommy and Daddy were clueless. All they could do was follow me to the airport as I took my trips to Atlanta to see my husband year after year. It stopped me from stealing; maybe that was a good thing. As time went by, I stopped seeing the detectives as they watched. I'm sure they had other pressing cases, besides, life goes on, this missing child was now labeled a "Cold Case."

19

I knew O was in the hole because the phone calls and letters suddenly stopped. I hated that shit, not knowing what was happening to him. Picturing him in a cell, isolated with no sheet or blanket, the only light by day filtered through a window. At night, just the light from the door sill. Exercise and a shower were allowed every other day. He was alone with his mind and trying hard not to let that play tricks on him. O had let his temper get the best of him. Time was added to his sentence for a brutal assault on another inmate. I was devastated.

I flew to Atlanta for his hearing. They brought him to court in an orange jumpsuit, handcuffed and shackled at his waist and ankles. He shuffled as he moved his feet, like Mommy used to do when she was on Thorazine, but he held his head high. He was a present-day slave, just to the government. He saw me in court; we weren't allowed to speak, only exchange quick glances. At least he knew I was there.

His only request when we spoke was that I didn't fuck anyone that he knew and still hold him down. I could've walked away, but I would've been leaving my heart behind. Every now and then, I'd take a cruise, alone, to Jamaica or St. Thomas to discreetly get my back blown out.

On one particular trip, I ran across a handsome young man from Colombia; his skin was black to the bone with the most beautiful green eyes. I slipped him a note through my waiter. We spent three nights together, two strangers willing to please each other in every way. He wanted me to send for him, help him get a green card, and a place to stay in America. The dick was on point, but I was a married woman; no need to lead him on. I couldn't help him with none of that, nor did I want to. I left without so much as a telephone number, relieved of stress with a smile on my face, and caught a flight from Miami to Atlanta to see my husband. Seems like I was finally becoming that "Bad Ass Bitch" that O said he would make me.

*　　*　　*

Summer 1984

O had been home for about two years. We were on an extended honeymoon for the first six months.

"Baby, look what I found in the attic, a black light and a Zodiac sex positions poster!" I exclaimed while reading the caption at the bottom of the poster like a commercial. "How cool is this shit?" I said immediately looking for my Zodiac sign. Needless to say, we explored a different position each day. We'd be fucking with the birds singing in harmony at five in the morning. I crawled out the bed, bone-tired, forcing myself to slowly get to my feet, walked to the bathroom in the dark feeling my way with my eyes closed, sat on the toilet and damn near fell in catching myself just as my ass touched the water.

"O, you left the fucking toilet seat up, again!" I screamed, totally awake now.

"Sorry, baby," he said with a deep hearty laugh. Cut the light on next time," he said, still laughing.

"No, your ass is home. You need to break that habit, quickly!" I said, briefly annoyed. I could never stay mad with him too long. I crawled right back in the bed and straight into his arms.

We slept in. Around noon, I showered and dressed and went downstairs to fix a picnic basket for a date in the park with caviar and unsalted crackers, not my favorite but his; strawberries, grapes, fried chicken wings, and potato salad. I put my entire foot in that shit! I took a bottle of champagne from the refrigerator and placed it in the weave basket—no need for ice; between the two of us it would stay chilled just long enough for us to punish. I reached for several cloth napkins, utensils, plates, and two champagne glasses placing them in the basket as well.

The blanket and cassette player were already in the trunk. We were on our way to our favorite spot by the water, not far from Haines Point. I liked to see the sunlight shimmer on the ripples in the water and watch the airplanes fly overhead. We weren't far from the house when I gave him a look and said, "Pull over."

He did as I asked. I reached over and unzipped his shorts and gave him head until he was hard, and then climbed on top and rode him until he came. I saw the police officer as he walked toward the car, just as I opened my eyes. I quickly dismounted and O zipped up his shorts, right before he knocked on the window. O rolled the window all the way down.

"You two okay?" he asked as he looked at O and then at me. *Thank God we didn't light the joint yet,* I thought to myself.

"You know you can't park here," the officer said mean mugging and about to write a ticket.

"No problem, Officer. My wife and I were just leaving. We were having a deep conversation. She's trying to drag me to marriage therapy," O said with a loud sigh.

"You know that helps. My wife and I went a few years back," the officer said with a smile.

"Thank you, Sir. We might just have to try it; we'll be on our way now." O started the car, put it in reverse, and we headed down the parkway.

"We're far better at the drug thing than fucking in the car. Marriage counseling, right!" I said shaking my head as we both burst into laughter.

"How did you let him walk up on us? You were supposed to keep your eyes open woman! This one's on you!" he said, still laughing.

"I hate it when you're right!" I said, giving him an elbow to the ribs.

We found a parking spot close to our favorite place. We took the picnic basket, blanket, and cassette player from the trunk of the car and walked toward the water. I smoothed the blanket out on the grass under a huge Weeping Willow tree, one of my favorites. O popped the cork on the Mumm Cordon Rouge, with me tilting the glasses one for him and one for me. We touched the glasses together as O said, "Here's to eternal love." We both took a sip. He played some Roy Ayers, "Everybody Loves the Sunshine." I lay back on his chest while we smoked a joint and sat quietly watching the water.

"Amber, do you remember that day you bust me out about me wanting you from the very beginning?" O said stirring up old memories, some good some bad while he played with my hair.

"Yeah, I remember; why?" I asked not knowing what he was about to say.

"I used to ride around your neighborhood, just checking things out. I rode up a side street and all the young boys were on their front porches, all eyes were glued in the same direction. I slowed down and looked over to my right to see what had them all so mesmerized. There you were in a Hawaiian print bikini, all shiny from the sun tan lotion, laying on a blanket on top of the garage sunbathing. I found myself pulling over to the curb, just as you sat up and applied more lotion, oblivious to all those watching. I saw your dad come out and say something to you that made you laugh; you laid right back down and continued to work on that tan. I wanted to snatch you off that roof, drape your body with the blanket so no one else could see what was meant to be mine. I knew right then and there that I wanted you. That night at the Go-Go just made me know it even more, I had to have you." He kissed me on the cheek and I smiled.

"Daddy used to tease me and say, 'Girl, I don't care how long you stay up there on that roof; you'll never get as dark as me.' We'd both laugh and he'd go back in the house," I said. "I'm glad you told me, because that makes us even. I knew I wanted you from the first time I saw your photograph," I added, now sinking deeper into his chest. We were so in love. Little did I know that trouble was on the way.

Not only was I enjoying my husband loving up on me every day, I also wanted a baby. I should've been pregnant ten times over by now. Something was wrong. I started feeling depressed every time I came on my period, as if the cramps weren't bad enough. I felt as if my life was incomplete. Ms. Lola helped me find a fertility doctor. I made an appointment.

O grew restless being in the house. He started gambling again. Staying out until the wee hours of the morning, sometimes not coming home at all. He was trying to play catch up with all that he'd missed while being incarcerated. I'd heard you can never catch up on lost years, only go forward. I guess he didn't get that memo.

"I have an appointment in the morning. The test results are back. I'd like you to go with me. You mind staying home tonight?" I asked in a soft non-aggressive voice.

"What time is the appointment?" he asked as he checked his watch.

I stared at him long and hard before answering. "I don't need any added stress, wondering if you're going to be here in the morning," I said as I tried not to lose my temper.

"No problem, baby; I'm all yours," he said ignoring his pager blowing up every hour on the hour.

At the doctor's, O held my hand as we sat in the waiting area. The nurse opened the door and called out our name. We entered the examination room. Dr. Harris walked into the room about five minutes later, shook O's hand, and introduced himself.

I watched as Dr. Harris opened my file.

"Mrs. Jones, the good news is I know why you've been having problems getting pregnant. You have a condition called endometriosis. Do you suffer from extreme cramps before and during your menstrual period?" Dr. Harris asked.

"Yes, I have extreme pain. Sometimes it would be so intense that I would be bent over in pain and would stay in bed the first day of my period." I answered.

"Scar tissue is blocking your fallopian tubes. You'll need surgery to even have a chance of becoming pregnant."

O and I looked at each other not expecting this news.

"Mr. Jones, I will need you to provide a sperm sample to determine your sperm count. My nurse will provide you with a cup, label, and sterile wipes," Dr. Harris said as he continued to look through the paperwork.

"Ain't nothing wrong with my sperm count," O said, seemingly annoyed with the suggestion.

"I'm sure you're correct, but we want to make sure your count is where it should be. Just following the checklist.

"Mrs. Jones, the surgery will be In & Out. I'll make a small incision right below your belly button, and go in and remove the tissue. I'd give it six weeks, and then you two can start trying to have this baby you want so badly. You'll need to take your temperature every day and make sure to record your temperature on these charts."

I reached out my hand to take the papers from Dr. Harris.

"You'll be able to see the fluctuation in your temperature. When it peaks, that's when you're ovulating. These are the days that you'll need to have intercourse. This is a very important step in our journey," he said. "Mrs. Jones, we can get you on the schedule as soon as next week for the surgery," he added, already in motion of calling his scheduling nurse.

"That's fine. I'm ready," I said, squeezing O's hand. He looked at me and smiled.

"The sperm count. I can do this at home or I have to do it here in the office?" O asked with an inquisitive look.

"Mr. Jones, you can do this at home, but it will need to be returned to the office immediately after," Dr. Harris said, displaying frown lines as if O's question was hitting a nerve.

"No problem," O answered, looking a little uncomfortable.

"No worries, baby, I'll help you," I said with a sly smile.

The following week, I was prepped for surgery and wheeled into the operating room. I awakened from the anesthesia and O was right there holding my hand. Dr. Harris came into the room and said, "The surgery was a success. Just follow the rules that we discussed, and soon you'll be pregnant."

The weeks seemed to pass slowly. I was in pain and counting the days. I almost didn't care that O was ripping and running the street. I needed six weeks to heal. I damn sure didn't want him laying all up under me, patting and feeling, asking if enough time had gone by for sex.

O was making a ton of money off of a crystal form of cocaine called rock. Rumor on the street was just one hit and you'd be hooked. It was complete madness for consumers chasing that high, but it was a drug dealer's answer to all prayers. You never knew how deeply this shit would affect people. Some were stronger than others. I saw it first-hand turn folks' lives around in a week, giving up the deed to their homes, signing over the title to their cars, and I'd heard, in some cases, selling their children for the right price, just for another hit. This wave crossed every social scale, from CEOs to junkies on the street. It rose to epidemic proportions in a matter of months, spreading across the country. The murder rate began to creep upward.

The bitch had a connection in California. She turned O on to his first hit, in hopes of pulling him away from me. Every ounce of larceny that ran through his blood lying dormant came to the surface. He was far worse on the rock than he ever was on heroin. He ran through significant amounts of money week after week, going on binges that kept him out for days, quickly depleting our bank account.

He was doing his usual this afternoon as he tried to slip out the front door without hearing my mouth.

"O, I'm ovulating. I need you to take care of this pussy before you leave," I said with no emotion.

"Baby, I'll take care of you later; I promise. I'm coming back home tonight," he said in a rush. I blocked the doorway.

"I only need your assistance for ten minutes," I said as I stepped out of my skirt and panties, reached between my legs, and began to masturbate while he watched. He quickly gave in. I could see the lust in his eyes as he turned me around to face the front door and entered me from behind. I kept him a little longer than he wanted, but I got what I needed.

20

I was actually gaining weight with this pregnancy. I was eating healthy and doing all the right things, except I was stressing big time. O had fucked up with his connects. They refused to deal with him, only me. I cut back on the numbers because O was lunchin, and Fats and Desi were more so competition at this point. This caused major arguments.

"I know I had some money in here," he said as he rummaged through his closet, tossing shoe boxes and checking shirt pockets.

"Nope. You came and got the rest of that night before last, and before you ask, I don't keep any money here," I said as I lay on the bed and watched his every move.

"So what are you saying? You're not going to get any if I ask?"

"What I'm saying is don't ask. I'm waiting for you to come to your senses so we can get back to a normal life. This baby will be here before you know it!" I said not amused with his actions.

"Do you remember those diamond studs you gave me last year on Valentine's Day? I can't find them. I've looked every-where," I said.

"Are you accusing me of stealing your earrings? Fuck it. I'm gone!" he yelled, as he walked out the bedroom door and headed down the steps.

It took a few minutes before I heard the front door slam. I didn't give it much thought. He didn't need an excuse to leave. That rock was calling his name. He had to figure out his next move. I had a strange feeling in my gut that wouldn't let me rest. I got up and went downstairs to the Cedar closet just to check. My silver fox was gone.

"This motherfucker took my coat!" I screamed out loud, now smoldering.

The next day, I called Chloe. I wanted to vent and get out of the house. We were riding down 4th Street in the Edgewood neighborhood when I saw a young lady walking down the street in my fur.

"That bitch has on my coat! Pull the fuck over, Chloe!" I said with my hand already on the door handle.

"Amber, I'm not pulling over. She don't have nothing to do with O selling your coat. She just benefited from the transaction. Besides, you're pregnant. I can't let you fight. You got plenty of furs; put a lock on the closet or better still put them in storage, so he can't get to them there," she said as she tried to talk me down. She was right, but I was boiling on the inside as she continued to drive down the street.

Seven months pregnant! I couldn't believe I'd made it this far. I thanked God each and every day. I drove to Ms. Lola's for a visit. As I stuck my key in the door, Desi swung the door open wide.

"Ms. Lola here?" I asked, sounding dry with a tight face.

"She took Ma to the store. They should be on the way back. You're more than welcome to come in and wait." He was being far too polite. My inner senses were telling me to turn around but I walked through the door and took a seat at the dining room table, flipping through the pages of a magazine.

I could feel him watching me.

"So, Amber, how's your marriage?" he asked, already knowing that my marriage was falling apart. O kept choosing the rock over me.

"None of your business," I casually replied, with no eye contact.

"Oh, it's like that, huh? I bet I can tell you some shit about your marriage that you don't know. Like you're not the only one having his baby."

I looked up from the page. He had my attention now.

"Desi, why would you tell her that shit?" Fats said coming up the stairs from the basement.

"You knew?" I said looking toward Fats with hurtful eyes.

"Everybody keeps dancing around her ass like she's some kind of princess! She act like she a gangsta, then she needs to hear the truth and handle that shit!" Desi said, happy to be the one to break the news.

I was stunned. I could feel my mouth ajar. I started gasping for air. I ran from the house, down the stairs, toward my car. Cody had just parked and was now walking toward me. I never stopped running. He knew me well enough to know that something was wrong. He jumped in the passenger seat just before I pulled into traffic, going around the car in front of me, on the wrong side of the road, flying down the avenue.

"Amber, can you please slow down and talk to me? Where are you going?"

I headed straight for 9th Street, not uttering a word to Cody as if he wasn't even in the car. I did slow rolls through the stop signs and stopped briefly for red lights before going straight through, heading to my destination.

I saw O right in front of me about thirty yards away, crossing the street at the corner of 9th and T. I stepped on the gas and steered the car straight toward him. He wasn't paying attention, probably high. Cody grabbed the steering wheel and laid on the horn. O jumped back up on the curb, staring at me in disbelief as we rode by. I slammed on brakes as the pain hit me hard, stopping in the middle of the street.

"I'm in labor. I can't have this baby now; it's too early!" I said crying and holding the bottom of my stomach. Cody jumped out the car, picked me up in his arms and placed me in the passenger seat. He drove like a madman to the hospital.

"Please, someone help me! She's in labor!" I could hear Cody yell as he ran from the car toward the Emergency entrance.

Two attendants and a doctor ran from inside the hospital and put me on a gurney, while checking my vitals. I was wheeled to the maternity floor and after examination given shots to slow the contractions down. Dr. Harris was paged to the floor.

"Mrs. Jones, I just saw you last week. What happened?" Dr. Harris questioned with a furrowed brow.

"I got some very disturbing news today," I said as I tried not to relive the conversation with Desi in my head.

"Is that why your blood pressure is through the roof? You knew from the beginning that this was a high-risk pregnancy. We've gone through too much to get you to this point. This baby is not coming today. If the injections don't slow down the contractions, we'll simply sew up your cervix. You'll remain here in the hospital for the next two months with your feet up and your head down," he said as a declaration, without any discussion. He reminded me of my father with the bulging vein at his temple. I knew to remain silent.

If it wasn't bad enough that I had to lie in an uncomfortable position, they made me wear a bra around the clock. I was miserable and still having contractions. Dr. Harris finally scheduled the surgery.

My status for the dietary department was now NPO, which meant nothing by mouth after midnight. I was pregnant and food of any kind was abruptly taken away. I was a soldier; I really thought I could do this with no problem. My surgery was scheduled for noon. By the time it got to be around 2:00 p.m., I was about to go fucking ballistic! I was pressing on the bell for the nurse's station, again.

"Yes, Mrs. Jones, how can we help you?" the clerk said, sounding annoyed.

"I was supposed to go to surgery at noon. No one has come to get me. Could you please check to see what's going on?" I asked, trying to stay calm.

"I'll let them know," the clerk replied.

I was raised right. I knew you could never be mean or disrespectful to anyone who worked in a hospital. These are the people that take care of you and nurse you back to good health, but damn!

It was now 3:00 p.m. I kept watching the clock on the wall. The shift was changing. I was having hunger pangs and contractions, and the baby was kicking all at once, and still no sign of anyone to take me to surgery. I hit the button again.

"Yes, Mrs. Jones. What do you need?" the voice on the other end sounded young, pleasant and truly not ready for me.

"I'm seven months pregnant. I was supposed to go to surgery at noon today. I'm starving and nobody has come to get me!" I said, sounding a little troubled, rubbing my belly and cursing under my breath.

"Mrs. Jones, the nurses are doing rounds. I'm sure yours will be there shortly. Please be patient," she said, trying to hide her irritation.

I began calling my doctor's office and leaving messages. Somehow, I slipped through the cracks. Dr. Harris called me at 11:00 p.m. My words were unintelligible. "Amber, I need you to calm down. My apologies for the mix-up. Another doctor on the team was supposed to cover for me. I was delivering babies at another hospital. I'm on my way to you now. Stop crying please. If your blood pressure is elevated, we won't be able to do the surgery," he said in an unwavering tone.

It was midnight when I was wheeled into the operating room. I was all cried out. Dr. Harris was playing Marvin Gaye, "Dance with Me." The anesthesiologist was just about to administer the medication.

"You're positive it's not going to hurt my baby?" I asked wide eyed and concerned.

"I'm certain that your baby will be fine," he said as he rubbed my shoulder and smiled down upon me.

Just before I went under sedation, I said out loud to anyone listening, "Sing it, Marvin!"

I opened my eyes after an unrestful night. Don't let anybody tell you that you get any semblance of sleep in a hospital. The nurses are poking and prodding, taking your temperature or your blood pressure every two hours on the hour and the food sucks!

O was right there next to my bed. I smacked his hand. His eyes flew open, awakening from the first good sleep he'd probably had in days.

"Baby, are you okay? Is my son good?" he asked with apprehension.

"Didn't I try to run your ass over? What the fuck are you doing here?" I yelled, forgetting that I didn't leave a message with the desk that my husband wasn't allowed.

"Amber, you're fucking crazy, but that doesn't stop me from loving you. Is my baby okay?"

"Which one?" I said with pure malice.

He sat back in the chair with a baffled look, wondering who told me.

"I need you to leave. I'm not wasting anymore tears or energy on this bullshit. I'll handle everything after the baby's born," I said. Each word was meant to stab him in the gut.

He got to his feet, looking utterly deflated and left the room, choosing not to argue.

I can't say two months went by quickly, it was the complete opposite. I'd lie in that same position, sometimes feeling as if the blood was rushing to my head. At least the hospital staff was accommodating, adjusting the bed just a little. Each and every nurse or assistant tried their best to make me comfortable with a smile. Donna was my favorite nurse. Her smile lit up the room. She would make me laugh, even when I didn't want to. We had long serious discussions about men and never settling for less.

She made me feel like life was worth living and that I needed to get prepared for the little one that I was about to bring into this world. Nothing else really mattered.

The contractions began quickly in the early morning hours and soon were five minutes apart. I was wheeled into the labor room, where an anesthesiologist administered the epidural. I was left alone, yelling and swearing to the top of my lungs. I tried to hold it in, but I couldn't. I was embarrassed, but quickly realized that I wasn't the first woman to give birth and scream and curse to the heavens; my lower back was giving me the blues. It was sudden pain and then it would go away as if it was never there. I was exhausted, but I would take short deep breaths to try to make it through the pain.

When the nurse came back to check on me, she exclaimed quite loudly, "He's coming. I can see his head!"

I barely made it to the delivery room. I was transferred to yet another bed, gave one more push and he was here. Anjelo Dominguez Jones, Jr. had arrived, and he was the spitting image of his father. I watched as the umbilical cord was cut and Dr. Harris jumped out of the way as the placenta gushed out and landed on the floor.

"Mrs. Jones, you have a healthy young man—ten fingers, ten toes, and great lungs!" Dr. Harris said as we all could hear my baby let the entire ward know of his arrival into the world.

It was love at first sight. I knew right then and there I would do whatever it took to protect him and love him more than anything else in this world. I watched attentively as the nurse took him away to be cleaned, weighed, and measured. An ID bracelet was placed around his tiny little wrist, although I'd never forget that face; they could never mix my baby up with another. His tiny face would be forever ingrained in my memory and my heart.

21

I'd been home from the hospital for barely a month when I got a strange phone call.

"Hello," I said as I answered the phone.

"Is this O's wife?" the woman said on the other end.

"Yes, this is her," I said.

"You need to get to Howard University Hospital right away. Your husband is about to get locked up for raping my niece. My name is Anita. I'll be waiting," she said as the phone line dropped.

It was cold as a witches' tit. I drove to the hospital thinking what the fuck has O gotten himself into this time. I parked on the lot, stopped to button my coat, and wrapped my scarf around my neck as I walked into the emergency room entrance. A woman stood and walked toward me. She was an older chick with an excessive amount of makeup plastered to her face. It looked like if she smiled too hard it would crack.

"You're O's wife?" she asked.

"Yes," I said

"I'm Anita. You're not what I expected. You're young and pretty," she said.

"Thank you, but I don't think you called me here to talk about my looks. You want to tell me what happened?" I asked, ready to hear everything she had to say.

I looked around the waiting room as she spoke. Everything about it reminded me of the night DJ died. I could feel myself getting agitated but decided it was important to hear what she had to say. I made myself calm down and focus. This just might be what I needed to finally walk away.

Anita was talking up a storm, she was telling it all, not just about the alleged rape but information about O and the Bitch.

"She has an apartment in Glen Arden and a house on the Avenue. He invites everybody to one or the other. He has keys to both. They like to entertain and get everyone fucked up and let them spend every dime of their money right there with them. He made it seem like you and him weren't together anymore," she said, just spilling all the beans.

"Really? That's interesting," I said, wanting to hear more.

I glanced up and saw a detective come out of the hallway that led to the examination rooms. Just then, O came through the automatic door, walked straight to me, gritted on Anita, and took me by the arm and pulled me outside.

"You got five minutes to explain," I said with my arms folded, as I tapped my foot on the concrete walkway.

"Amber, I didn't rape that girl. I promise you I didn't," O said looking like his life depended on me believing him.

"I'm listening," I said.

"That old broad in there has been trying to get at me for a long time. She wanted me to go with her last night. I shut her down. I don't want her old ass. She's mad about that shit; that's why she's running her mouth trying to come between us," he paused as he looked around the parking lot, showing signs of paranoia, and then he continued.

"The girl in there that said I raped her is Anita's niece. She bought an eighth of coke and asked me if I had somewhere to go where we could smoke. I just wanted to get high. I took her to my friend's apartment. He let us in and we went into the bedroom. While she was in the bathroom, I stole the coke from her purse and snuck out the bedroom window. I left her there alone with them. They must've fucked her. She and her Aunt are trying to blame that shit on me for some payback," he said.

"You always doing some dumb ass shit behind that fucking rock!" I swung before I got the words out good.

He grabbed me and held on tight.

"Amber, please don't do this. I need you to go talk to the detective. Tell him I would never rape anybody. I'm not going back to jail behind this lie. Do this for me, please," he begged.

"Let me go!" I said as I snatched away and walked back into the hospital waiting area.

I looked around for the detective. I spotted him in the corner, "Excuse me, Sir. Could I speak with you for a moment please?"

The detective stepped back out of earshot and let me approach.

"My husband has been accused of raping the young lady in the back. He's far from perfect, but what I do know is that he'd never rape anyone. We've been married for a lot of years and just had a baby boy a few weeks ago. I feel so bad for her. Is there any way I can go back to see her? I'd like to apologize for what she's been through. I don't wish that on anybody, even though my husband didn't do this," I said with sincerity.

"She's in room number three," he said and stepped off to the side.

I walked down that hallway thinking about how I was going to apologize to this woman for the pain, the trauma, and the humiliation she was going through. I knocked on the door and entered.

"Hi. I'm O's wife. I just wanted to say . . ." I stopped in mid-sentence. The look she shot me was one of contempt.

She had large passion marks that started just below her earlobe and disappeared underneath her hospital gown. I knew that wasn't my husband's work.

My question to her was, "So how long you been fucking my husband?" I didn't wait for an answer. I'd seen that look too many times before.

I went to the detective and said, "The rape kit will not show any sign of my husband's sperm. The young lady is lying."

O dodged a bullet with this one. I got in my car and went home without him.

* * *

A few weeks later, I took Anjelo for his first doctor appointment. Chloe came along; she was getting quite attached, spoiling him rotten. He was dressed in one of several outfits that Chloe stole the day before. We passed right by where the bitch lived. O's silver BMW was parked right out front. He sold the Jaguar to flip some money and keep getting high. I took all the titles to the vehicles, keys and the deed to the house to Mommy's and placed them in the safe. I'd been riding past that house for days, but seeing his car parked right out front, the anger rose from the pit of my stomach.

We were sitting in the waiting room, waiting to be seen by the pediatrician, an older woman with a contagious smile, who had a way with babies, named Dr. Lancaster. She came highly recommended by DJ's mom.

"Today is the day I'm going over there," I said looking at Chloe while peeling a mandarin, putting a slice to my mouth and taking a bite.

"What are you talking about?" Chloe asked as she placed Anjelo over her shoulder and began patting him on the back, listening for a burp.

She looked at me and saw my face all screwed up and then she knew.

"Oh, you mean her place? Does she have a name?" Chloe asked.

"Yeah. Bitch!" I said bluntly. To be honest, he never said her name and I never asked. "She's just been a thorn in my side."

"Mrs. Jones, no eating in the waiting area, please," the receptionist stated solemnly, pointing at the sign on the far wall. "The doctor will see you and the baby now."

We both rose from our seats. I opened the door and Chloe went through with the baby.

There was no rhyme or reason as to why I decided I was going to confront O today. He'd just been to Mommy's the day before yesterday to spend time with the baby and steal glances at me. In fact, I followed him out of the house when he left.

"I'm going to change the locks if you steal one more thing out of the house," I said walking behind him.

He turned and faced me and said, "Amber, that's my house and I've bought a lot of that shit you wear, jewelry included."

"Once we got married, all that shit became community property. It's not just your house anymore," I said.

"I'm not arguing with you today," he said.

He gave me his back again and continued to walk up the street to his car. I took off my mule slipper and threw it as hard as I could, aiming straight for his head. He turned abruptly, like he had eyes in the back of his head and snatched the shoe out of midair and threw it into the bushes half way down the block. He got in his car and as he drove by he yelled out, "Have fun looking for your shoe." I was pissed. Just then, two young boys came riding toward me on their bikes. I grabbed the handle bar on one. The other young man stopped.

"The first one to find my shoe in those bushes gets twenty dollars," I said pointing down the street. They both slammed their bikes to the sidewalk and took off running. I hobbled back to Mommy's house and sat on the concrete steps. My new found friends came flying back up the street. One was waving the shoe and yelling, "I got it! I got it!"

"Thank you," I said while examining my shoe. I reached in my purse and gave each of the boys a twenty-dollar bill.

"Thanks, Lady" they both said simultaneously as they jumped on their bikes and continued on their way.

I think just seeing his car parked in front of her door was the deciding factor.

"He's a handsome baby," Dr. Lancaster gushed while examining Anjelo from head to toe.

"He looks just like his father. I don't see me anywhere," I said as I peered around the good doctor searching for a tiny piece of me.

"Am I going to meet Mr. Jones in the near future?" Dr. Lancaster asked.

"We're not together," I said with a hardened voice.

"You might want to work on that. I can see in your eyes that you still love the man. Anjelo deserves a good home with both parents," she said, still playing with the baby. I had no comeback as I looked to the floor. She was right; I did still love him.

After the appointment, I rode up the avenue, and saw O's car still parked in the exact same spot.

"Chloe, take my baby to Mommy," I said with anger.

"Amber, I don't want to leave you down here by yourself," she said.

"Chloe, do as I say, please." I was already in motion opening the door and exiting the car.

I could see her eyes following me in the rearview mirror as she headed up the Avenue. I walked up the stairs at a steady pace. I was ready to handle my business. I knocked on the door. I could hear O's voice as he walked toward the door, speaking to someone inside. He looked out the peephole.

I heard him clearly say, "Oh shit!" I knocked louder.

"Open the door, motherfucker! You're coming outside to talk to me. I ain't going nowhere until you do!" I screamed at the door. There was complete silence. I banged on the door again, loud and hard.

"Either you come outside to talk to me or I'm calling the fucking police. I don't think you want that shit," I said angrily, feeling beads of sweat forming on my forehead as I paced, ready to go to war.

I heard tires squeal next to the curb. The cavalry had arrived. Chloe must've told Ms. Lola; she brought Fats, Desi and Elena.

"Amber, if you don't bring your yellow ass down those steps! You know O ain't worth this shit! We need to leave and we need to leave now before we all get locked up on some bullshit!" she said, madder than a wet hen.

"No disrespect, but I'm not going nowhere until this bitch ass motherfucker comes outside to talk to me!" I screamed, staring at the door.

"Everybody's talking about your ass. You're just adding fuel to the fire with this shit." Desi said, shaking his head and looking at me with disgust.

"Shut the fuck up, Desi! Now is not the time! She wouldn't be down here if it wasn't for your ass!" Ms. Lola said as she jumped between the two of us. I was already down the concrete steps, in motion, ready to rumble!

"No, let her ass swing. I have no problem whatsoever smacking the shit out of a woman, especially her ass," he said as he stepped around Ms. Lola.

"So what, we ten all over again? Desi, I can't let you hit her," Fats said, as he pulled Desi away.

"Desi, you weren't raised to put your hands on a woman. You know she's not herself," Elena said, cautioning her son with her eyes.

I caught a glimpse of this fine ass negro checking me out as he walked past on my left from inside the house. I was enraged, but I did a double take as he slipped by. I watched him acknowledge Fats as he disappeared down the block, got in his car and left; I was still spewing obscenities without stopping to take a breath.

"Well, look who decided to finally come outside," Ms. Lola said, lighting up a cigarette, inhaling the smoke long and deep.

O walked up to me and said, "We can talk, just not with an audience," his eyes were big as saucers, darting nervously from left to right. He looked as if he just hit the rock right before he came outside.

"Can you all sit in the car? I won't be long," I said, sounding a bit calmer.

They walked toward the car, but nobody got inside, not trusting me. At least they gave us some privacy.

"Is she having your baby?" I asked in a hard-bitten voice.

"She never said it was mine," he said as he looked everywhere except at me.

"That's some lame shit," I said, shaking my head. "You weren't even man enough to tell me. I had to hear that shit from someone else, someone that I dislike with a passion," I said all up in his face looking up into his eyes.

"I'm leaving here tonight. Got some shit I need to handle. I need time to think," he said as he backed away, not knowing if I was going to swing. "Go home." Then he turned and went back into the house.

I walked down the steps and picked up a brick out the yard and threw it toward her car windshield. Fats knocked it out of my hand, leaving the brick to fall heavily to the ground.

"Amber, I'm not spending a dime of my hair, nail, or massage money to pay for no windshield cause I know you ain't paying for that shit! Pick her ass up, Fats; we're leaving from down here now!" Ms. Lola barked as an order.

Fats grabbed me and threw me in the backseat with Ms. Elena stuck in the middle, a barrier between Desi and me. Stevie Wonder's song "Go Home" was playing on the car radio. Any other time, I enjoyed listening to that song but those were O's last words to me as he walked away. It was tearing at my heart. Everyone had an opinion about the situation on the ride home, but I was in deep thought; I only heard bits and pieces. When I looked up, I was being dropped down the block at my parents' house.

Daddy was waiting. He watched me walk up the steps. I tried to focus on anything else but him.

"Amber, I rode up and down Georgia Avenue looking for you. I can't believe you were embarrassing yourself in public behind this man!"

Daddy was about to blow a fuse. I could tell he'd been crying—his eyes were red and his rage was hard to conceal, and the vein on the side at his temple was bulging.

"That's my husband! I had every right to go there!" I protested.

"Make this your last time going anywhere chasing after a man, husband or not! You got a baby upstairs who needs his mother. Grow up!" Then he stormed up the stairs without looking back. I sat on the living room couch, my ass sinking deeper into the pillows as I cried and rocked, rocked and cried, just like Mommy.

Fats delivered the message. "O got an unpaid bill. That nigga is gonna kill him if he don't pay. Just letting you know cause you need to keep your distance and know this, I don't give a fuck what happens to that man."

He walked out the door as quickly as he entered.

O called not long after. "Amber, I want to see my son," he said with a strange sense of urgency.

"You can't see your son until you handle your bill." I said.

"Amber, I don't have the money. I fucked up," he said, sounding lost with nowhere to turn. A silence followed by heavy breathing.

"How much do you owe?" I asked.

"A hundred grand."

"You couldn't have smoked that much shit. Is there money still out in the street?" I asked, having trouble understanding.

"I fucked it up. Does it matter how? I'm tired," he said, I could hear his voice crack.

"You need to go into a rehab out of the city, get yourself straight, and give me some time to settle this matter. There's a facility about two hours away. A friend of a friend put his wife there years ago; it's pricey, but it's worth it if you're ready to get clean," I said.

"I appreciate you, Amber. I know after everything I've put you through you don't have to do this," he said.

I was quiet as my mind flashed back over the years to all the fucked up shit we'd been through but remembering that there were just as many good times as bad.

"I need you to disappear off the streets. Call me every day and I'll let you know when it's a go. We'll figure out how you'll get there. I won't be able to visit. I'm sure I'm being watched, waiting for you to show," I said, as I tried to think things through in my head.

"I love you, Amber," he said.

I had no response as I placed the phone on the receiver ending the call.

To make matters worse, Anjelo had colic. He would ball up in a knot, turn red in the face, and scream for hours as if someone was sticking pins in him. Mommy would take him from my arms to give me a break, then Daddy. We played musical chairs for the majority of the night, handing off the baby to whoever was up next. I was exhausted. I couldn't go home. I was too scared to be alone with my son.

Chloe came to spend the night to help with the baby. She watched me pace back and forth, covering the four corners of the bedroom.

"Here, Amber. Take a hit of this coke. It will put some pep in your step, make this situation a little bit more manageable," she said, offering me the package.

"Girl, I don't want that shit! You know I don't do drugs!" I said moving out of her range, as I rubbed Anjelo's back and hummed in his ear as I tried to soothe him.

By 3:00 a.m., that package started looking more and more desirable. I was dog-tired while I watched Chloe wide awake, dancing around the room with the baby. I took a hit and then another. It was as if someone stuck safety pins through my eyelids. I felt a sudden surge of energy, it was almost euphoric. Chloe left the rest of the package with me.

Later that day, I took another hit; if it kept me moving and doing what I needed to do what was the harm? O called Mom's when he didn't reach me at home. I sniffled once or twice during the phone call.

"You alright? Are you catching a cold?" he asked, never suspecting the worse.

"No, my allergies have been really fucking with me lately. Where are you staying?" I asked, quickly changing the subject.

"I'm down Big Tony's. He said he'll get me to the place whenever you say it's cool," he said, sounding a little jittery.

"I'm on it. I should know something before this evening. Call me then," I said.

"Why are you at your Mom's?" he asked knowing that I normally didn't stay there overnight.

"Your son has colic and keeps me up at night. I need the family's support to get me through."

"Damn, baby, I wish I could help."

"I know."

A week later, O was in rehab. "Big Tony" called to give me the number to the fine ass nigga to settle the bill. I dialed the number.

"Hello. This is O's wife Amber. I need to meet up with you to take care of some things for him," I said directly.

"I'd really like to take you out. You're breathtaking," he said that shit as if he wasn't just on the verge of killing my husband.

"Thank you for the compliment, but no thanks. I'm good. Where do you want to meet and what time?" I asked.

"Tonight at 8:00 p.m. Belford Towers, end of the parking lot on the right before you get to the dumpsters," he said.

"What will you be driving?" I asked.

"An Alfa Romeo, dark blue. And you?" he asked.

"I'll be in a black Camaro." I had a rental for this occasion. "See you then," I added.

"He doesn't deserve you. Let me know if you change your mind. You got my number." The phone line went dead.

I hung up the phone, immediately dialing Fats. "I'm meeting the dude tonight to take care of O's bill at 8:00 p.m., Belford Towers, end of the parking lot on the right. I need you to have someone there by 7:00 p.m. to watch my back. I don't think he's stupid enough to try anything, but you just never know," I said with angst in my voice.

"That motherfucker don't want no war. This ain't about O; this is about you," Fats said. I took a deep breath and exhaled. I knew he had me. Then, I took another hit of the powder.

The drop went seamlessly. He rolled up and I handed him the bag without exiting the car, all in a matter of minutes. He knew the money was correct. When it came to a matter of life and death and an effort to correct a wrong, there was no room for error.

22

Dr. Lancaster put Anjelo on some expensive formula that helped put an end to the colic. God knows I was relieved. It suddenly hit me that paying O's bill, the rehab, taking care of others, everyday bills at the house, along with living an extravagant lifestyle had put a dent in my pockets. The hospital bill still needed to be paid.

I started selling ounces, breaking them down to grams when needed. I was so out of my league. At least the quality was still exceptional. I found myself in a strange position, a boss with no workers. I had too much pride to go to Fats.

Mommy didn't mind keeping the baby. She loved him like he was her own. Besides, she wouldn't let me take him home. I'm sure she just wanted to make sure he was really okay. No one complained. Anjelo kept her busy, no time for the voices in her head, at least not today.

I continued to stay at my parents' so I could be near my son. I'd make trips home daily to check on the house and get more fitted clothing. The pregnancy weight dropped off quickly. I had a lot of free time. Chloe and I started running the street going to the Go-Go, clubbing, hitting the after-hour spots and snorting cocaine.

On this particular night, Chloe and I were in an after-hour spot on Missouri Avenue. I saw a few of O's associates so I knew not to do anything out of order. It might come back to haunt me later. I went to the bathroom to take a couple of hits and then back to the bar to get a drink. I'd just walked out of the stall and was checking my nose in the mirror. A woman walked right past me, opened the bathroom door, looked back at me and said, "Your husband got some good dick." As quickly as she said it, she was gone.

I could feel the red blotches creep up my neck. I was infuriated as I quickened my steps. I watched her join her friends at the end of the bar. She picked up her wine glass and took a few sips. I walked right up on her and stole her ass, hard and close. She was so confident that she didn't see me coming. I totally caught her off guard. She fell backwards from the bar stool and hit the floor. I stood over her as I pulled my Luger from my purse and said, "Looks like you get a pass. I'm in a good mood. You get to see another day, but don't ever disrespect me again."

"Come on, Amber, let's go!" Chloe said as she pulled me by the arm. I placed the Luger back in my purse and we left to find another spot to chill.

We would be so tired coming in at 6:00 a.m. that we would disrobe, throw our outfits on the bed, put on pajamas, and jump under the covers. By the end of two weeks, the bed was covered with clothes. We would just crawl underneath and pass out.

Daddy was pissed when he knocked on the door and saw the room in disarray.

"I'm sick of looking at you and Chloe with that mess on top of the bed. Clean this room up today! Don't even think about leaving here until it's done!" He motioned to close the door and opened it again. "One more thing, cook dinner before you leave," he said as he slammed the bedroom door tight. I let out a long sigh before we both turned over and went right back to sleep.

I picked up my keys off the coffee table and was heading out the door when Chloe popped down the steps saying, "I'm going with you!"

"You don't even know where I'm going. I could be going to hell in a handbasket, for all you know, but I see your ass is willing to follow," I said laughing out loud.

"I do know where you're going; you're going to check on the house! I need to peruse your closet. I want to wear something really cute tonight and you need something too! Besides, I don't feel like boosting today," she said.

"Why do I need something really cute?" I asked, as I looked around for my purse, tapping my forehead with two fingers, just as I remembered I'd left it on top of the pile of clothing on the bed.

"We're going to a party with an uppity crowd tonight. You've got to mix it up every now and then," she said.

"Chloe, you know I don't like being around bougie motherfuckers, staring as if they ain't got no home training, looking down their noses, acting like they better," I said with an air of disapproval.

"These people aren't like that. They got money, but they're cool. You'll see," Chloe said on her way out the front door ahead of me.

We pulled up to the garage. I opened the doors and we drove in and parked right next to the Cobra. I barely looked.

Chloe burst out laughing as we entered the living room.

"What the hell is so funny?" I asked as I looked around the room.

"You remember the day that couch was delivered? You ordered it from High Point. I can still see the look on O's face when he walked over to sit down. You told that nigga don't even think about sitting on that couch!" Chloe was still laughing as she spoke. He'd asked, "Why did you purchase a couch that I couldn't sit on in my own home?" You said it was cream, linen, and leather. Not for his ass or anyone else as a matter of fact. That's when we started calling the room 'The Museum.' 'Don't sit. Don't Touch. Just look.'

"Damn, Chloe, you don't forget shit!" I said now laughing along with her.

We went up the stairs to the bedroom. Chloe took several outfits from my closet and placed them on the bed while removing her clothing.

"Why do you have on mix match underwear?" I asked as if she had committed a cardinal sin.

"I put on what was clean," she said with an antagonistic air.

"You know Mommy always said when she was in her right mind . . .?"

"I know the rules, Amber," she said, interrupting me before I could finish my sentence. She began to recite the list from memory.

"First impression is the last impression; bath or shower daily. No one else should have to endure your funk, not even you. Apply deodorant every day. Brush your teeth and your tongue, floss and gargle; nothing worse than a cute bitch with bad breath. Apply Vaseline to lips daily; no cracked lips—who would want to kiss you! Wear matching underwear without any holes in case you get in an accident and have to go to the hospital or in case you find that man that you want to get naked for, but for now, keep those legs closed."

Chloe was so animated I couldn't do anything but laugh. She was acting and sounding just like Mommy. I jumped in and we played tag team.

"No ashy knees, elbows, and feet," I said.

"No snags in your pantyhose," Chloe said.

"Drink plenty of water, so your pee don't stink," I said laughing.

"Speak intelligently, especially in front of adults," Chloe said.

"Always keep a five-dollar bill in your wallet in case you need to call a cab; no chipped nails. Excuse yourself from the table to the ladies' room to reapply lipstick, never in public and shave under your arms and your kitty kat," Chloe said, determined to finish last.

"You got a lot going on down there. I can see that from here," I said pointing at the hair escaping from the sides of her panties. "What if a man wanted to fly you away to an impromptu island vacation? You should always be bikini ready," I said from experience.

"Well I ain't got no passport like a certain person I know, so that shit won't be happening anytime soon, and if I did, I would just buy a razor when I got there."

I looked her in the face as she displayed that smug smile. "Well, it's the truth!" she said.

"Aren't we snippy today?" I said while I shifted my shoulders and wrinkled my nose.

"Sometimes I get tired of you acting holier than thou!" Chloe spoke with an exaggerated motion waving her index finger in my direction.

"You're such a flower child. Free love!" I said while walking the length of my closet looking for an outfit. "You're always meeting men at the Go-Go and going home with them, like it's nothing, night after night, complete strangers. It wouldn't be so bad if drugs weren't involved. That shit scares me, Chloe."

"Look who's talking. You met O at the GoGo, went home with him, and stayed for an entire month. Who does that shit?" Chloe said.

"That was different."

"How so?"

"O is my soulmate."

"Is he? I see the way you look at Fats," Chloe said, picking at her nails without a care. "Admit it! You were tricking, bitch! Shit just worked out for your ass," Chloe said as a dismissal.

I didn't respond. She left me to ponder on that one with my feelings slightly bruised. She saw the expression on my face and realized she'd gone a little too far.

"I know why O let you stay all them days cause you got that good good. You know they say crazy pussy is good pussy. Why do you think your dad is still with your mom after all these years," she said more of a statement than a question. We burst into laughter and just like that the tension was gone.

"I think I want to wear this one right here! I've got the perfect shoes to match!" she said admiring herself in the mirror.

She had on the beige jumpsuit that I wore the night O took me to dinner at Old Ebbitt Grill for the very first time. The jumpsuit had sentimental meaning to me, but Chloe was my best friend and besides she was wearing the hell out of it, almost as good as me.

The party was off upper 16th Street on one of those flower streets, Geranium or was it Juniper, I can't remember which. We made sure to clean the bedroom and I cooked a roast, mashed potatoes, string beans, and baked a cake from scratch before we left. Daddy loved a bowl of ice cream every night. He'd be happy to see cake to go along with the ice cream when he arrived home late from working his endless job.

I found a parking spot at the bottom of the driveway. "Where's the package, Chloe?" I said.

"I thought you got it from under the pillow," Chloe said while searching through her purse for her phone.

"No. I was kissing Anjelo goodnight. Damn!"

We sat there for a minute, carefully considering our next move.

Chloe spoke up first, "Let's go inside, party for a little while and then leave early."

"That's cool. I'm tired for real. We've been going pretty hard," I said, pulling down the visor, taking one last look in the mirror.

"Yeah, but we've been having big fun!" Chloe said, showing all thirty-two like a mischievous twelve-year-old.

"Chloe, do you ever get the feeling after snorting that shit your heart is about to burst through your chest?" I asked.

"Yeah, girl, all the time! Remind me to give you some valium. It'll calm you down and help you sleep," she said.

We exited the car, walked up the driveway lined with neatly manicured trees with high top fades, and headed toward the house.

"Knock. Knock. Knock."

A handsome older guy opened the door and said, "Well, hello ladies! Welcome to my home."

It was a huge house but sparsely furnished. Something seemed a little amiss. He ushered us into the dining area. There was a heavy wooden table with intricate carvings on the legs that seated eight people. Each seat had a glass pipe strategically placed in front of each chair. We were the last guests to arrive. The host came out of the kitchen with a large piece of rock and began to cut it with a razor blade, laying pieces on top of each pipe. I looked at Chloe trying not to catch an attitude; she was oblivious to my stare. Everyone began to smoke except for me. Chloe got to her feet and began to dance, slow and seductive, while the others watched.

The older gentleman said to me, "You're not partaking in the festivities?"

"No, that's not my thing," I said.

"I understand your fear of the unknown. This is the best high on the planet. You like that powder?" he asked.

"I do, but this is different," I said, wanting to leave.

"The key to rock cocaine is to make sure you eat healthy, take your vitamins, exercise, and drink plenty of water. You're in control of this; it's not in control of you. I've been doing this drug for over a year. I think I look damn good!"

Everyone laughed at his comment.

Chloe found her way back to the table, and sat back down in the chair next to mine.

"Amber, just try it once. If you don't like it, you never have to do it again," Chloe said, handing me the pipe.

"After I take this hit, we're leaving right?" I asked.

She nodded her head yes.

I took the hit. Everything in the room was heightened, the song on the stereo, the conversations in the room, I could hear bells ringing, not loud or disturbing but soft and calming, like the sound of bells when you meditate. I closed my eyes and took it all in; before long I took another hit, and then another. None were like the first, none would ever be. How could anything so perfect be recreated? I looked to my left and watched Chloe take a hit that could surely have been broken down into several.

"Chloe, your hair is on fire!" I screamed.

She continued to take the hit, focused, not even her hair burning could stop her. She finally put the torch down and patted the front of her hair. No one seemed to care except for me, definitely not Chloe.

I looked at my watch, and it was 4:00 a.m. Chloe was busy scraping the pipe and the screen for residue. She took that one last hit. All the guests were gone and so was the rock. Chloe got on her knees and proceeded to search the floor, running her hand over the surface looking for crumbs and maybe even a piece of rock dropped in haste. I was more than ready to go after watching her behavior.

"I'm going to the ladies' room, and then we can leave," Chloe said as if she'd just suddenly snapped back to thinking clearly.

The sun was just beginning to rise when we finally walked out the front door. When we got to the car, Chloe pulled rocks out of her ears, pockets and even her belly button.

"I got some for when we get home," she said, still geeking.

"I'm going home to my baby. Where do you want me to drop you?" I asked, starting to feel guilty.

"You can take me up by Soldier's Home. Are you sure you don't want to come?" She asked, displaying the rocks in her hand.

"No, I'm going home."

After dropping Chloe off, I went to Ms. Lola's house. I still needed to come down from my high before going in the house.

I put the key in the door and walked upstairs to Fats' studio and surprisingly found him hard at work.

"You been in here all night?" I asked as I walked over, stood behind him looking over his shoulder.

"I got in late. I couldn't sleep, so I came in here and started on a new painting. Where are you coming from?" he asked, never taking his eye off the canvas.

"Hanging out with Chloe. When are you going to paint me?" I asked as a diversion, I didn't need him asking me for details.

He stopped what he was working on, moved to a blank easel and said, "We can begin now, while I'm in the mood."

"You mean now, like right now?" I asked, looking confused. "Where do you want me to sit? Is this outfit okay? What about my hair?" I said looking around the room in search of a mirror. The one question I didn't ask was 'Do I look as fucked up as I feel?'

"You're fine; just one thing, I need you to take off your clothes."

"Why?" I asked, not understanding his request.

"I need to capture the real you," he said as he looked into my eyes.

I stepped back and stripped down to my bra and panties, crossing my chest with both arms.

"Amber, I need you to take everything off. You trust me, don't you?" he asked.

I dropped my arms and removed my panties and bra. My actions said everything.

"Where do you want me to sit?" I asked for the second time, looking for a chair.

"I want you to stand right there. Show me what you're feeling inside. I need to peel away the layers. I don't need clothes in the way," he said as he began to paint.

I stood for hours on end, shifting my weight as I grew tired.

"I'm almost done. Come back tomorrow and we'll continue," he said.

"Can I see?" I asked as I stepped into my panties and hooked my bra.

"You can see it when it's done," he said as he walked to the sink and started cleaning the brushes.

I came back every day for a week until it was finished.

"You can look now," he said, rising to his feet, stretching his arms out wide, opening his mouth wide followed by a yawn. He stepped back so I could move in close. I stared at the woman on the canvas. It was my exact likeness, except her color was blue.

"Fats, why did you paint me blue?" I asked with a perplexed look.

"I paint what I see," he said with his back to me as he walked to the sink once again to clean his brushes. I looked at the canvas one more time. It was finished, no question about that. He'd signed it and gave the piece a title. He called it "Indiscretion." Warm tears ran down my face as I gathered my things. "Yearning for your Love" by the Gap Band was playing softly on the stereo in the background, Fat's subtle innuendo.

Chloe was missing in action, again. She finally called around 9:00 p.m. with another story.

"Hey, Amber."

Just those two words, slow and prolonged, letting me know she was high on that horse.

"What's up, Chloe?"

"Girl, let me tell you what I went through today. I've been spending the last few days with the guy up near Soldier's Home."

"Where I dropped you off, right?"

"Yeah, the same place. Well, today my shit started itching. My first thought was I know this negro ain't give me no crabs, but the itching continued to get worse.

"So did you go get something to get rid of that shit?" I asked.

I went to the Peoples Drug Store, walked up to the cashier and quietly asked, "What aisle is the RID on please?" She promptly said, "I don't know, but wait just one minute and I'll find out for you."

The bitch went on the intercom and said, "A customer needs assistance. What aisle can she find the RID please?"

"Amber, when I tell you I could feel people staring a hole through my ass. I don't get embarrassed about much, but that one did it for me. I wanted to punch her funny looking ass in the face!"

She was talking up a storm, and then there was complete silence.

"Chloe, are you still there?"

I knew she was nodding.

It was torturous sometimes trying to hold a conversation with her ass when she was fucked up. I usually tried to read my book in-between our on and off conversations, but tonight, she had my total attention.

"What happened next?" I asked, prompting her to talk, anxious for her to continue.

"Sorry, Amber. I put that shit on before I called you. Girl, why am I combing my pubic hair like it said to do on the directions and I can see the crabs jumping off and all up in the comb? Amber, this shit is moving; they're crawling down my thigh."

I dropped the phone for a minute, ran around the room shaking my hands with my fingers spread wide in total disbelief, as if that alone would allow me to unhear what she'd just said. I had a visual and it wasn't pretty. I picked the phone up and put the receiver back to my ear.

"Hey, Chloe. Sorry, I thought I heard the baby crying," I said with chills rubbing my hand up and down my arms.

"Amber, I think it's time for me to go rinse this shit off. Oh, and before I go, I haven't forgotten about returning your jumpsuit, I just need . . ."

I cut her ass off in mid-sentence. "Girl, I wouldn't think of taking that jumpsuit back from you! It looked so much better on you than it did on me. I'll talk to you tomorrow okay," I said hurriedly, hanging up the phone, still cringing as if something was crawling on me.

23

I woke up the next morning with every intention of going on a mission. I dressed in baggy clothes and a head-wrap, sliding on dark shades and gold hoop earrings, got in the Ford Focus, and drove straight to the paraphernalia shop on Benning Road to purchase a pipe, screens, and a torch. I was hoping that no one would recognize me. I slipped in and out without being noticed.

Once I got back to the house, I cooked up a gram of Peruvian flake as I'd watched Chloe and O do on numerous occasions. I stared in shock at the size of the rock that came back in the water. I broke it into tiny pieces, snuck in the bathroom and locked the door as if I wasn't home alone.

I took one hit and was paranoid as fuck! That shit jumped on my ass with a vengeance! I unlocked the bathroom door and walked to the window to peep out the blinds, needing to see if the sirens that I could hear in my head weren't right outside. I didn't see any police cars, as I continued checking the lock on the front door again and again, and then just standing there as if my feet were immobilized. Thirty minutes must've passed before I could take a step. OCD and overthinking to the 10th power was my routine during my paranoia, but it didn't stop me. I finally talked myself into walking back to the bathroom. I closed the door, turned the lock, took another hit, bigger than the first, and started the same insane madness all over again. It was like being in a nightmare with my eyes wide open. This time, I gathered everything up and placed it under the sink and closed the cabinet door. Taking a seat on the floor with my back against the cabinet, waiting for the police to come through the door any minute to arrest me. The sirens in my head were much louder this time. I must've walked back and forth to the front window twenty times, peeping out the blinds and then being stuck. The phone rang and I almost jumped out of my skin, ignoring the ring, covering my ears hoping it would stop. I thought I could hear Anjelo crying but I was too afraid to come to his aid. I stood from my seat on the floor and walked to the bedroom closet where I had stashed an ounce of powder. I damn near ran to the bathroom where I flushed the entire ounce down the toilet. It was nightfall the last time I peeped out the blinds.

I took a valium. Still no sleep. Two hours later, I took a pain pill and fell into a deep slumber, dreaming again, but this time I was drowning in the pool at the old house. Zeus was standing at the edge of the pool watching me go under struggling to catch my breath, not willing to help me because I didn't save him from O. My eyes flew open, suddenly awakened by a cold wet feeling, pulling back the covers I saw that I had soaked the bed and was lying in my own urine.

*　　*　　*

Chloe was renting a room in a house on Missouri Avenue. I'd come up with a plan to get paid real quick before O came home. I needed her assistance. I dialed her number.

"Hello," she said, answering the phone while still sounding sleep.

"Hey, Chloe. What are you doing?"

"Just lying in bed."

"You trying to get some money?" I asked knowing she wouldn't say no.

"You better bet it! What do you need me to do?" she eagerly asked in response.

"Come to the house so I can explain my strategy," I said, wanting to speak to her face to face. In the meantime, I called Chili and asked for a huge favor.

"So, what you're saying is we're going to get a room at the Motel 6 for two days, sell a ton of cocaine and heroin at a reduced price like a thirty percent off sale at the department stores from 9 a.m. to 9 p.m., get the money, and bounce!" Chloe repeated my words to me.

"Yep, that's my plan in a nutshell. We'll pay Chili back first for fronting the drugs and then split the money 60/40. You good with that?" I asked not expecting any pushback.

"I'm good," she said, anxious to get started.

"One more thing, Chloe, no dipping in the product and no shaving off the top. No getting high for two days. I need us both to be on point," I said.

"You can depend on me. I might make enough money to get my own place," she said with a gleam in her eyes.

"No doubt. Let's get this money!"

We raised our right hands in the air giving each other a high five. Then, we jumped in the Ford Focus. I dropped Chloe at Mommy's to watch Anjelo and I went to meet Chili.

Once I got back, I called all of O's clients and some of my old clients. Chloe had a few folks who would be interested as well. We set up appointment times and pre-orders. I made it clear to everyone that if they missed their appointment time, it was a done deal. I didn't want anyone seeing who was who. This operation was going to be run professionally, hopefully with no hiccups. I needed some security. Cody was the first person to come to mind.

I pulled up on him down DJ's mom's.

"Hey, Ma!" I walked over to give her a kiss on the cheek and a big hug, immediately turning to wash my hands in the sink, tearing a sheet of paper towel, hurriedly drying my hands, lifting a fried chicken wing out of the aluminum pan.

"Oh shit!" I exclaimed, juggling the wing between both hands, while looking around for a paper plate; it was piping hot.

Ma was shaking her head and laughing at my predicament, "I could've told you they were hot. They just came out of the frying pan. You so pressed," she said, adding more wings to the hot grease.

"I haven't had your wings in a minute, pressed I may be!" I said admittedly, taking a bite, looking for a napkin.

I spotted Cody sitting in the corner, away from everyone else, watching television. He didn't talk much, but was loyal to a fault. He grew up in foster homes, so he never really got attached to anyone, but just like DJ, he had a special place in his heart for me. He was a natural born killer and would be the perfect security for Chloe and me.

I walked over, took a seat next to him and spoke quietly, "Cody, could I speak to you in private, please?" I said rising from the couch, stepping outside, with the half-eaten wing on the paper plate. I walked down the steps to the sidewalk as I took another bite of the wing. He followed.

"What's up Amber?" he said, minus a smile, all business. I told him about my plan.

"If you decide to help me, you can't tell Fats or Desi. They wouldn't be down with this move. I'll pay you out my share. Just let me know your price up front," I said.

"Amber, you're my girl. I got you! Your secret is safe with me. I still got mad respect for you. Not many women would have held it down the way you have over the years," he said with a smile.

"Thank you, Cody. I'll see you on Friday morning, unless I need you before," I said with a wide grin as I walked back to the car.

I knew I was all the way wrong storing drugs in my house. O would always say, "Don't shit where you eat."

It was a bold move on my behalf, but everything about this was. I was a hustler and scared money don't make no money. Cody, Chloe, and I weighed and packaged the drugs to fill the orders in preparation for Friday and Saturday morning. Cody escorted us to the room with his hidden weaponry. We sat up shop and let the day unfold, eating meals and snacks out of my favorite picnic baskets in between serving customers. The sun was setting as we served the last customer. It had been a very profitable day.

Saturday morning was overcast with gray clouds, just a hint of sun peeking through every now and again. Today was busier than yesterday; no time for a full game of spades, as I walked to the door, looked out the peephole, and threw a few green grapes in my mouth as I answered the knock. It was one of Chloe's boosting buddies, the last customer of a very long day.

"Amber, I don't have any cash but can I trade you this bag of diamond rings for the coke?" she said, having been used to doing business with my husband.

"It's not that kind of party—no fronts, no shorts. I'm only accepting cash; besides, I'm not trying to run all around town trying to sell that shit!" I said aggravated, looking at Chloe with pursed lips.

"You know your husband bought a lot of your jewelry from me over the years, nothing but high quality gems. I didn't charge him top dollar cause me and O are cool as shit! Come on, Amber; help a sista out," she said, as she stated her case.

"Helping you is making more work for me," I said while examining the rings through the clear freezer bag. The room went silent, waiting on my decision.

"Give her what she wants," I said as I placed the gems in my Chanel bag.

God must've been on my side because my two-day sale went off without a hitch. I met up with Chili on Sunday morning to square up the money that I owed him. He sat behind the steering wheel and watched me walk toward his truck with two black duffel bags. I opened the door and got inside.

"Senorita. I'm amazed at how you pulled this off in such a short time frame. I'll partner with you any day," he said with a look of admiration.

"Thank you, Chili. I appreciate you for trusting me. Oh, by the way, would you like to buy a ring for someone special?" I said pulling out the bag filled with diamonds.

Chili bought two rings. I didn't ask any questions; I was just glad to make the sale. I opened the door and returned to my car, leaving the Wheaton Mall parking garage, heading back to D.C. with a smile. Next, I met up with Cody to pay him his share.

"Amber, I think that might have been the easiest money I've made in a long time. It's a pleasure doing busy with you," he said as he climbed out of my car and walked back to his and disappeared from sight.

I went to Chloe's room and hit her off. She was giggling like a little kid.

"When is the last time you've had this much money from putting in two days' work?" I asked.

"Never," she said as she hugged me real tight and put the money in the safe.

We decided to grab a meal and celebrate. I pulled on the corner to run into Mommy's to get Anjelo when Desi approached the car with an intimidating look and snatched the car door open on the passenger side.

"That bullshit that you two pulled off this weekend, cut into me and Fats' money. Don't do that shit no more!" he said, addressing us both.

"I needed money to get my own place," Chloe said as if she owed him an explanation.

"All you had to do was come to me. I would've given you money to get an apartment," he said and went in his pocket and started peeling off one-hundred-dollar bills. Once he got to a couple of grand, he handed her the cash.

"Your girl's going to get you hurt. Watch yourself, Amber," he said as he looked in my direction.

"Is that a threat?" I asked. He'd struck a nerve. But he just turned and headed back to Ms. Lola's house without a response.

I quickly jumped out of the car following his ass. "Chloe, can you get Anjelo please? I need to have a very short conversation with Desi."

"Desi, hold up a minute. I need to talk to you," I said with piercing eyes as I followed him up the steps.

"It's obvious you're trying to come between Chloe and my friendship. Good luck with that. You want to threaten me? I think you've forgotten I held you and Fats down while you both were in; ya'll came home straight as a motherfucker! So, if I cut into a small portion of your profits for two days, I'll take that shit as a tip. Now you can run and tell Fats about my actions this weekend, or he can find out on his own and I'll deal with that, but if you tell him, then you'll give me no choice but to let him know why we have such contempt for each other, the truth. I remember seeing you and the Picture man as if it was yesterday. I have no empathy for you. I tried to help; you shot me down, so I guess once a bitch always a bitch!"

I watched his eyes narrow as he made a closed fist, I could see the veins protruding on his hand, while he took quick shallow breaths.

"Go ahead, swing. You've been wanting to do that shit for a long time. I'll buy popcorn and soda later to watch Fats whip your ass. I bet we'll see then where the loyalty lies. Nobody likes your ass. You've always been in Fats' shadow, wishing you were him, but you'll never be able to step into his shoes. If I was you, I wouldn't make any more idle threats. You might want to continue figuring out how to tolerate me cause that's about all you can do. Have a good day!"

I turned and walked back down the steps, leaving him simmering on the porch.

∗　∗　∗

Chloe, Anjelo, and I drove to Georgetown, heading to Houston's Restaurant.

"Chloe, jump out and put our name on the waitlist, please, while I park the car. Hopefully, the wait won't be too long," I said looking around for a parking space on Wisconsin Avenue. Houston's was a popular go-to for folks in the life. You never knew who you might run into while waiting on your table, hopefully no one you had beef with. I saw the fine ass dude from Baltimore as soon as I walked in the door while carrying the baby. He rose from his seat, and walked toward me.

"You need help?" he said, reaching out to take the diaper bag off my shoulder.

I felt the electricity go through my body when he touched me, my nipples were hard. I was embarrassed because he noticed. Chloe stepped up and took the bag out of his hand.

"Thank you," she said as she walked back to her seat, never taking her eyes off of him.

"That's his aunt. She's overly protective. We got it," I said, wanting to disappear into thin air. O taught me to never sit with my back to the door as I looked around for a space to sit down. It was packed, standing room only. One of his friends came out to say their table was ready. The entire space cleared. I was able to sit down with Anjelo, facing the street, and motioned for Chloe to come sit next to me.

"Who the fuck was that? He's fine as shit and obviously got a hard on for you," Chloe said, speaking quietly.

"That's the guy that was going to kill O," I said, sitting Anjelo down on the seat to my right.

"Damn! I know you wished you didn't still love your husband," Chloe said in typical Chloe fashion.

"You're right, but I do." I said, never shocked at the shit that came out of her mouth.

Chloe's name was called much sooner than I expected but I was really happy, hoping to eat before Anjelo woke up demanding to be fed. He had quite an appetite now that the colic episode was over and done. I opted out on breastfeeding; you would think that with all the shit that I've experienced in life that something so simple wouldn't scare me so bad, but it did.

The waiter came to take our order. He looked to be around thirty, with the body of a runner, with a curious smile.

"My name is Solomon. I'll be your server today. Can I get you ladies a cocktail before taking your order?" he said in an attentive manner.

"I'd like a margarita on ice please," I said.

"Salt around the rim?" he asked.

"Yes please."

"What can I get for you?" he said as he stared into Chloe's eyes. She locked in on his gaze.

"I'd like a French martini," she said, low and sexy.

"I didn't quite hear your order," he said.

"You can come closer," she said, obviously flirting. He leaned in and she whispered the order in his ear. Solomon stepped off to get our drinks. I just shook my head.

"Damn, Chloe; I thought you were getting ready to strip," I said giggling.

"Did you see his body? Boyfriend looks like he might be working with something," she said, as if she was going to check that out and report back later.

Chloe ordered the Hawaiian steak and I got the baked chicken. I managed to make it through the meal and was requesting a box when Anjelo began to stir. I headed to the bathroom with the baby and the diaper bag. I couldn't help but glance at the table with the fine ass dude and his crew, they were loud as shit! Throwing down shots and having a celebration. He watched me walk by and gave me a wink. I turned back straight and kept walking. By the time I returned to the table, Chloe had packed up the boxes and was ready to go, leaving Solomon a nice tip and her phone number on the back of the check. The fine ass dude and his boys were just leaving.

He paused at our table. "It was nice seeing you again, Amber. Until the next time," he said as he continued walking toward the exit.

"Are we ready to go?" Chloe said, getting to her feet and gathering the bags.

"No. I need to feed Anjelo; plus I want him and his friends to be gone by the time we leave.

"You really don't want no parts of him, huh?" Chloe said while scrutinizing every waiter within close proximity with her eyes, searching for Solomon.

"No. I don't!" I said, done with the conversation. Just then, Solomon walked up to the table.

"I'm going to call you later if that's okay. I get off at 10:00 p.m. tonight," he turned and walked away to another table to take orders. I watched another young lady as she stared into his eyes.

"Looks like your boy gets a lot of play," I said jokingly, knowing that it didn't matter to Chloe about other women; she would be waiting on that call. She had a pocket full of money and could buy all the get high she wanted, so a new dude just for play was right up her alley. I would have to remind her we needed to go apartment shopping and pay the rent in advance for at least six months before she blew all that cash.

We left Houston's, dropped Anjelo off to Ms. Lola, with his tiny little toes wiggling and her tickled pink grin as she took him from my arms. Chloe and I headed to Georgia Avenue to hit a few salons. I needed to sell the rest of the diamonds.

I saw Julie, the receptionist, through the front window as I parked on the Avenue. I exited the car and entered the salon.

Chloe rolled down the window and spoke, "Amber, I'm going to wait in the car this time around."

"No problem," I appreciated her keeping me company.

"Hey, Julie! Is Ms. Beverly working today?" I asked with my eyes darting around the waiting area, checking out the caliber of patrons waiting to get their hair styled. It was the first of the month; never know who might want to spend that check on a ring.

"Hey, Amber! She's upstairs. Go on up," she said, taking a credit card payment from a customer. I climbed the steps lined with exposed brick. Ms. Beverly was set up in the back where she had a clear view of her stylists.

"Hey, Ms. Beverly. Can I interest you in a diamond ring?" I said pulling the freezer bag out of my oversized purse. She immediately put the curling irons down.

"Come here, baby. Let me see those a little closer," she said, reaching out for the bag with a gleam in her eyes. "Excuse me. I need to step away for a minute," she said, gently touching her client's shoulder. She walked to her office and unlocked the door with me on her heels. I knew that walk meant she was more than interested. I took the bag out of her hands and laid each ring on her desk for inspection.

"Can I try this one on?" she asked, staring at a large square Princess-Cut.

"Of course. That one's nice. I've tried it on a few times, and then I had to remind myself that this right here was about me making my money back," I said knowing I needed this sale.

"How much do you want for this one?"

"A third of whatever the tag says.

"So that would be around $1,700?" She asked.

I looked at the tag and whipped out my calculator. "It's a little cheaper. $1,666.00."

She put the ring to the side while continuing to try on the rest. Her eyes kept going back to that ring.

"Ms. Beverly, why are we doing this? Just like the clothes I bring to you, I know what you like. I know your style. You know you want that ring and besides you left your customer in the chair, remember?" I said hoping to help her make up her mind a little faster.

"Alright, Amber, you've convinced me." She slid the ring on her finger one more time and then headed to the safe where she took out a stack of bills, counting out the hundred-dollar bills on the desk in front of me. She went in the pocket of her smock to get the sixty-six dollars. I gathered the rings and placed them one by one back in the freezer bag.

"Did you put the ring in the safe? You don't need to be wearing that while you're doing hair," I said.

"I did. Thank you, Amber. Let me get back out here before my client walks out the door. See you next time."

24

Spring of 1987

I awoke with the birds, showered, dressed in a hot little mini dress, and drove out 50 toward the Annapolis Bridge. I was on my way to pick up O from rehab. The sunrise over the water was magnificent. Mommy always said, "Appreciate everything around you that's free." I was taking it all in as I drove across the bridge, with both hands on the steering wheel, playing a CD, needing the continuous music to keep me calm. I had major issues with driving over bridges and through tunnels.

"Does this shit ever go away?" I said out loud as I tried to stay focused on the music.

I pulled into the compound, feeling an instant sense of calm and tranquility. There were numerous brick buildings surrounded by lakes, cement paths lined with trees and flowerbeds. It felt peaceful and untroubled. I followed the signs to the administrative building, parked, and walked toward the entrance. After showing my identification, one of the counselors went to get O.

When he walked through the entrance, he held his arms open wide and displayed that smile that I'd missed. I ran to him, wrapped around his waist, and held on tight. He'd gained his weight back, his eyes were clear, and he was ready to go home.

"Thank you so much for helping him," I said to the director, just a little misty eyed.

We walked out the building together. He put his bag in the trunk.

"You want to drive?" I asked handing him the keys. He smiled and got in on the driver's side, adjusting the seat and mirrors, no longer looking like the shell of a man he'd become but now the strong black man that I fell in love with so many years ago.

We were right outside the compound gates when O began searching the radio stations. Michael Henderson's song "At the Concert," featuring Roberta Flack, came on the radio. I touched his hand.

"Baby, that's my song. You've got to pull over," I said with expectation in my eyes.

"Amber, I'm ready to go home. Your ass likes every song that comes on the radio," he said, keeping his eyes on the road.

"O, I want to dance with you, please," I said with puppy dog eyes. He took one look and caved, as he pulled the Range over to the curb. I turned the radio up and rolled the windows down. We both got out of the truck. He took my hand and we began to hand-dance on the sidewalk. It reminded me of happier times as he pulled me in close and we started to bop, smooth and easy, morphing into a carnal slow drag with his hands on my ass and me pressing up against his hardness.

"Hey, O! I see why you were in such a hurry to go home," his young roommate yelled from the back of a station wagon.

"Have a good life. It's been real!" O raised his hand in the air, acknowledging the young man, as the car sped by.

"Baby, you got any money on you? I want to get a room," he said with desire in his eyes.

"I thought you were in such a hurry to get home," I said teasingly.

"Woman, don't play with me."

We both laughed as we got back in the truck in search of a hotel.

"You lucky I don't take that pussy right here," he said driving down the highway, stealing glances in my direction.

"You know we don't do good fucking in anything that moves."

We both laughed out loud.

We found a hotel with a vacancy. After checking in, I handed the key card to O to do the honors. I let him shower first, faking important phone calls that needed my immediate attention. The truth was I was nervous as hell. It was like being with him for the first time all over again. He stepped out of the shower, drying off with a towel as he walked toward me. I could see his lips moving but I swear I couldn't hear a word he was saying.

"My turn," I uttered while ignoring his naked body as he dropped the towel to the floor. I moved right past him heading to the bathroom as I stepped out of my sandals, removed my dress and underwear, and pulled the wet towel on the floor closer to the tub as I climbed in the shower. I stood very still underneath the shower head and closed my eyes. I cleansed my body with circular motions, rinsing the soap down the drain just as I heard the shower curtain ripple. My eyes popped open as O stepped back into the shower.

"Did you really think I was going to wait? We've been apart way too long. I need what belongs to me," he said gently kissing my neck, as he placed my hands against the shower wall. Then, he slid between my thighs with intention and purpose as he plunged deep inside my twat, encompassing every thought; my legs were weak. He carried me from the shower and laid me on the bed, kissing me slowly with a burning desire. His lips tasted sweet like fruit punch. He was now licking between my breasts, sliding down toward my stomach, circling my belly button, slowly moving to my clit, leisurely caressing my inner sanctuary. He felt my body start to tremor, on the brink of an orgasm. He held my hips and plunged in deeper as I screamed out loud, shaking uncontrollably.

"Can I have my pussy now?" he asked with reserve as if I could refuse, nodding my head yes, still trembling, not able to speak. O entered me over and over, slowly satisfying my every need. Chest to chest, our hearts beating as one.

We laid in each other arms, not saying a word listening to the tempo of our uneven breathing.

"I know this might not be the right time to ask, but I've thought about it a lot while I was in rehab. Will you be able to accept the baby?" He held on to me tightly, expecting resistance as he spoke, but there was no need. I didn't pull away or hesitate in answering.

"I'll love the baby as if it were my own. Babies are innocent; they're born into confusion. They need to be nurtured and loved," I said from my heart. He kissed me deeply and we made love one more time before heading home. We were going to try to make our marriage work.

It's a good thing I got some dick on the way home because O was enamored with his son. He wanted to bathe him, feed him, and even change his diaper. He talked to Anjelo like he was a grown man, getting the biggest kick out of our infant son grasping his finger and squeezing real tight, until they both were worn out. O fell asleep with our son on his chest. It was priceless to watch.

I was feeling antsy; thoughts of getting high crossed my mind, but I fought off the urge. I didn't know how long I was going to be able to pretend to be his perfect wife. I'd already proven how fast I could fuck up and show out, my track record was blemished while hiding the fact that I was now an addict with integrity. I always paid my drug bills on time and still had all my connects. I'd fuck up my money with the quickness, along with associates that promised to pay at a later date, taking them at their word, but realizing too late that they were just along for a free high. All the responsibility fell on me. I was still learning shit the hard way. I would have to maneuver around O, carefully.

*   *   *

O, Anjelo, and I were going to an annual picnic in Rock Creek Park, given by some of the OGs for families and close friends. It didn't start until 2:00 p.m. I was already dressed. I looked at the clock and it was now noon. I'd cooked the night before so I didn't have much to do but pick up Anjelo from Mommy's. O already left to help set up.

One little hit shouldn't hurt. I'd be straight in an hour and be on my way. I took my paraphernalia into the bathroom, moving too fast, forgetting to lock the door. I had the pipe to my lips and was just about to place the flame on the rock when O burst through the bathroom door. He was livid as he knocked the pipe out of my hand; it shattered into tiny shards of glass across the tile, sparkling like diamonds. He snatched me out of the bathroom and slammed me down on the couch with both hands. I was petrified. I could see the tears staining his cheeks. It took a few moments before he spoke.

When he did, all he said was, "Why?"

My words began to regurgitate as if I'd eaten something bad.

"It started while you were in rehab, not the rock, but the powder. Anjelo had colic and I was sleep-deprived. I told you that," I said, folding my hands inward, clicking my fingers together nervously.

"Then Chloe offered me some powder so that I could get some energy, you know, so I could stay up and deal with the baby," I said with apprehension, scared to death of what he might do next as I twisted and pulled at my wedding ring as I spoke.

"Mommy was keeping Anjelo and I had a lot of time on my hands. I went to a party with Chloe one night and I tried the rock," I said, not once looking in his eyes.

"I should've known that bitch Chloe had something to do with this shit. She's the common denominator in each scenario, rotten to the fucking core. I don't know how I let her stay around this long," O said, his voice was cold. "She's no longer welcome in our home," he said, leaving no room to counter.

"I'll help you get the food together. We'll pick up Anjelo, and then we're going to the picnic as planned. Today is family day. We'll table this discussion until tonight."

I couldn't tell if it was the sun or O's eyes burning a hole in my back as we walked from the car. I found myself longing for the shade. Rare Essence was cranking. I danced as if I didn't have a care in the world, just like I did on those school nights, knowing Daddy would be mad as shit because I stayed out past curfew. Just like back then, I'd deal with the consequences when I got home.

I could feel O watching me. I blew him a kiss. He ignored my gesture and continued on with his conversation while holding the baby. It was at that very moment that I knew our tabled conversation wouldn't go well.

Once we got home, O went to lay the baby down; he'd fallen asleep. It was past his bedtime. I saw my opportunity to run. I slipped out the garage. Damn if I was going to stay and take the chance on him slipping back into that nigga that whipped my ass. He still had a temper. I drove through the neighborhood, heading for New York Avenue. O was calling my cell phone no sooner than I hit the corner. I ignored his calls.

As I drove, I allowed my thoughts to go back to the time when I saw white dots falling from the corner of my eye. I went to see an ophthalmologist. The dots were called floaters. My diagnosis was a detached retina from all the blows I'd endured over the years from O's anger. I could have easily lost my eyesight if the condition had gone undetected. Laser surgery was needed to seal the tear. Fuck if I was going through that shit again. I pushed down on the gas pedal and drove even faster.

I got a motel room, not the cleanest, but real cheap because the air conditioning was broken. I called Chloe to come meet me. I was calmer when hitting the pipe when I had some sort of distraction. Chloe and I would play spades for hours on end.

It was hot as shit. We stripped down to our bra and panties but neither one of us complained. I finally turned my phone off; I was tired of O calling. We made several trips to the ATM in the middle of the hood in the wee hours of the morning. Before you knew it, the sun was rising. Every time I entertained the thought of going home, I'd just take another hit.

I gave Chloe money to go buy more rock and fast food, which I hardly touched. By the fourth day, we'd smoked all the rock.

"Here, Chloe. Go get us another eighth please," I said, going in my purse and handing her money.

"You go, Amber. I'm going to take a nap," she said as she curled up under the covers and closed her eyes.

Following her directions, I made a wrong turn and ended up in a cul-de-sac. Jump Out with long straggly blond hair and dirty clothes had some teenagers lying face down on the sidewalk with their pockets turned inside out. The baggies were spread out in clear view on the hood of the car. The young men were hand-cuffed, waiting on the paddy wagon.

"Ya'll some dirty motherfuckers! You ain't even find shit on me!" one of the teenagers yelled from the ground.

The police were still searching the car for more contraband or planting drugs that were never there before. O would tell me stories about crooked cops who would do all kinds of shit, from setting folks up to be murdered or robbing drug dealer's homes and never turning in the drugs or the money to evidence. O had police on payroll who kept him informed.

I drove around the circle of homes, as the police watched, finally finding the right street, two blocks over, parked, walked up the steps and rang the doorbell. A tall svelte guy with mixed gray hair opened the door.

"Hi. I'm Amber. Chloe sent me," I said looking past the gentleman at the nicely furnished living room.

"Come in and have a seat. I didn't know you and Chloe were friends. You O's wife, right?" he asked, already knowing the answer.

"Please don't let him know I'm here," I said as I jumped straight to my feet from a sitting position.

"Baby girl, I'm not calling O, but I'm not selling you shit either! I got much respect for your husband. We were in together. All he talked about was you. If he got wind of this right here, he'd probably shoot up the entire block behind your pretty little ass. Does he know you running with Chloe?" he asked.

I was still stuck but managed to mumble, "She's my best friend."

"She might be your best friend, but her best friend is that rock. Best believe. When Chloe came here last night, she sucked my man's dick right here in front of me and then took him in the back and gave him some pussy for a discount, and then offered me up next. I'd be scared to stick my dick in her; my shit might fall off. Did she give you any money back?" he asked.

I just stared in silence.

"I didn't think so," he went on. "She's a party girl and will do anything for a hit, and I mean anything. It's a side street about five blocks away where the truck drivers park their tractor trailers. The young boys up the block tell me she be out there at 5:00 a.m. going from truck to truck sucking and fucking. That ain't nobody you want to be hanging around. She'll set your ass up. You'll be all hemmed up in some shit you don't know how to get yourself out of for real. Go home. Don't come back here," he said, opening the front door. I slipped past him heading straight for the car. It was time to go home.

We drove to Mommy's.

"Chloe, I'm going inside to get Anjelo. You might want to wait out here on the porch," I said as I put the key in the lock. I crept up the stairs, hoping to dodge all the creaks in the wood. I peeped into Mommy's room. Anjelo was asleep. I walked toward his crib and Mommy came from out of the shadows, swinging a baseball bat at my head. I was tired but my reflexes were good. I dipped, came back up and grabbed the bat. We wrestled briefly. I was able to get the bat out of her hands and threw it across the room.

"Get the fuck out of my house, trying to steal my baby. Bitch, I'll put your ass six feet under," she said moving toward the hedge shears on the dresser.

"Mommy, it's me," I said crying and still trying to get to the crib.

"You're not my daughter. Get the fuck out of my house!" she yelled loudly.

Anjelo was screaming, awakened by the yelling. I ran out the room, down the steps and out the front door. Chloe followed.

We had to knock on Ms. Lola's front door. My exit was in such haste, I dropped my keys. She opened the door with a look of relief quickly replaced by rage. Chloe hid behind me as if that would make her invisible to Ms. Lola's fury.

"Mommy won't let me get Anjelo!" I said, crying hysterically.

"Leave that baby where he is for now. Where the fuck have you two been? Everyone has been worried senseless! Your husband has been here several times. You know it took a lot for that man to come here, but he put his pride aside for you. He's worried sick. I don't even want to talk about your father." She paced as she spoke. I'd never seen her quite this upset before.

"Ms. Lola, I'm sorry," I said.

"Shut the fuck up. I'm still talking," she said with fire in her eyes.

"Fats and Desi have been in the streets looking for you both. Ya'll look like shit! Amber, don't let me see you with a fucking scarf tied around your head ever again. When did you decide that you wanted to start getting high and lunchin? That shit is not even in your makeup. You've always been strong and a boss. Who started you down this path of destruction?" Ms. Lola asked just as Fats and Desi walked through the front door.

"I want to hear the answer to that one," Fats said looking like he wanted to wrap around my neck and squeeze real tight.

"Chloe and I went to a party one night," I said, staring down at my hands.

"That morning you came in here and asked me to paint you. I thought your ass was high but I was second guessing myself," Fats said. Then he asked, moving toward Chloe with a menacing look, "Chloe, you turned her on to that shit?"

"I didn't put a gun to her head! She's a grown woman!" she said without remorse.

Ms. Lola stepped in front of Fats and smacked the shit out of Chloe so hard she almost lost her balance.

"Get out of my house. You're dead to me and to the rest of this family. Don't bring your no-good ass around here no more," Ms. Lola said with disdain. Chloe turned with tears in her eyes and fled out the front door.

"Cut your phone on and call your husband to let him know you're alive. I'll call your father," Ms. Lola spoke as if she was ready for me to be out of her eyesight, at least for now.

The phone rang once; O answered.

"Amber, are you alright? Where are you, baby?" he said, sounding frantic.

"I'm okay. I'm at Ms. Lola's. I'm coming home," I said hoping he would forgive me.

"I'll be waiting."

I pulled up the driveway and opened the garage, and O was standing there waiting for me as I pulled into the space. He opened the car door. I climbed out, not knowing what would happen next. He put his arms around me and held on tight, as if he'd never let me go.

"I wanted to come home but I was scared," I said, fighting back the tears.

"Scared of what?" he asked as he stared into my eyes.

"I thought you were going to hit me," I said.

"Amber, you left because you thought I was going to put my hands on you? I just wanted to talk," he said. "I watched my mother and father fight constantly as a child, until she finally left him. I was already in the street when she got with my stepfather. I didn't care about anything or anyone outside the two of them. Then I met you. I didn't know how to handle real love. I'd never allowed myself to feel this way before. The times I was around my parents as I got older, I watched how my stepdad loved my mother. He was good to her. She deserved to be loved like that. I think I got that relationship thing all twisted and fucked up because of what I was exposed to growing up, the good and the bad. I didn't know how to separate it in my head. When you told me about the detached retina, I knew I would never hit you again. I don't care what happens. I'm not ever putting my hands on you. I don't want you to be afraid of me," he said with tears in his eyes.

"I went to get Anjelo at Mommy's and she tried to hit me with a baseball bat. She wouldn't let me take him. She said I wasn't her daughter," I said realizing that I had been away from my son for four days, feeling crazy.

"I just took him to your mom's this morning. We can go get him now. I know he misses you," he said.

"I need to take a shower and change my clothes. I don't know if I'm ready to face my father," I said.

"I'll be right there with you," he said. "Amber, she had the baby this morning," he said in a rushed voice, sounding like he just needed to get it out.

"Did you go to the hospital?" I asked, never turning around.

"No. I was too worried about you," he said as he walked up behind me and wrapped his arms around me.

"What did she have?" I asked, taking a deep breath.

"A girl," he said.

I had mixed emotions, but I would abide by my words and love her as if she was mine.

I stripped in the living room, throwing my clothing in the trash. I walked into the bathroom, closed the door, and stared at myself in the mirror, disappointed in the person I saw staring back. I took the scissors from the cabinet and started chopping at my hair, watching the locks fall at my feet. O came into the bathroom in the midst of me cutting.

He spoke with a crooked smile, "Good thing I learned how to cut hair when I was in. I guess I'm going to have to straighten that up for you, huh?"

"I could use some help," I said as I pulled at the uneven strands. I felt a tear trickle down my face.

"I got you, baby. Now and forever," he said.

O and I walked into my parents' home together. Strangely enough, Daddy just hugged me; there was no lecture to follow. Mommy came down the steps, stopped midway, and let out a harrowing scream when she saw my haircut.

"Amber, what have you done? Hayden, do you see this child's head?" she said, addressing Daddy with displeasure.

"I think it's cute! It brings out her eyes," Daddy said, giving me a wink.

I walked up the stairs toward Mommy to get Anjelo. She touched my head. I kissed her cheek as I ran past, so happy that she finally recognized me. No one gave me a hard way to go, wondering if I was having some sort of breakdown.

Two weeks later, O surprised me with a new pair of diamond stud earrings to replace the ones that disappeared.

"We're going out tonight. I'm taking you to the club. My man is having a birthday party. I want you to wear something short and tight to match that hair," he said as he hit my ass before he walked up the stairs. I smiled. We were in a good place again.

I think I exceeded his expectations with a pale peach spandex dress, five-inch heels, platinum blond hair and the recent gift in my ears. He stared as I walked down the stairway. I felt good. He still loved me.

We arrived at the club. There was R&B, hip-hop, jazz, and even house music pumping on various floors. There was an intimate lounge, with low lighting for conversation. O and I spent hours snuggled up, laughing and talking, reminiscing about the good times. He took me to meet the "Birthday Boy." It was the guy from N.E. We both played it off like we'd never met.

"It's a pleasure meeting you, Amber. I've heard a lot of good things about you," he said as he kissed my hand.

"It's nice meeting you as well," I said, smiling graciously and so appreciative that he never told O that I tried to buy drugs from him.

I wanted to dance; EU and Trouble Funk were scheduled to play first. Lil Benny and Chuck Brown would be closing out the party. I took O by the hand and led him toward the stairs. I saw the fine ass dude from Baltimore at the top; he paused when he saw me, watched my every move as I climbed the stairs, never taking his eyes off me, ignoring O as if he wasn't there.

He spoke just as we were passing, "Hey, Amber."

I didn't even acknowledge his presence with a "Hello." I knew he was being disrespectful. I was holding on to O's hand just a little tighter, as if to say, "Not tonight, baby."

When we reached the top, O quickly pulled me in a corner.

"You had some dealings with that nigga other than when you made the drop?"

"Hell no! Why would you ask me that? You know better," I said.

"I saw the way he looked at you. Did he try to hit on you?" he asked. His eyes were beginning to darken.

"Baby, let's go home," I said, never answering his question.

We left the club. We drove in silence.

When we arrived home I asked, "Why are you so angry with me?"

He finally spoke, "I'm not angry with you. I'm angry with myself. If it wasn't for me, you never would've met that nigga; besides, why wouldn't he want you?" he said lovingly.

"He don't know what a handful I am; you do and you still love me in spite of it all. Take off those clothes. He ain't messing up my night."

25

Three months had passed. I was in the kitchen cooking dinner. Anjelo was in the playpen trying to get my attention. O was sitting in the nook reading "Native Son" by Richard Wright. I turned the evening news on just in time to hear, "Baltimore drug dealer found shot to death in car." The reporter spoke with enthusiasm as if it was the lead story of the day. O and I both looked up just as his picture was being displayed on the television screen. I looked at O; he went right back to reading his book, expressionless, as if we'd just watched the weather report, predicting another day of rain. There was no discussion. I knew not to ask and it was better for me not to know.

O was back on top. Buying toys, not only for Anjelo and me, but also for himself. He purchased a boat with sleeping quarters because he loved the water. He came home the previous night on a BMW motorcycle, followed by two of his men, one in a BMW 750i sedan and a hoopty following behind the BMW. I could hear him coming down the street before he even got to the garage, popping a wheelie with the front tire in the air.

I met him at the door. "Do me a favor and don't kill yourself on that shit," I said with a frown and one hand on my hip, letting him know I was serious.

"Woman, I've been riding since I was eleven, if not younger. You don't have to worry about that one. I'm not going out like that!" he said, taking his helmet off, standing back admiring his new possessions. The BMW was special. O had hidden compartments built inside the doors for transporting drugs from state to state.

He walked in the house taking off his riding jacket, washing his hands in the kitchen sink, and swooping up our son into his arms, planting a big kiss on Anjelo's cheek. His cell phone rang. I could tell the call was serious. He put Anjelo down and walked out the room.

When he came back, he spoke deliberately and to the point, "That phone call was about Cody. They dug up Gina's body; his DNA was found. They'll be making an arrest soon," he said.

"O, is there something you can do? Cody's not going to jail for life. He'll go down in a hail of bullets before doing that time. Can you get him out of the country?" I asked, praying that he would say yes.

Cody never worked for O, but they had mutual respect for each other, and O knew how much Cody meant to me.

"I know someone who can probably smuggle him into Cuba. Amber, he won't be able to come back. You do understand that? There will be no more contact," he said.

I stared off into space, taking it all in. "I understand," I said.

"Let me make a phone call," he said.

I rode with O to Miami. This was far from being a pleasure trip. We waited in the dark of night, with hundreds of stars above our heads for light. The water was pitch black as we listened for the boat, just O, Cody, and myself, not saying a word, quiet as church mice. I turned toward Cody and hugged him with my eyes. I was sad because this was like losing another brother, never to be seen or heard from again. But the outcome was far better than him spending his life behind bars or dying at the hands of the police. I could hear the sound of the water beating against the rocks. The boat came in with no lights. Cody climbed aboard. I waved as the boat vanished from sight into the murky waters. O and I made our way back to the car, mentally preparing ourselves for the long ride home, carrying thirty kilos of cocaine. There was a drought back home, and O said he couldn't turn down the price.

"You want to flip a coin to see who drives first?" I said throwing a quarter in the air. O just looked at me and smiled.

*   *   *

We'd only been back home for a few weeks. I was back to disappearing for days at a time. I knew folks all over the city so it was easy for me to get lost in the projects in dead S.E. and not even come up for air. I had a young friend named Noah, who cooked rock for a living. I used to serve him. Always gave him a good deal on the price. He didn't mind me hanging out with him and his girlfriend, Sandy, and I didn't have to spend a dime for what I smoked.

I got high by candlelight on a blow-up mattress next to the window with the leak. A helicopter was flying overhead searching, its light crossing the window in repetition. Gun shots could be heard ringing out close by. Police sirens wailed in the distance. The rumbling of a nearby train passing by rattled the dishes in the kitchen cabinets.

Sandy would play spades with me for hours on end, while I played Luther Vandross' song "Wait for Love" repeatedly.

"Damn, Amber. I love me some Luther but can we listen to another song?" Noah said standing over the stove, watching the powder turn to rock.

"My apologies," I said, finally coming down from the last hit.

"I'm tired, Amber. I'm going to bed," Sandy said while gathering up the deck of cards in her hand, returning them to the old tattered box.

"I'll be right behind you," Noah said. Amber, you're more than welcome to stay. Just no more Luther."

All three of us laughed.

The house was finally quiet. I was just about to take another hit when I heard a tapping noise in the kitchen. I put the pipe down, got to my feet, and slowly tipped toward the noise. A large rat was running across the kitchen floor with a chicken bone in his mouth from the trash. He disappeared through a hole in the wall. I forgot all about taking that hit. It was time for me to go.

I knocked on the bedroom door.

"Noah, come and lock the door behind me. I'm going home," I said as I put my purse on my shoulder and my bag in my hand. No sooner had I stepped onto the sidewalk than several men ran past as if the devil was on their heels. I saw the barrel of the guns as the tinted windows rolled down, front and back. Bullets rang out. I got down low close to a parked car as I saw one of the guys scream out and fall to the concrete. I waited until the car with the shooters turned the corner, and I jumped to my feet and hauled ass to my car and drove in the opposite direction with no lights.

I was lost for a minute. I had to get my bearings. I reached inside my purse while driving, feeling for a gram of coke that I always kept with me. I took a hit just as I was passing the 7th District Police Station just to calm my nerves. I glanced in the mirror and swiped at the blood dripping from my nose. I pulled over to the curb to look for some tissue in the glove compartment, cupping my hand underneath my nose to catch the blood. I stuffed my nostril with the tissue and laid my head back on the headrest and closed my eyes.

I jumped as I heard someone tap on the glass. It was a policeman. I rolled down the window and removed the tissue.

"Are you okay?" he asked.

"Yes, Sir. I had a slight nose bleed. I'm okay now. I think it stopped. I'm heading home. You be safe in these streets," I said as

I waited for a car to pass before I pulled out of the parking space and headed home.

I must've been really fucked up when I got home. I fell asleep with all my clothes on. The last thing that I remembered was getting out of bed to pee. When I opened my eyes I was laying on the bathroom floor in a pool of blood. I hit the floor with no warning. I don't know how long I had been laying there. I got up, cleaned myself up, and took some ice from the freezer for my face. My head was throbbing, my throat was dry, and I felt like shit. Maybe this was a sign that I needed to slow down.

O would always take me back, but this time it wasn't with welcome arms. He was giving me the silent treatment just like Daddy used to do when I fucked up. I disappeared again a week later. This time when I went to the ATM in the middle of the night, high and alone, there was no money in the accounts to withdraw.

I said to myself out loud, "O took all the money. What the fuck am I going to do now?"

I'd already pawned my jewelry. I needed the cash to get it out before they sold my shit. I was going to have to go home and face O. The house was empty when I entered. I went through all my hiding places. I couldn't even put my hands on a dollar bill. I got back in the car and drove to 9th Street. I saw him having a conversation with a few of his friends. I double parked and blew the horn. He turned and stared. I rolled down the window and called out his name.

"O, I need to talk to you, please," I said in a raspy voice.

He walked across the street to the car. He looked down on me with a sullen face.

"O, I pawned my jewelry. I need to get it out today or they'll sell it. Can you give me the money, please?" I asked, trying not to look in his eyes.

"The first thing you ask me is can I give you money. You didn't even ask about our son. What the fuck is wrong with you, Amber?

You're letting this shit take you somewhere that you might not be able to come back from," saying so, he turned to walk away.

"O, please; don't do this."

He spun around, stuck his hand in his pocket and started throwing hundred-dollar bills in the car as he spoke, "I bought that fucking jewelry for your ass; now I have to give you money to get it out of the pawn shop. Make this your last time asking," he said in a menacing voice.

I watched the money slowly drift at a snail's pace, as it fell in my lap, on the console, the passenger seat, and on the floor of the car. I could hear people laughing. I was embarrassed as I rolled up the window. I made a left on U Street and headed straight for the pawn shop. I had to get there before it closed.

A few days later, O moved out. He got an apartment in Silver Spring. He stayed away for three weeks, no phone calls, no contact, just visiting Anjelo at Mommy's. My heart was broken.

The radio announcer's sexy voice came across the airwaves, "You're listening to one of my all-time favorite songs, Michael Jackson's "I Can't Help It." I'd just finished washing a few dishes in the sink. As I dried my hands, I began to snap my fingers while listening to the song on the radio. Michael had something special with this one. He was letting the whole world know that he was all grown up. I thought about how much I was missing O. I picked up the phone to call him but thought better about making the call. I couldn't handle hearing disappointment in his voice, not today. I placed the phone back down on the receiver.

Knock. Knock. Knock.

I quietly tipped to the door. Not wanting to be heard by some overzealous salesman. I looked out the peephole and there O stood. He was as handsome as the first day we met. I opened the door standing to the side because I was half dressed.

"I'd like to see my son. I went past your mom's but he wasn't there," he said.

"Ms. Lola took him to the beach house," I said.

"When will he be back?" he asked.

"Tomorrow," I said.

"Okay," he said and glanced at his cell phone as it rang, ending the call without answering.

"I think I left my watch upstairs in the safe. Do you mind if I take a look?"

I stepped back and opened the door wider so that he could enter. I watched him walk past, across the hardwood floor and up the stairs. I closed my eyes and wished that he would never leave, although I knew there was no chance that he would stay.

He came back down the steps twirling the watch around his finger. "Send for Me" by Atlantic Starr came on the radio.

"I love this song," I said as I closed my eyes and moved my head from side to side. I opened my eyes just as I heard him lay the watch on the counter. He turned and walked toward me. I closed my eyes again as he took me in his arms and we began to dance. I could smell the light scent of his Polo cologne, and felt his breath on my neck. He held me tight. The song came to an end far too soon. He kissed me lightly on my cheek and then turned and walked out the door. All I could do was cry.

I started getting high early the next morning, right after I got out of the shower, in just my tee shirt and panties. There was no one to play spades with so I played solitaire for hours. I tried to pull it together by evening, throwing on a black and blue wool dress that was hanging in the closet straight out of the cleaners and some black knee high leather boots. I was still high, but I got in the car and headed to Mommy's. I felt like I needed to see her. I lucked up on a parking space two doors down. I got out of the car and went into the trunk to get the gift I'd bought for her weeks ago and kept forgetting to drop it off.

I heard tires squeal as O whipped a u-turn and pulled up on the corner. He jumped out of his car yelling my name, "Amber!" I turned around and saw his jaw clenched as he stared me down through angry eyes.

"I just went past the house. I forgot my watch. You left the pipe on the kitchen counter. I've had enough of this bullshit. Look at you; you're high right now! You're going to rehab and you're going today! You've been putting this shit off for too long!" he screamed with fire in his eyes.

"O, I'll go, but not today. I need to take Mommy her gift and then I have to go shopping, Anjelo is outgrowing some of his clothes." I was grasping at straws as I spoke, making things up as I went along, avoiding his stare. He grabbed me by both arms. I tried to pull away.

"Amber, you saved my life. Please let me save yours. I love you."

"I love you too, baby, but I just can't go today. I've got a lot to do and it's getting late," I said as he held me tighter. "O, let me go! I can't do this with you today!" I screamed as we began to struggle.

I felt something pierce my shoulder, as if someone had thrown a sharp edged rock at my back. I'd been shot, but I didn't feel any pain. The bullet went straight through me and struck O in the chest. A pool of blood began to soak through his shirt. He fell to the ground, pulling me downward with him. I felt a burning sensation as I cradled him in my arms, screaming, "Somebody call 911, please!"

Tears poured down my face as his blood mixed with mine. My dress was saturated. "Please don't leave me, O. I'll go to rehab. I swear I will. Just don't leave me. I can't imagine life without you. You're my rock. Anjelo needs his father. Baby, we've been through so much. We'll get through this too," I said as I touched his face and kissed his lips. He never said a word. I watched the life drain from his eyes as they fluttered and closed. He bled out on the cement with me still holding him close, still kissing his lips as he died in my arms.

I could hear people running toward us, sirens and flashing lights. I wouldn't let anyone near his body. "Get the fuck away;

don't touch him!" I fought the paramedics trying to take me from the scene. My hands were drenched with his blood.

"Amber, you've been shot. You have to go to the hospital. You're losing a lot of blood," Ms. Lola said tearfully. I looked into her eyes. I could probably count on one hand the times I'd seen her cry.

"I can't leave him," I said while rubbing his beard with my bloody hand.

"Amber, there is nothing more you can do for him now. He knew how much you loved him. Please get in the ambulance," she said while lifting me off the ground. She stayed right by my side on the ride to the hospital. I could hear someone screaming but the screams were so loud I thought they belonged to someone else; all along, it was me.

Two weeks later, I found myself at a familiar place, planning a funeral, this time for my husband. Ms. Lola stepped up and made all the arrangements with just a yes or no from me. Mommy sunk into a quiet place. She stopped talking altogether, not even engaging with the voices. Anjelo kept crying, not understanding all the new faces trying to console him and me.

I had a private service. O wasn't coming back from the spirit world haunting me because I had this grand funeral with a bunch of onlookers and people he didn't know, just trying to be seen. We'd discussed our wishes in case of death because of the business we were in and he expressed that he wanted to be cremated. I did as he asked, hoping to take a trip to Cartagena when his son was old enough, so we could spread his ashes in the blue water amongst the coral reefs. He loved diving and swimming amongst the fish, so I felt that would be appropriate. He would be at peace.

I stayed between Ms. Lola's and Mommy's for weeks on end after the funeral. Everything at the house reminded me of O; I couldn't handle any of it for now. Someone got word to me that the Bitch had moved out of town with O's daughter with no following address. I never got to see his daughter. Maybe it was for the best. I didn't feel strong enough to take care of two children. I could hardly take care of me.

I fought depression like I was going twelve rounds in the ring against a worthy opponent. On the bad days, I could hear O's voice screaming, "Get the fuck out the corner! Get off the ropes!" I listened. He never steered me wrong.

I put the pipe down, although I still snorted the powder on days that it was too hard to cope. Fats was there, not in my face, but in the background, giving me time to grieve. I knew I could just reach out if I needed him.

I finally convinced everyone that I could handle going home. I walked straight to O's closet, pulling his shirts close to my nose. I went from one to another before slowly sinking to my knees as I began to scream his name. Depression wasn't going to let me go so easily.

I wasn't sleeping. I couldn't turn off my thoughts. Memories of our life together raced through my head like a never-ending movie. I felt as if someone had stuck a needle in my arm and drained every bit of energy from my body. During waking hours, I found myself crying on and off throughout the day. The only time I ate was when Daddy, Ms. Lola, or Fats came by and forced me to eat. They would bring Anjelo along for a visit. My son would make me happy but only for short increments in time. Four months passed and I knew I needed help.

My eyes flew open. I thought I heard O's voice ask if I had seen the moon tonight. I longed for his voice. I could always hear him in my dreams. I decided to go for a walk. I glanced at the clock on the wall. I didn't realize it was 11:15 p.m. My days and nights were turned around. I changed my mind. That would make me as careless as the women I'd seen jog in Rock Creek Park, alone after dark, with headphones on their ears listening to music in a predator's campground, oblivious to danger. I wondered how they felt safe. I carried a gun everywhere I went. What was their defense?

I decided to go to the liquor store instead. It closed at midnight. Maybe a drink would help me sleep. I jumped in the shower, threw on some clothes, and drove to the liquor store. My friend Jay would always have a smile and inspiring words for me no matter how long the line at the drive-through. He waved from the window and went to get me a bottle of Dom, my usual, but I didn't want that tonight.

"Amber, where have you been? It's been months since I've seen you last," Jay said peering inside the car.

"I gave up drinking for a while," I said thinking that I'd given up on a lot since O's death. "Jay, I'd like a bottle of Remy Martin V.S.O.P please," I said.

"Amber, you not drinking your bubbly tonight?" Jay said, showing me the champagne bottle that he had sitting at the cash register, waiting for me.

"I'm not feeling bubbly tonight. I need something to go along with my mood," I said.

"Don't make this a habit," he said as he tapped his watch. I looked at the clock on the console and then lowered my head like a child being reprimanded. He took the money and handed me the bag while staring long and hard.

"It's late. You go straight home," he said. I managed a smile as I drove off. I did what I've always done, masked the pain with a smile.

Once I arrived home, I opened the bottle of cognac and took two shots. I then went up the stairs and pulled down the ladder and climbed up into the attic in search of my bible, a gift from one of the nurses at St. Elizabeths. I found it in a cardboard box in the far-left corner, right on top. My life was on tilt. I wanted God to help me make things right. Isn't that what we sinners do? Turn to the church. I decided to skip that bullshit and go straight to the source. I needed a one-on-one with the man.

I climbed back down and placed the bible on my bed, before heading back to the kitchen to pour a real drink. I took that shit to the head and poured another. I went up the stairs to the bedroom with my drink in one hand and the bottle of cognac in the other and placed them both on the nightstand. I took off my clothes and put on a pair of pajamas from the dresser drawer. I put on Curtis Mayfield's song "(Don't Worry) If There's a Hell below We're All Going to Go." I climbed into bed and reached for the package of coke inside the drawer of the nightstand, opened the aluminum foil, and took a couple of hits.

I opened the bible, turned to a random page, and began to read out loud, "Luke 12:2-3: For there is nothing covered, that shall not be revealed; neither hid, that shall not be known. Therefore whatsoever ye have spoken in darkness shall be heard in the light; and that which ye have spoken in the ear in closets shall be proclaimed upon the housetops."

I took another hit as I turned the glass up to my lips and drank hard and fast as if I was gulping a cold glass of water on a hot summer's night. I read the passage again this time to myself over and over. Mommy would always say, "What is done in the dark will come to light." I tried to read another passage but it wasn't clear; in fact, it was downright confusing.

"God, I talk to you all the time. It's so much easier than trying to read this bible. If it's your word and it's for the people, why is it so hard to understand?" I said out loud, my voice beginning to slur. In my fucked-up state of mind, I was determined to figure it out, alone and bewildered. Two hours later, out of total frustration, I hurled the good book against the wall, feeling downtrodden and lost. The devil was busy this morning. I watched it as it fell to the floor with a thump. The tears flowed from my eyes down my cheeks and around my chin before wetting my pajamas like water from a leaky faucet. I stumbled over to the floor where the bible landed and bent down and almost toppled over. I picked up the bible and stumbled back to the bed, sat on the edge, opened the drawer to the nightstand, and placed the bible and the coke inside.

"Forgive me, God. I know I've sinned. Everyone thinks they can fuck up and ask for your forgiveness and keep doing the same shit over and over and keep getting a pass. That's not what you meant; at least I don't think that's what you meant. I'm confused," I said through trembling lips.

"On second thought, don't forgive me yet. I know I'm not ready to make that change and I don't want to run out of passes. I'm not taking any chances. At least I got out of bed. Thank you for allowing me to do that."

I cut off the music, took a valium, turned off the light, and hoped for sleep.

∗ ∗ ∗

Winter 1987

I got an unexpected phone call from Chloe's boosting buddy. "Amber, I know you might not give a fuck, but Chloe is sitting in the McDonald's at Georgia and Peabody with just a sweater, no coat. She's not herself. I tried to talk to her, but she acted like she didn't know who I was. I didn't know who else to call."

Surprisingly, I didn't hesitate to drive to McDonalds. Would I ever get over seeing Chloe fucking Fats as some sort of payback from being alienated from the family or forgive her for holding on to the key to the apartment? Never, but I couldn't leave her despondent and wandering the streets in the cold. She'd been my friend since childhood.

My eyes swept the McDonalds from front to back, as strangers in pea coats and wool caps stared back at me. I even checked the bathroom. Chloe was nowhere to be found. I drove down the Avenue scrutinizing every block between Peabody and Randolph. I made a right on Randolph and then a right on 14th Street and started my search again. I don't know what made me ride up Upshur Street by our old high school, but I could see her sitting all alone in the bleachers staring at the field. I pulled up the driveway and parked, climbed down the bleachers toward her, and took a seat right next to her.

"It's cold out today." I said rubbing my hands together. I could see my breath as I spoke. "We had some good times in these bleachers at the football games, especially the championship games. You remember the cheerleader with the big ass titties that we use to bet on how long it would take for one of them to slap her in the face while she was doing her routine?" I asked, thinking that I saw a gleam in her eyes; it definitely wasn't a smile. We sat there quietly for at least fifteen minutes.

She finally spoke, "Desi gave me . . . . " Then, she abruptly stopped talking.

"Desi gave you what, Chloe? I asked with concern.

"Nothing. He never liked me anyway. I have to go."

"Is there somewhere I can take you?" I asked, rising to my feet just as she did.

"No."

"At least let me give you my coat. There's some money in the pocket," I said as I took off my coat and laid it over her shoulders. She turned and started to climb the bleachers.

She stopped at the top, looked back at me and said, "I'm sorry." As quickly as she spoke, she hurriedly walked away, heading toward the bus depot.

26

I drove back to Ms. Lola's. Parked outside on the corner, contemplating how quickly my life had changed. My inner circle was getting smaller. I went inside the house, cut on the television, and there was an old rerun of "Lucy" on. Desi stuck his key in the door. I could tell it was him by his footsteps. I never turned around.

"It's quiet as shit in here. You got the house all to yourself?" he asked while removing his coat and laying it across the chair.

"Ms. Lola is at the beach house. Your mom is in Atlantic City for the weekend. Fats said he was taking care of some business. He went to meet one of your connects, which I clearly don't understand; it's a drought. Fats always said, 'Sometimes you just need to be still.' How did you convince him to go against his own advice?" I asked in a serious voice.

"The move was beneficial for us both. I didn't think I'd make it back in time from Philly," he said while sorting through the mail. He headed for the basement steps.

"Make sure the windows and doors are locked while you're down there, please. One less thing for me to do," I said watching Lucy and Ethel. I was usually laughing like shit at their antics but not today; my mind was somewhere else.

"Amber, it's habit. You know I've had this job since I was a little boy," he said with his chest out, seeming proud.

He'd been a little nicer to me since O's death. But I took it as some temporary bull shit. I didn't care one way or the other. I still disliked him with a passion. I wanted to ask him about Chloe but I didn't feel like arguing with his ass. I just wanted him to leave.

He came back up from the basement and asked, "You staying here tonight?"

"More than likely. Why?" I asked, looking in his direction, away from the television as he placed a piece of mail in his coat pocket.

"No reason. I was just asking. I'm out," he said as he closed the front door behind him.

Fifteen minutes later, Ms. Lola was coming through the back door.

"You came home early? I didn't expect you back until Monday," I said getting up out of the chair to help her with her bags.

"I wasn't feeling good. I decided I wanted to be in my own bed tonight," she said, moving a little slower, with noticeable dark circles under her eyes.

"Do you need me to get you anything?" I asked, gathering her bags to take up to her bedroom.

"Can you go get my prescription filled, please? I'll leave it down here on the dining room table. I'm coming up right behind you. I need to lie down," she said as she climbed the stairs holding on to the rail. This was the first time in my life that I could remember her looking fragile. She was always such a strong and commanding woman.

I took the prescription from the table, folding it once and placing it in the zipper compartment of my purse. The temperature had dropped a few degrees since I came in earlier. I buttoned my coat, wrapping the scarf around my neck tightly, opened the car door, and quickly turned on the heat, shivering just a little. I couldn't help but think about Chloe. "I wonder what Desi gave her that she didn't want to talk about." I realized I was speaking the words out loud, hoping she would be okay.

I drove downtown to get Ms. Lola's prescription filled. There was a long line at the pharmacy. I checked my phone a few times for any unanswered texts. I was hearing from people that I hadn't seen in years, checking on me to make sure I was good.

Finally, it was my turn.

I handed the gentleman the prescription stating, "I'd like to wait on that please," I said.

"Let me ask the pharmacist if we have this in stock. I'll be right back," he said as he walked away with a slight limp. He looked too young to have hip problems, but I quickly turned my head in the opposite direction as he came back to the register.

"You can take a seat right over there. The pharmacist has a number of prescriptions ahead of you."

"Thank you."

"No problem."

I walked around the store instead, stopping to look at the nail polish, not able to decide on a color. I read a few articles in *Vogue* magazine and then I did the same with *Cosmopolitan*, putting each one back in its proper place. I heard Ms. Lola's name called and made my way back to the counter.

"Do you have any questions for the pharmacist about your medication?"

"Yes. Just one."

"You can step up to the window right around the corner to your right. The pharmacist will be with you shortly."

I watched the pharmacist finish a call and then walk toward the window.

"Can I help you?" the pharmacist asked as she looked down, placing a black pen back in the pocket of her white smock and then focusing on me with an attentive smile.

"What is this medication for, please?" I asked.

"It's a cancer drug," she said. I stared at the bag, wanting to drop it as if it were on fire. I felt flushed.

"Miss, are you okay?"

"Yes. I'm fine. Thank you," I said as I left the store in a daze.

I walked in the opposite direction of where I'd parked the car, turned around, and found my way back. I climbed inside and sat motionless thinking, *Why didn't she tell me? Fats can't possibly know; she's his world. He couldn't have kept that to himself, without me knowing something was wrong. I've been so damn preoccupied with everything that's going on in my life. I should've paid more attention.*

My cell phone rang.

"Hello."

"Amber. Thank God!"

"Daddy, what's wrong?" I questioned sensing the relief in his voice after hearing mine, but only for a second.

"Where are you?"

"I'm leaving the drug store. I had to get a prescription filled for Ms. Lola.

"I need you to come home right away," he said.

"Daddy, tell me what's wrong."

"Just come home," he said, ending the call.

I could see the flashing lights of the fire engines and police cars from a block away. I pulled the car to the curb and ran up the street. Daddy was on the front porch, screaming my name, but I ran right past him, never stopping. Pushing through the crowd of bystanders, a detective dressed in an off the rack pin striped suit with trousers kissing the ground grabbed me as I ran up the stairs, blocking the entrance to the house.

"Let me go! I need to go to her! Get the fuck off of me!" I yelled, twisting my body trying to pull away.

"This is a murder scene. I can't let you inside the house."

I let a total stranger hold me as I wailed uncontrollably beating on his chest as I fell to my knees. Daddy picked me up off the cold concrete. He wrapped around me as if I was still his little girl, his arms were comforting. My feet were moving, but I couldn't feel them touching the ground. He took me to the house, removed my coat and scarf, took the throw from his favorite chair, and placed it around my shoulders. I was still shaking, trying to process it all, the cancer, the murder, and my own selfish feelings of loss.

The detective found his way down the street, knocking on the door. I could hear bits and pieces of their conversation, quietly and softly, not wanting to disturb me or Mommy.

"There was a violent struggle. She managed to shoot one of the intruders; there was a trail of blood going out the back door. She was brutally raped, beaten beyond recognition and thrown from the second floor. Her neck was broken on impact. It's been a long time since I've seen an assault and murder like this one. This was personal. Did she have any enemies, someone that might want to see her dead?"

Daddy's response was, "Lola had no enemies. She was always giving back to the community. She helped me raise my daughter; my wife, her best friend, has been sick on an off for years."

"At some point, I'd like to speak with your daughter," he said.

Daddy and the detective stepped out on the front porch for the remainder of the conversation. I'd heard all that I needed to hear.

I could see Mommy out of my peripheral vision. She had a blank stare and a nervous tic at the corner of her mouth. "Mommy, I'm so sorry for your loss."

She looked in my direction for a brief second, as if to acknowledge my words, and then returned to the blank stare, the tick more noticeable than before.

I had to tell Fats. I dialed his number. No answer. I waited five minutes and called again. Still no answer. I paged him 911. Still no call back. I dialed Desi. The phone just rang. Something wasn't right.

I got the phone call from Fats around the same time the coroner arrived to take Ms. Lola's body to the morgue.

"Hello."

"I'm locked up. I need you to call my lawyer. I got some money in the safe, but it's not enough. You might have to ask Ma to give you some money." I could hear the frustration in his voice.

"Fats, I don't know how to tell you this . . I broke down as I began to speak. "Your mom was killed tonight. It was a home invasion," I said through nonstop tears. I could hear heavy breathing on the other end of the phone as he tried to hold back the tears. I questioned if I'd made the right decision to tell him or if I should've waited until I was able to visit him at the jail, but there was never a right time to deliver bad news.

"Call my lawyer." And the phone went dead.

I needed to get some money and I needed to get it fast. I was sitting on the sofa with both hands on my face in a praying position contemplating my next move. I thought about Fats' paintings in the studio, especially the nude painting of me in blue. I searched the yellow pages looking for art dealers. Why not? It was worth a shot.

Two weeks had passed and today was Ms. Lola's funeral. I knew in my heart that my tears would overflow. I would cry not only for Ms. Lola, but also for the boys missing her going-away celebration and all the loved ones that I'd loss, especially my husband. She was like a mother to me. I felt empty inside. I was so grateful for Elena. She kept me strong before and during the funeral. There was still no word from Desi. The judge sat right next to me on the front row, rubbing my hand gently, sometimes squeezing it tightly. Ms. Lola's death had aged him overnight; he was still handsome, but his blue eyes were somber.

Fats not being able to attend his mother's funeral was killing me inside. I couldn't imagine what he was going through. I thought about him throughout the service and cried just a little bit more. After the burial, we returned to the house. I watched the judge as he looked around the room at the small personal gifts he'd given her over the years. He picked up a sterling silver lighter from the mantel, rubbing his fingers across her initials engraved on the side. He didn't stay long after that.

"Amber, don't be a stranger," he said.

"I won't," I said as I hugged him tightly. I totally understood. He needed time to grieve alone. Elena came down the steps with a suitcase. I was baffled.

"Amber, I'm going back to the beach house with the judge. You can handle things here. He needs me more than you right now," she said as she placed the suitcase on the floor and hugged me like she'd never see me again.

I walked out the door right behind them, deciding to go check on Mommy. She still wasn't talking. We'd just buried her best friend. I needed to let her know that I was here for her. I'd gotten used to our one-sided conversations. I'd barely put one foot in front of the other when it hit me like a ton of bricks. Ms. Lola's casket had just been lowered in the cold ground, now covered with fresh dirt. I could envision her banging on the casket, clawing at the top, wanting to get out because Elena was going home with her man.

"He needed her," I said out loud with disgust, rubbing at the corner of my mouth, smearing my lipstick. "This right here is why I don't trust women."

And then, speaking in the third person, I said, "Okay, Amber. Maybe I'm reading this all wrong; after all, Ms. Lola did win Elena from the judge in a poker game. Maybe she was just going back to what she knew as home. Going back to cooking, cleaning, and maybe giving up a little pussy this time around; everybody needs somebody."

I was having another conversation in my head with just me. Then I thought about Gina's message, "Watch those who are close to you."

My head started whirling. Elena was much too calm not to have talked to her son in two weeks. She knew he was safe. This was Desi's master plan gone wrong. He was eliminating each one of us one by one, or so he thought. He had DJ killed, gave Chloe a drug that fucked up her mind. I was supposed to be at the house that night, not Ms. Lola. He sent Fats to make a move with his connect, during a drought. He probably orchestrated the bust with the police on payroll. Mommy always said that money was the root of all evil.

I spun around, walking at a brisk pace toward the judge's car just as he was backing out of the alley and driving toward the corner. He rolled down the window.

"Can I talk to you for a minute? I'd almost forgotten. Ms. Lola expressed to me some personal things that she wanted me to convey to you in case she passed before you. It would help put my mind at ease if I told you now. Elena, I won't keep him long."

"No problem. I'll be right here," she said affectionately as she laid her hand on his coat sleeve. He stepped out of the car and we walked a few steps down the block.

"What do you need to tell me, Amber?" he asked, taking my hands in his, holding on tight.

"Please don't show any signs of anger with what I'm about to tell you. Elena is watching. I think Desi arranged the home invasion. He came by the house the night Ms. Lola was murdered. I was there alone. He went down the basement. I asked him to make sure the windows and doors were locked, as he always did. The police said the killers gained entry through the basement window. She wasn't supposed to be home. Remember, she was at the beach house with you? She came home early, said she wasn't feeling well. I left shortly after to get her prescription filled. Desi was trying to kill me, not Ms. Lola. That's why he's gone underground. He knows that he fucked up. He got Fats locked up, gave Chloe some bad drugs, had DJ killed, all so he could be the man. Please don't let on to Elena that you know any of this," I said as I hugged him tight.

"He robbed me of the last few months I had with the love of my life. That can't be forgiven," he said with anger in his eyes.

"Just remember that I love you. Keep your eyes open and be safe," I said. We hugged again as he turned and walked back to the car adjusting his leather gloves and tightening the scarf around his neck.

I went to sit with Mommy, waited until dark, and went to the house where I dressed in all black. I was back in the car thinking about all those nights we played hide-and-go-seek as kids at the beach house. I knew every nook and cranny. If Desi was there, I'd find him and I was going to kill him.

The beach house was a two-hour drive from DC. I was in the only car on a long stretch of lonely road. The corn fields were unrecognizable at night, covered by yesterday's sudden snow shower. The trees were bare, with stripped bark, ice glowing on the limbs the color of silver spray paint. I was getting lost in the right to left movement of the windshield wipers, almost missing my turn. My drive to the beach was with landmarks, never a map. I parked a mile away from the house, not wanting to be seen. I slipped a few times as I zigzagged across the yard, inching my way from the side of the house to the porch. The wind was brutal, clipping my face with a barrage of sand and snow. I heard a shotgun blast and a woman's scream. The front door was ajar. I went inside, tipped toward the screams with my gun drawn, as I peered around the corner. Desi lay on the kitchen floor with half of his brain splattered on the wall. The spattering of blood, skin, and brain made the perfect collage for his death. Elena was on her knees near his body screaming and praying, as if that was going to bring him back. The judge stood back at a distance saying, "I thought he was a burglar." There was no remorse in his eyes. I left without being noticed.

*　　*　　*

I got a phone call from an art dealer a week later.

"Hello."

"May I speak with Mrs. Amber Hayden, please? "This is Julius Southerland," he said.

"Speaking," I said, trying to contain my excitement.

"My associate showed me the painting that you brought in about a week ago. The artist is extremely talented. Does he have other work that we can see? He may possibly have a very bright future," he said.

Once again, I was moving without Fats direction or approval. At least I had the money to pay the lawyer. I was there for his trial date. The judge threw the case out. The supposed cocaine was bath salts well packaged in plastic shrink wrap. Fats was arrested before he got a chance to test the product. I don't know if his lawyer could have gotten him out of a murder charge so easily.

$$* \quad * \quad *$$

Eighteen Months Later

The weather report was deceiving. Water was still lingering on the leaves from last night's rain. Dandelions were swaying in the breeze with half eaten heads. There was no rain in sight, as predicted. Fats and I brought Daddy to visit Mommy at St. Elizabeths Hospital. I watched Fats play touch football with Anjelo in the grass. He was really good with him.

Daddy exited the hospital saying, "Amber, you can go see your mother now."

"Thanks, Daddy. I'm going to stop and see Chloe first; I won't be long," I said, rising from the bench, walking toward the front entrance.

I gave the receptionist my driver's license and signed the visitor log and proceeded to the fourth floor. Chloe was dancing in the corner to music in her head. I watched her for a few moments before approaching. It was obviously Go-Go; I could tell by the way she moved.

"Hey, Chloe. You good?" I asked as I danced with her like we used to do. She smiled. "Come sit and talk to me for a minute," I said, moving to a vacant table with a deck of cards, taking a seat, pushing the cards to the side. She didn't follow. I walked back toward her saying, "I'll tell the nurse to let me know if you need anything. I'm going to see Mommy."

She kept right on dancing as I walked toward the locked door.

I took the elevator down to the third floor. Mommy was sitting in a chair staring off into space.

"Hi, Mommy," I said as I kissed her on the cheek and pulled up a chair right in front of her. I plunged right into bringing her up to speed.

"The crocuses Daddy planted in the front yard are beginning to bloom. They're really pretty and purple this year. Your grandson thinks he can tell me no. I swear I need you to come home. You know I don't do well in the discipline department. Fats said to tell you 'Hello.' He'll come up to see you next week. Chloe's here on the fourth floor. She set the drapes on fire in her apartment with a torch. They had to rescue her from the flames. The side of her face was badly burned. I just left her; she's in good spirits." I thought I saw a movement in her eyes. I kept talking.

"You're going to be a grandma again. Fats and I are having a baby. I'm excited."

Still no response as she continued to stare. "I finally turned my life around. I'm clean and sober. I got my GED and I'm working with kids at a Mental Health Center. You know I'm still a free spirit! I snuck them off campus to a movie in my own personal vehicle last Monday. You know that's against the rules. They enjoy the trips and I like the rush, almost as good as stealing.

"Look at my new tattoo," I stretched out my arm so she could see it clearly. "It's a dragonfly. It represents the transformation in my life. You've watched my ass go through a lot of shit. I finally made it to the other side. I came in from the cold," I said.

I sat for a few more minutes in silence, looking out the window, and then back at Mommy. "They still haven't found O's killer," I added with watery eyes.

Mommy turned toward me and leaned in close. She touched my face as only a mother could and looked deep into my eyes. I could feel the love that I'd longed for as she whispered in my ear, "I told you I would never let anyone hurt you."

*This is my dedication to Chuck Brown the
Godfather of Go-Go – Rest in Paradise*

*Thank you for starting my everlasting love
affair with this genre of music.*

To all the Go-Go Bands established or up and coming, keep it rockin!

*Go-Go has a way of taking over your body like a holy roller at a
Thursday night revival, totally out of your control. Erotic tendencies
are set free as soon as you hear that beat. The cool flow of the rhythm,
engulfing your spirit, your soul and your mind. Your fingers begin
to snap while raising your arms high in the air. I could feel the
percussion in my chest; I laid my hand across my breasts to keep it right
there if only for a minute. My head began to rock, my hips began to
sway; I had my own style, not to be copied. It was so relaxing but yet
uninhibited, a safe haven from all the problems at home. If you wanted
to bend over and shake your ass, it was cool—there was no judgment.
I forgot who I was dancing with, losing myself totally in the music.*

About the Author

Eva S. Pinkney is the self-published author of Crazy Is As Crazy Does Part 1, the novella and Part 2, the novel. Both are based partly on Pinkney's own experiences dealing with her mother's mental illness.

She is a native Washingtonian, who now resides in Camp Springs, Maryland, but will always remain a DC girl at heart and can be reached on Instagram @talkingparrotmedia or at www.talkingparrotmedia.com.

www.ingramcontent.com/pod-product-compliance
Lightning Source LLC
Chambersburg PA
CBHW072102300726

48975CB00003B/673